Snug Harbor Series

Book II

The Cruise

F. L. H HUDKINS

This is a work of fiction. Names, characters, Places and Incidents are the product of the author's imagination or are used fictitiously, and any resemblance to actual persons, living or dead, businesses, companies, events, or locales is entirely coincidental.

ISBN:0692261974
ISBN-13 9780692261972

DEDICATION

This book is dedicated to the men and women of the United States Navy and Marine Corps who sail the seas and serve in foreign lands to defend fellow citizens of the United States.

Other Books in Snug Harbor Series:

Book I   -- The Launching

Book III -- Fiddler's Green

CONTENTS

ACKNOWLEDGMENTS

Julian H. Hudkins for his praise and critique after reading the rough draft of the first book in the Snug Harbor Series, *The Launching,* when he, too, was a sailor.

Wilson O. Hudkins Caceres who provided encouragement in publishing this book and for his gift of a new computer and manual on self-publishing.

Agueda Tonie Hudkins-Teague who provided valuable information in final preparation of this book.

Bill Leaseburg, *The Starving Artist,* who illustrated the cover of this book from nothing more than a rough idea from the author.

CHAPTER ONE

ARRIVAL

The official deck log of Naval Air Station Santa Cruz Spain for 30 November reads:

United Airlines Military Charter, flight 521, from Philadelphia, Pa., touched down 0901 local time. All passengers, less one, safely debarked and duly cleared Spanish customs. Reporting personnel met by respective command sponsor. Aircraft towed to apron adjacent to Hanger Three for fueling and servicing prior return flight scheduled 1800, 01 December. Flight crew transported to Hotel Cordoba. Master Chief Henry C. Berkeley transported to Naval Hospital for medical evaluation after being rendered unconscious aboard aircraft. Reason unknown. Master Chief Berkeley insisted he was not ill, refused on-scene medical attention and refused to enter ambulance. Subject transported via Navy sedan. Wife, Patricia L. Berkeley, accompanied husband. Command sponsor, Master Chief Hector D. Seeley and wife, Lisa Ann, followed in POV.

This Flail-Ex, which caused me to look like an understudy to an idiot, began with a question session initiated by my wife concerning the submission of travel claims, for transportation of our bulldog and cat from Big Otter, West Virginia to Puerto Santa Cruz, Spain. The discussion occurred as the aircraft was swinging into its final approach.

Shortly after our engagement and gearing up, teeth, hair and eyeballs, to become a model Navy wife, my prospective bride purchased a sea bag full of naval texts from the *Navy Institute* and boned up on Navy customs, traditions, rules, regulations and history. Her intelligence was such that her knowledge of obscure topics often surpassed my own. I was proud of her, but her questioning Navy related happenings became something of a pain in the stern. I had, on occasion, threatened to conduct a book-burning!

The conversation that caused the flail-ex went something like this:

"Clay, I have been studying this manual on Navy travel regulations. It is clear that we cannot claim travel expenses for Jarhead and Blue Suit, even though we will pay for their transportation to Spain when they follow via a civilian aircraft."

"So?"

"So, darling," she said, in a little girl voice, "Can one claim a stowaway? And I want you to remember that I love you desperately."

"A stowaway?" I asked, wondering what desperate love had to do with a stowaway

She took my right hand and placed it on her lower mid-section. *"This* stowaway, dearest."

That revelation caused me to faint and make a spectacle of myself in front of God and everybody -- just as the aircraft touched upon the soil of Spain. It also told me the reason for various occurrences since we married almost three months prior.

Why the alleged ghost of the first Berkeley matriarch, Margaret Louise (Tinny) Berkeley kept tripping around our farm house in West Virginia smiling at her. Why Patty insisted we bring the cradle in which Berkeley babies had bedded down since the year 1710. Why she insisted her parents visit us in July. Why she had recently been extraordinarily amorous, even for *her*, a one hundred-pound sex kitten.

Patty Lane was **PREGNANT!**

The doctor poked and prodded at me for a good fifteen minutes, making odd sounds of dismay as he discovered various and assorted dings and zippers that adorned my beat-up carcass. He then strapped me on an EKG machine that looked like something Doctor Frankenstein used to zap bolts of lightening into his monster. Finally, after uttering a sea bag full of hems, haws and hums, he pronounced my heart that of a healthy teenager and declared me fit for full duty, which was exactly what I had told the hospital corpsman who wanted to prod at me in the air terminal.

Fainting from shock is not uncommon, certainly not when one's bride of not yet three months announces her pregnancy in a sneaky way in front of God and everybody when no such thing was even suspected, and absolutely not desired -- by me!

What a way to report to a new command! Such an omen would have caused a superstitious person to catch the next flight out of Dodge.

"My usual procedure is to proceed to the waiting room while my patient dresses, or is transported to a room, and reassure those concerned about the person's well-being. Not *this* time, Master Chief. You are on your own! I do not wish to speak with your protective wife, not after the fit she threw when I refused to let her inside the examination room." the four-striper doctor exclaimed, with no room for argument in his voice.

"I can understand why you might feel that way, Captain."

Patty must have gone totally off-plumb when I sagged in the aircraft seat. When I regained consciousness, she had removed her seat belt and was kneeling on my lap thumping on my chest and trying to give me the Kiss of Life and scream, all at the same time. Despite her being not much larger than the average mouse, it took considerable effort of three flight attendants to get her off my lap and back into her seat.

She went into a Mark One - Mod Zero rampage when the doctor would not permit her to enter the examination room. She poked him in the chest with her tiny finger and called him names which were very harsh, and which probably derived from her reading of Shakespeare. Her actions were quite out of character, considering my shy, young, farm girl wife did not know any really nasty words -- 'Damn and Hell', being her strongest cuss words. Missus Seeley resolved the situation by taking the slack out of her towing hawser and hauling Patty out into the hospital waiting room, belligerence radiating every step of the way

Patty probably still did not realize her: *I will slip my pregnancy to Clay gently* tactic caused the entire series of events.

Patty struggled from the heavy arms of Missus Seeley, dashed across the nicely waxed deck and threw herself against my chest with force enough to knock me backwards.

"Oh, Clay-honey!" she sobbed against my now rumpled khaki shirt that would have been rejected by a San Francisco wino as casual attire.

I kissed the top of her wavy-curly head. "I'm fine, Kitten, just like I told that corpsman at the airport. The doctor said I have the heart of a healthy teenager."

"Oh, I am so glad! I would *kill* myself if something happened to you!" she exclaimed, then locked her big, gray eyes and gave me one of her penetrating looks. "If you are okay, then why did you faint on the airplane? Are you certain that mean doctor is competent? Should we get a second opinion from a Spanish doctor? Are they well-trained? Should you--"

I caught her by her little shoulders, set her down in a blue, plastic chair, bent over and said, softly, for her ears only, "I passed out because of the shock of learning you're pregnant and for no other reason. What is done is done, and I'm not being critical, but you should have waited until we got to the hotel, then told me straight out and up front. Actually, you should have told me when you first learned of it. I couldn't have been more shocked if you'd announced you'd taken up with a barfly and wanted a divorce!"

"A *divorce*? You will *never* get rid of me, Henry Clay Berkeley!"

"The shock would have been similar. Speaking of pregnancy, should you be walking?"

"I am in no way *damaged*. I am only pregnant. I am a strong, healthy girl."

"You can walk around and . . . everything?"

"Certainly! I learned of my pregnancy only days ago, but I have seen an obstetrician and I am in excellent condition to carry a baby." She muzzled my ear and whispered, "*Everything* is possible until the seventh month. Isn't that great?"

It was -- then again, maybe not, depending on how many amorous sessions in a given day and night her pregnancy generated. No normal male could hack the degree of conjugal attention she had whipped on me over the last few days -- teenage blood pressure and heart aside.

The *Playa de la Sol* hotel had been remodeled and was even fancier than when I was last in Puerto Santa Cruz. The lobby, which also provided entrance to the bar and restaurant area, was thick with potted plants, heavy Spanish furniture and wee cubbyholes fitted with a table and two chairs. The floor was covered with glazed, reddish tile. The white, stucco walls were decorated with arts and crafts and paintings of Spanish scenery. There were the usual swords, battleaxes and halberds on the walls commonly seen in Spanish establishments, but no weaponry such as jawbones of asses, dried kitty cats, dogging wrenches and the like.

Master Chief Hector Seeley, our sponsor, had done himself proud in selecting our beach front room. Patty fell instantly in love with the large, airy room the moment she stepped through the door.

That was good, considering we had to live there until the current occupant of our cottage-to-be transferred.

Patty bubbled on and on as she swept through the room, touching every piece of furniture as she went. "Oh, Clay-honey, look at the painted tiles running along the wall! Look at the spacious bathroom! Look at the French windows overlooking the beach! Look at the size of that bed! Oh, we have a TV. I can learn Spanish and look at the lovely beach and ocean at the same time!" She hugged herself, cocked her wavy-curly, taffy haired head toward her left shoulder and gave me a sly, broad-toothed grin. "We have been awake for hours on that darned airplane while flying across five time zones. Clay-dearest, let us take a nap!"

We did . . . but not directly. The little minx's rambunctious maneuvering in the huge bed told me she no longer believed I'd almost slipped my cable and shifted my flag to The Big Canoe Club in the Sky a couple of hours earlier.

Patty fell instantly asleep once she turned loose, but I lay there with both portholes wide open, worrying. My concerns when initially contemplating making love with Patty were two fold and for those reasons I had kept my hands off her, more or less, for about three months after we met.

Things she said shortly after we met led me to believe her knowledge of birth control consisted of avoiding cabbage patches and locking her knees together to prevent storks from landing. I surely did not want a little Berkeley-Patterson wood's colt crawling about the terrain, although that would have been in keeping with Berkeley family tradition.

Issues of the first Berkeley couple in our family line were certainly wood's colts. That couple formalized their marriage vows in 1709 by jumping over a stick behind tobacco bales on a Norfolk, Virginia dock before heading out, flank-speed legs, toward the mountains of what was then Western Virginia. Their trek to the rugged, almost uninhibited mountains was necessary to prevent a Tidewater planter from taking custody of Margaret Louise Tinny as an indentured servant. The fact that both had arrived on the morning tide, but in different ships, and had not previously met, did not affect their forming a lasting relationship even though there was no record of their marriage having been formalized by clergy. They produced a baker's dozen children, built their first plot of land into fair-sized holding and lived together in harmony for eighty-one years. They died one day apart.

The second concern was that Patty was so darned tiny! She was not skinny, but well-built with every part of her beautiful body having been fabricated by God's people fitters in miniature. It seemed impossible for a woman of her size to successfully carry a baby to term, let alone give birth

The first concern sorted itself out nicely; she did understand birth control despite her obvious innocence.

The second concern disappeared, at least in my mind, when I informed Patty that I wanted children about as much as I wanted a third Purple Heart. Her desire to have children surfaced again after she claimed sightings of an old lady ghost milling about smartly in our orchard and bedroom. These occurrences followed directly after she had read old family journals and my mother's diaries, which Patty said contained entries of similar sightings.

Supposedly my mother had seen an aged female ghost holding a cradle and smiling at her just before she learned she was pregnant with me. The same ghost, thought by my mother to be the Matriarch of the Berkeley Clan, mustered in and smiled at Patty one night. If the old gal was holding a cradle, Patty *neglected* to tell me that part!

Nosy darned ghosts! If they were so concerned about maintaining the Berkeley Line, they should have put more heat on their descendants to be fruitful and multiply. Natural death and death by disease, injury, war, and an inordinate number of female births caused the number of Berkeley males to fall to where I was the last of the line.

In keeping with tradition of a sponsor, Hec and Lisa Ann Seeley took us to the Sea Dragon Club for supper that evening. It would have been normal for them to have taken us to the Chief Petty Officer's Club, except Naval Station Santa Cruz had no CPO club. CPO and officer's clubs, unlike clubs for lower-ranking personnel, are not fully supported by the Navy and cease operations when they do not sustain at least a tiny profit. The officer's club reduced in size to a room in the Bachelor Officer Quarters and the CPO club was turned into the Sea Dragon Club, for the four top enlisted ranks -- an all-ranks club in actuality. The CPO's reserved one room with a tiny bar for their private use so they could weep, wail and gnash their teeth without junior personnel overhearing them.

Patty, frothing at the mouth to experience Spanish culture, expressed disappointment when I told her where they were taking us. She perked up and appeared quite pleased when she viewed the club's Spanish decor. The immaculately covered tables with heavy silver cutlery and a multitude of crystal goblets were exactly as she'd seen depicted in books about Spain

The kind and friendly Spanish waiter, quite adept at recognizing a total greenhorn, took Patty under tow and steered her toward paella -- a dish of meat, seafood, rice and vegetables. Patty dug in and gobbled her paella with gusto.

Hec ordered a good sherry to polish off our meal that had already encompassed a number of glasses of superb local wine. Patty went deep in conversation with Lisa Ann concerning the care and feeding of a house in Spain. I feared much of what Patty learned would fall by the wayside before morning, her being tipsy on one glass of wine and a sip or two of the brandy.

I'd heard pregnant women should not drink alcohol and so informed Patty soon after we sat down. That caused Lisa Ann to take me to task and inform me that Spanish women drank wine with every meal and their children were born quite healthy. She backed up her argument by stating the infant death rate was much lower in Spain than in the United States. I, being wise, at times, shut the hell up!

"Clay, I'm retiring from this billet." Hec said, after we finished our meal. "We're going to use our retirement to sail around the world in a small yacht we had built in Cadiz. I have to take delivery soon. When can you relieve me?"

I, having had a tad more wine than I needed, faked a salute and said: "Master Chief Seeley, you stand relieved!"

CHAPTER TWO

REPORT FOR DUTY

I'd visited Naval Communication Station Santa Cruz to iron out long-haul communications problems when I was aboard *Forrestal* in the Mediterranean, so I was marginally familiar with the command. I mustered in at the quarterdeck, gave my service record and orders to the female first class petty officer standing officer of the deck watch. I then went to the operations department office where I found my new boss already at her desk. Strange that. Really strange, considering that it was not yet 0600.

"Good morning, Commander. I'm Clay Berkeley, reporting for duty."

"I gathered that, Master Chief. Welcome aboard! I'm Lucy Stoutmaster. Would you like some coffee? I just brewed a pot." the Lieutenant Commander said, rising from behind her desk.

"I'd love a cup of java -- two or three, in fact, it being zero-dark-thirty." I said, smiling at her. My initial impression was that she exhibited considerable class. Her uniform appearance was immaculate. She was a mite overweight, but pretty. I was fairly certain I was going to like this woman.

We had a cup of coffee, then another, while discussing the department and the command, during which she asked something odd. "Both Master Chief Seeley and Captain Keene know you, Master Chief. I've heard many good things about you. And some not so good concerning your escapades ashore. I do have one question. Are you on a twilight cruise? I mean, did you come here to retire?"

"I have sixteen years plus in the Navy, so I will have about twenty years of service when my tour here is up. I don't intend to retire until I serve at least thirty years."

"Wonderful!"

Damn strange comment, that.

Hec mustered in at 0755, briefed me on the department, showed me where the publications, instructions and document files were kept, told me what a great billet I had and how easy I was going to have it compared to sea duty. He then conducted his personal abandon ship drill. I could not help but think he resembled a Nazi leaving Germany in 1945. I thought it quite odd he did not provide information as to his daily routine and made no mention of situations that were hanging fire.

I expended the entire morning checking myself into various organizations and departments aboard the Naval Communications Station and Naval Station Santa Cruz of which the communications station was a tenant command. There were so darn many of them: disbursing, that kept my pay record and paid me up to date; hospital that kept my medical records into which they filed the consultation sheet from my reluctant visit the previous day; dental department, that immediately scheduled me for a checkup appointment; supply department so they would readily recognize the new official thief in town; morale, welfare and recreation department, in case I wanted to take tours, ride horses, utilize hobby shops; and a host of places not likely to see me again until I checked out of the command three years later. My last stop aboard the naval station was to the senior chaplain who gave me a stack of brochures that discussed booze, drugs, cussing and other items of a nasty nature

I returned to the communications station around 1300 to meet with the executive officer and commanding officer.

The XO, a full commander, was likely on his last tour of duty considering he was many pounds overweight, wore a mussed uniform, hadn't shaved particularly well that morning and was, in general, a wreck! He didn't appear to be making any great effort to move paper through the command, not from the stacks and stacks of documents littering his desk.

"My name is Harlan Webster. I understand you just completed a successful tour of recruiting duty. Tell me, Master Chief -- do you know anything about shore communications?"

There were a couple of little dings in my transfer evaluation that suggested I was less than perfect at carrying out recruiting directives, but nothing that showed I'd been fired for inadvertently informing God-world that Navy recruiting procedures was a "Joke." The XO had apparently not picked up on the dings, they being sort of buried in verbiage that suggested I could walk upon water without sinking past my ankles. But his comment told me he had at least scanned my service jacket.

"I'm no expert at shore communications, Commander. Most of my billets were at sea. This is my first communications station, although I've worked closely with stations world-wide to get the support I needed at sea."

"I expect you to shake down quickly, Master Chief. There are serious, serious problems in operations department. I expect you to resolve them ASAP!"

"What sort of problems, Commander?"

"For one, the department does not support me as it should. Your boss, Lieutenant Commander Stoutmaster, seems not to understand her responsibilities. She is never prepared for the morning briefing. Another problem is rampant fornication among the young sailors results in a significant number of pregnant, unmarried females. This problem exists throughout the command, but your department has the highest percentage of pregnant, unwed females. I contribute this to a distinct lack of moral leadership on the part of your boss. The drinking of alcohol is also a problem."

I'd have been mighty shook up if I had some pregnant *males*! I'd also have been concerned if the young sailors were not concerned with lust and liberty. Drinking could be a problem, if carried to excess. I had my qualification sheets signed off on that!

"I'll work on the pregnancy and drinking problems. The relationship between you and the department head is between you and her, whatever it is you perceive."

"I do not perceive anything! I know! Tell me, do *you* approve of females in senior billets?"

"Do we have a choice? There is not a great deal of interest among young men to join any of the services and many are rejected for mental, moral or medical reasons. There are simply not enough qualified males running loose to man the Navy. I know that, having just spent two years trying to beat qualified male recruits out of the brush. DOD did a study that showed only about one-third of age-eligible men qualify for the services, many fail because they're obese. Females are more prone to enlist than males and more are qualified education-wise. Women do well in the Navy. I've not worked many female sailors, but those I did were four-oh, really outstanding. Good leaders too."

"I do not agree! Women do not have the fire in their guts to perform as well as males in extreme situations. They simply do not have the male 'strap on the sword and charge' attitude! I am uncertain what *your* attitude is, but I expect to see some fire lit beneath the operations department and I expect it near-term!

"I believe it stupid, detailing a female to a billet that rightfully belongs to a male!" The XO launched into a tirade concerning women in the Navy and why he did not consider them suitable for anything except clerical duties. He abruptly stopped his rant, laid a sour look on me and said, "The captain has spoken of you. He declined to discuss what his ship accomplished while you were aboard, but implied it was highly classified and important to the national interest. I suspect it will be old home week between the two of you, but I want you to understand that your being buddy-buddy with the commanding officer will cut no ice with *me*!"

That was a two-way street; he cut no ice with me either.

The captain came from behind his desk, grabbed me by the hand and slapped me on the back. "Welcome aboard, Master Chief! We've sailed many a mile since the good ship *King*! I have been looking forward to your arrival. We badly need your leadership and management skills in the operations department. Let me get you a cup of coffee. It's good Navy stuff, not that sissy designer coffee sailors in the New, Modern Navy want to drink.

"Oh, I have a copy of the citation for *King's* Navy Unit Commendation, in event you have not seen it. It contains a well-written lead-in paragraph, but the body of the citation says only: '*King engaged in classified operations at the direction of the Chief of Naval Operations, the Joint Chiefs of Staff and the President of the United States.*' That is all it says, but we know and can take great satisfaction in what our ship accomplished."

The captain and I had a nice chat about the highly classified mission our ship had conducted, where old shipmates were stationed, who had advanced and who had not, and for what reason. We basically held a gossip party, known in the Navy as scuttlebutt.

It *was* old home week, but the captain was a taskmaster who would never permit a less than competent subordinate to call in markers from a past working relationship. The manner in which *King's* crew carried out their duties was primary in the mind of the captain back then, and I had no reason to think it would be different in Santa Cruz. We were in total agreement on that point. The mission came first!

The next chuckhole in the path, the first being the XO, was when I attempted to get to know the operations department secretary, whose attitude was sulky. She enlightened me that she was not a secretary, but was an 'Administrative Assistant,' whatever the hell that was. All I learned was her name was Doris Harris and that she was a temporary hire, rather than a permanent employee. I wondered if she might not have had a close relationship with Hec Seeley, so I inquired as to how she was going to feel since he retired.

"I hardly knew he was here."

"What did you do for him? Filing? Typing?"

"He never bothered me!"

"Well, what *do* you do?"

"I do a lot of things!"

The grip and grin session with my administrative assistant being less than satisfactory, I prowled around the office reading various documents and gleaning through the file cabinets for the next couple of hours. No one came to see me about anything. I knew almost nothing about the 225 person department comprised of six divisions and an earth satellite station, but I knew it couldn't be operating that smoothly. Then Doris threw a stack of paper on my desk, all in a jumble. I was really learning to like this woman

"What is all of this?"

"The afternoon guard mail from ship's office. You initial it and then I take it to *Missus* Stoutmaster."

I wondered about the emphasis on the *Missus,* rather than her saying *Commander Stoutmaster,* but left that alone. "What do you mean, I initial it? Isn't it for me to take action?"

"Seeley just initialed it and I took it to her."

"Leave it here. I'll decide what to do with it."

"My work day ends at five! I usually leave early."

"Not today, Missus Harris. Not today."

She huffed back to her desk in a cubbyhole adjoining the room and started buffing her nails. She'd done that for a while earlier, followed that with addressing a box of Christmas cards, then engaged in a lengthy, tittering telephone conversation with an unknown party. Yep, I was becoming fond of Doris Harris.

There was nothing of earth destroying importance in the stack. There were a couple of request chits from sailors requesting advancement to seaman after having served their time in grade as seamen apprentice; a shore patrol report concerning a sailor found drunk and disorderly in the city of Jerez; a chit requesting Captain's Mast and a few other minor cats and dogs.

None of the request chits had been properly routed via their chain-of-command. Some were signed. Some were missing check marks and/or comments recommending, or not recommending, approval.

The chit requesting captain's mast did not carry the reason the sailor wanted a formal hearing with the captain. It was his right to request a mast and it was his right to withhold the reason why he wished to see the captain, but this never happened. The reason a sailor wanted to see the captain was nearly always to air a grievance and it was impossible to keep the nature of the complaint secret. Therefore, the sailor's supervisors would have known the reason and quietly passed the reason up the chain-of-command, either by note or telephone. Neither appeared to have happened and Hec had said nothing.

I wrote notes outlining my displeasure in the handling of the chits and called Doris to my desk. "These chits require additional work before being forwarded. Those that requested advancement appeared to have lurked in someone's basket for more than a week. That is not acceptable. All being equal, they should be advanced now. I'm sure the sailors could use the money. I've written notes on each chit, explaining the deficiency. I want you to put them in the guard mail . . . no, I want you to hand carry them to the divisions concerned and tell the responsible chiefs I want them back tomorrow morning. I'll call the chief who forwarded the one for request mast and the chief of the person on whom the report chit was written."

"Why don't you just give them to Missus Stoutmaster? Seeley did."

"Because, Missus Harris, it is not the commander's job to chase folks around. Items that go to her should be ready for final action. From now on, we'll ensure all is Bristol fashion before she gets paperwork of any sort. Speaking of which . . . you said you are an administrative assistant. If so, you should have noticed the discrepancies in these chits and brought them to the attention of those responsible. I would not expect that effort of a mere secretary, but I do expect it of an assistant."

"You are causing unnecessary work!"

"How so?"

"By placing an additional burden on me!"

"Gee, I'm sorry about that, but I'll be giving you a lot more work as I learn what is needed. Shouldn't be a burden as you seem to have a lot of time on your hands."

"I'll tell my husband if you overwork me!"

"And who, may I ask, is your husband?"

"He's the supply officer for Naval Station Santa Cruz. A full commander!"

"I'm greatly impressed. Now, run along and get the chits to those concerned."

I needed to look into this temporary hire thing, like ASAP. I knew it was virtually impossible to fire a civil servant, but wasn't certain where a temporary hire fit into the picture. I knew one thing. I wasn't going to put up with a lazy, incompetent secretary such as I had in recruiting. That one was the sole support of her family because her husband was flat useless and I didn't have the heart to fire her. Not this time, Buccaneer. Doris shared a commander's salary.

Commander Stoutmaster came into my office around 1630, looking rather agitated. "Where is Missus Harris? Did she leave to get her hair done, take her cat to the vet, or what?"

"I sent her to deliver some stuff. I don't expect to see her until quitting time. She had to take one item to the receiver site."

17

"Darn, she did not pick up the afternoon guard mail!"

"Yes, she did, Commander. I took care of it."

"*You* took care of it?"

"There was almost nothing ready for you. There were some improperly forwarded request chits that I had Missus Harris return -- and a chit requesting captain's mast with no word on what the sailor wanted or needed. I called the chief of that division, but she wasn't there. I told her leading petty officer the chief was to call me ASAP, ready to brief on the problem. I see no need to bother the captain if the problem can be rectified within this department. There was a report chit for drunk and disorderly on a girl who works in the message center. I sent that to her chief. If her record is clean, all he needs to do is counsel her, chew on her a bit maybe, depending on her attitude and past conduct. I'll schedule her for Drinker's Hack It School if she has a history of alcohol problems. Other than that, nothing but circuit continuity reports that showed no problems or outages. Those are in your basket."

"You bother with minor paperwork? Do master chief's do that?"

"I don't consider it minor. Sailors wanted something, or needed something. In my Navy, things are handled at their proper level. They only go up the chain-of-command as far as need be. Sending everything up the chain indicates things are not pusser in an organization. Is that the way you see it?"

"Why, yes it is! Keep doing as you just did. *Please!*"

The following morning, mainly to satisfy my curiosity, I came in at 0430, picked up a stack of messages that arrived during the night and gleaned through them. Certain people, including me, received a copy of every message addressed to the communications station and to those addressed to local commands for which we provided communications, except for Top Secret and highly sensitive messages, both of which were courier routed.

I found only two that required an answer from the operations department. I drafted what I believed to be appropriate responses and put the drafts aside. Several messages contained implications of forthcoming evolutions that could, or would, impact our command, so I wrote notes outlining the impact, what I recommended we do, and put them aside too.

The commander came tearing through the passageway hatch just before 0600. Suspicions confirmed; she was coming in at zero-dark-thirty every day. I poured her a cup of coffee, then another for myself and walked into her office, which adjoined mine. "Good morning, Commander. A bit early to work, huh?"

"It is not by choice! The XO requires I give him a briefing at 0800 daily before the regular department head briefing with the CO at 0900. He spends the entire hour nit picking and generally ruins my entire day. That never happens at the regular brief. The captain asks questions, gives orders and admonishes when needed, but he never nit-picks. The skipper offers guidance too. He is easy to work for so long as I give him a sincere effort. The XO . . . ugh!"

"Are you the only department head from whom he requires a separate briefing?" I asked, thinking I already knew the answer.

"Yes, I am. He claims I do not know my job. I didn't at first, but I do now. He seems not to like women and I sincerely believe he enjoys putting me in a corner and stabbing at me. I feel as helpless around him as Ferdinand the Bull in a bull ring. I *never* understand *what* the XO wants!"

"Well, look, Commander, I just went through the messages from last night. You get the same messages I do. Both of us getting the same messages is a huge waste of paper. So why don't you glean through your own stack this morning, look at what I pulled out of mine, what I answered, the notes on messages, and so forth. Let me know if we are on the same wavelength. If we are, we should work with only one stack of messages, rather than us both getting a stack. I'll make a fresh pot of coffee while you're doing that."

The Commander threw up her hands. "A master chief making coffee? *Imagine!*"

After about forty-five minutes, the Commander stuck her head out of the window in the bulkhead, grinning like a possum in a blackberry thicket. "I'll take another coffee, Master Chief, if you are still in the café business."

She took a sip of her coffee and said, "You noticed a message of importance I'd have overlooked. And I now understand each situation, thanks to your notes. Also, you answered one that I would not have, thinking it of marginal importance. I'd have been yelled at by the XO, for not doing so. You really know about things, don't you?"

"I know about *some* things. I know how briefings go, having given them to a commodore and an admiral while on their staffs. I'm no whiz on shore communications, so I could easily overlook something. I almost chucked the one about the space shuttle frequency change, then remembered hearing about emergency landing sites. I suspected the Naval Air Station runway was designated as an emergency landing site and checked with technical control. Sure enough, we are responsible for those transceivers."

"Well, I'm the best prepared for the briefings this morning than I've been. Thank you, Master Chief Berkeley. Thank you so very much!"

The commander came floating back into her office around 1030, simply bubbling! "Master Chief, would you like my autograph?"

"Say **Waaat**?"

"My autograph. You are looking at the female reincarnation of *Manolete*, a famous Spanish bullfighter!

"Oh, you should have seen it! The XO would charge, I'd take a quick look at the message concerned, glance at your note, and then stab him! Charge! Stab! Charge! Stab! Oh, I won every one this morning! He sulked throughout the CO's briefing

20

and tried to nit-pick me after the briefing and I stabbed him yet again! Master Chief, award me both ears and the tail!"

"Bravo! Ole! Good show! Whatever.

"Commander, I'm an early riser and an early to work sort. My wife says I am a Type A Personality, whatever that is. I'll be in around 0600 every day, so there is no need for you to do that. Fast as you digest what you read, you could come in around 0715 and have plenty of time to prepare for the briefs. You never know, you might get blessed and the XO will leave you alone, once he decides you have all your shi . . . er, stuff in one sea bag. What do you think?"

"I like it! We will try that tomorrow and see what happens."

"Same on weekends, Commander. I'll make a check of the messages and the night's happenings, or I'll designate a chief to do it for us. And, by the way, if you happen to have administrative work hanging fire that you haven't been able to get to, I suggest you stop being selfish and spread the wealth around."

"I'm going to *like* working with you, Master Chief. I believe I told you I never worked directly with a master chief before Santa Cruz. The captain is certainly correct. You are *nothing* like your predecessor!"

"I appreciate your comments. I believe the captain would tell you I'm not known for blowing smoke up anybody's as . . . er, blowing smoke, but I'm going to enjoy working with you too. All you need is a little help."

"You can say that again! Yes, you can certainly say that!"

I kept Doris Harris on the jump over the next few days. The woman was in bad need of positive direction! When I had nothing for her to do, I dreamed something up. She was never friendly, but she got out of her sulk. I never gave her time to sulk!

I met various chiefs in passing when I toured the work centers on my second day in the command, but I figured some of the CPO's barely knew who I was. There was a need to let them know how I operated to prevent misunderstandings that could cause hard feelings, or worse. I therefore scheduled a meeting with all of the CPO's on Friday afternoon.

I had three senior chiefs and eight chief petty officers in the operations department, four of whom were assigned rotating eight-hour shifts as communications watch officer. The others were in charge of divisions.

When they were all seated in the conference room, enjoying the sticky buns and coffee I'd provided, I started my spiel.

"Good afternoon, Ladies and Gentlemen. For those who have not met me, I am Clay Berkeley, the new-on-the-ground operations master chief. I've never served at a communications station, so a lot of this is new to me. I will, therefore, be calling upon each of you for advice. If you believe I am screwing up, tell me so. I may not agree, but I will listen. Be candid with me. Beat around the bush, or hide something, and I'll find a *real good* billet for you, like master at arms of the chow hall! Intentionally lie to me – you're gone!

"Because I will be calling on each of you for assistance, I need to know something of your background, past billets and such. Please do not use this as an opportunity to surface items you want in your next evaluation. Rest assured that I *will* know what to write in those! I will, of course, request your input when evaluations are due.

"I started my career in the Amphibious Force. I didn't love the Gator Navy! For those of you who served in the amphibious ships . . . well, there are destroyer sailors and then they are the others. I managed to ball suc . . . er, pardon me, weasel my way off gator freighters after I made second class. I then served in the destroyer *Frank E. Evans* as leading radioman under the firm direction of Master Chief Seeley, who was then a chief. I transferred to *Forrestal* in a technical controller billet as a first class. I wasn't aboard but a few months before I made chief and was transferred to the destroyer-leader *King*, where our CO was skipper.

"After *King* I served a tour working with the Spanish Navy in Madrid as a sort of liaison between our two navies, working out compatibility issues. I then went to Vietnam in a communications billet, but ended up driving PBR's. These are fast, heavily armed, river patrol craft, for those of you not familiar with PBR's. I had some months as communications officer for a destroyer squadron, spent a few weeks helping devise a course in Quality Control and Monitoring, then a year-long tour in a cruiser-destroyer group.

"Oh, I've been trying to forget! I served on recruiting duty before I came here. The one good thing that happened to me there was I met my first and only bride, who I married three months ago. In event any of you are thinking of applying for recruiting -- don't! Not unless you are deep into pain, such as engaging in acts involving the use of chains, bull whips, ice picks, vice grips and the like. If you enjoy such things you *will* enjoy recruiting duty."

That comment tore them up! The female chiefs were still giggling long after the males quieted down.

"Please stand, starting with the chief at your left, tell me who you are and what you've done since you first started sucking the U.S. Government sugar tit . . . uh, sorry, Ladies."

I was a mite disappointed when the chiefs finished giving synopsis of their careers. The eight male CPO's had a combined total of less than thirty years of sea duty; two had never served on a ship. One of the females had sea time aboard a submarine tender. I had to assume they knew their jobs as related to shore communications, but our ability to support the fleet was in question because so few of them knew much about how ships operated. I was surrounded by Shore Pukes!

"I'm not big on misunderstandings, so I am going to lay out how I operate and what I expect of you. I believe you will learn I'm easy to work with -- so long as you do what you are supposed to do, and take care of your people.

"Most of you have taken courses in leadership and management. Let me tell what everything you learned in those courses boils down to: *'First the mules, then the troops . . . then the officers!'* That quote comes from an 1883 book titled: *The*

Army Officer's Guide. If you first ensure the mission is accomplished, then care for your subordinates, and finally, take care of you own needs, everything else will fall into place. The Marines say it another way: *'Never eat before the troops eat. Never sleep before the troops sleep.'*

"I have learned in the field of telecommunications that nothing bad usually happens when it is busy. Bad things happen when it is quiet. That happens, I believe, because folks tend to kick back when it is quiet and fail to keep a firm grip on the tiller. This is serious, regardless of the field of employment, but screwing up in telecommunications can kill ships and people if orders are not delivered correctly and on-time. Lesser situations also occur when things do not happen in a timely manner. This has happened to me when I needed urgent support from communications stations and couldn't get answers after their working hours because no one with sufficient authority was around to make a decision. It is zero fun bobbing around the briny deep, needing support and not getting it. That tends to get the guns of your CO leveled directly at you.

"I expect communications watch officers to read every message addressed to this command and do a sampling of messages flowing over the circuits in case something hot is brewing.

"In case there is doubt about the chain-of-command, I am division officer for the Communications Watch Officers. If you can't contact me, contact Commander Stoutmaster. If you can't contact her, contact the XO or CO! If nobody can be found, make a decision, right or wrong, but make a decision!

"Same thing when you sample messages flowing across the circuits. If something is breaking loose in the fleet or elsewhere, it will likely impact this command. Do not fear to call the captain direct if something hot is breaking! You are his *personal* representative when you stand watch as CWO.

"I will be living in room 107 in the *Playa de la Sol* hotel, for the foreseeable future. Call me when you have any doubt at all. I will never repeat *never* chew you for calling me, no matter how ignorant a question may be or what time it is, day or night. To keep it simple -- if you have a nagging feeling you should notify or confer with someone, do it!

"Over the past days, I have seen God-World and one-half of Santa Cruz trooping into the commander's office to ask her something or tell her something. This stops *now*! All queries and problems will be routed via me. She ought not be bothered by anybody, except me, her division officers, and those above her.

"There will be weekends when, for whatever reason, I will task one of the day working chiefs to fill in for me to check messages and the night's happenings. Notify someone in authority if needed. Remember, when you act on my behalf, you speak with my voice and I will back you to the hilt. I served with our captain in *King* and I know he will do the same. Read the messages, take action as needed and notify someone if necessary.

"Questions?"

A skinny, runt of a chief stood and asked, "What if my division officer tells me to take something directly to the commander? What do I tell him?"

"Tell him exactly what I said. If he questions that, tell him to call me. He has direct access to the commander. If he deems it important enough to brief her directly, he can do it personally."

A female senior chief hit me right between the eyes with a shocker. "I can understand you wanting a weekend off, Master Chief, but why can't the commander come in and check the messages?"

It took a bit to get my gear locker re-stowed before I answered her. It was okay for me to come in on my off-time. It was okay for the commander to come in on her off-time. It was not okay for the senior chief to come in on her off-time. Her question put her directly into my sights unless I later discovered her question did not reflect her attitude. I'd keep an eye on her!

"Do you have a glimmer of how much the commander has on her plate, Senior Chief? Probably not. One of my main tasks, the biggest, is to support her so she does not need to damn near live in her office, as she's been doing. She should not be doing work below her level either. She operates at the executive level, not middle management where we fall. That means she makes decisions that impact on the mission of the station. Other than that and keeping those above her informed, she should be able to sit behind her desk and dream grand dreams!

"I thank you for being here today. Feel free to see me about anything -- business, personal, whatever. My hatch is open."

No one had mentioned Hec Seeley and I was beginning to wonder what he had done to earn his beans and bacon during his tour at Santa Cruz. I wondered if their silence had something to do with him telling me he had refused a formal retirement ceremony. I understood none of that. Hec was a top-drawer chief when we were in *Frank E. Evans*.

Patty and I had a great weekend visiting towns near Puerto Santa Cruz. We checked out an empty bull ring, four huge Catholic churches and toured towns, including *Jerez*, from which the English word *'Sherry'* is derived. There we observed the stages of wine fermentation in glass fronted barrels stacked in a pyramid, one on top of another and attended a short briefing and movie on the making of wine. I sampled the *copitas* of wine they offered in the hospitality room while Patty sipped only a tiny glass of a pale, dry wine.

We took our Saturday evening meal at one of the open-air, seafood restaurants that lined the waterfront of Cadiz. We ate seafood ranging from mussels to *langouste*. Patty was a healthy eater, but her pregnancy turned her into a real trencher-woman and she ate twice as much as I did. I started to pour her a glass of wine at the start of the meal, but she covered the glass with her palm. I reminded her that the naval station's OB-GYN doctor had confirmed that wine was good for her.

"Yes, he said that and Spanish ladies at the hotel lectured me on the value of wine in building the blood when pregnant. I believe all are correct, but wine does not taste good just now. Something to do with the baby, I suspect. Speaking of the bab --"

"Look! Patty, see that brass plate on the wall behind your chair? It says Columbus watered the *Santa Maria*, the *Nina* and the *Pinta* at this very quay wall. We could be sitting in the exact same spot as Columbus!"

Patty gave me a strange look, then turned at looked at the brass plate. "That is interesting, but I want to talk about the baby. There are many things we need to discuss and I --"

"Come on, Kitten. We have time to visit a huge department store just down the road. That store makes Macy's look like a village store in West Virginia!"

"I have never visited Macy's. I have never been to New York! I want --"

"You read a lot. You know what I mean. Come on!"

Patty trapped me in our huge bed that night, just after she took care of any lusty desires that might have been lingering in my overused body. She straddled me naked, and put her hands on both sides of my face, then shook my head to and fro. She sure was a strong little devil, for her size! "Clay, we must speak about our child!" She exhibited a weak, little grin. "Which do you want? A boy or a girl?"

Actually, I wanted neither.

"Clay! Which do you *want*?" she demanded, after I failed to answer.

"I really don't care, Patty. I've never given children thought, one way or the other. I'm happy that you are healthy, but I wish you were not pregnant."

"But . . . but, any healthy woman should be pregnant after as many times as we have, you *Know*! Children are the purpose for the basic act, not pleasure. Everybody knows *that*!"

"Maybe you're right, but most folks do not have children unless they want them, like I told you one night and again a month or so ago. If you hadn't checked your pills in the trash can, I wouldn't be going half-crazy with worry!"

Patty threw the rear of her right hand against her lips, a common Patty gesture when she was shocked or confused. "*You* want me to have an *abortion*, don't you?"

"No, Kitten, I would never ask you to do something that's against your beliefs. The baby is, I suppose, fact. We will have to live with that."

"Well, by-damn-in-hell, you had better believe we will!" Patty yelled, then did a pixie weight stomp into the bathroom.

I turned over and pretended I was asleep. I had, in fact, just fallen asleep when I felt a tiny hand running across my shoulder.

"Are you asleep?" Patty asked, in a soft, wavering voice.

"Not now." I said, turning to face her.

"Do you want a divorce?" Lots more wavering that time.

"Why in the name of John Paul Jones would I want a divorce? If there is anything in creation I want more than you, I'd like to know what the hell it is!"

"You are so unhappy about the baby, so maybe it would be better if you just got rid of me." No wavering that time. She had gotten the answer she was looking for.

I pulled her little head against my chest and cuddled her to me. "Look, you mouse-sized maniac. What I am worried about is you -- not the baby!"

"Women have babies every day -- millions per year. I do not understand your concern."

"Patty, honey, you do know how babies get into the world, don't you? The physical process?"

"I was raised on a farm!"

"What if the baby weighs more than a few pounds? What is that going to put you through? Is it even possible?"

"Of course it is possible! I believe the average weight is about six pounds. Thousands and thousands of small women successfully give birth. Why do you believe I cannot?"

"I worry about it. I was worried about making love with you the first time, for the same reason. You are so tiny. It hurt you, didn't it?"

"That was the greatest night of my life! It hurt only for a moment, after which it was glorious. Childbirth will be a much greater pain, but will be magnificent. Women who have given birth say they forget the pain as soon as they nurse the baby." Patty hugged herself. "Watching the birth of a lamb or a calf is almost too much to comprehend. The birth of a human baby must be mind boggling!"

I prayed she was correct, but the size of her waist and hips did not convince me. I, too, had seen animals give birth when I was a kid on our farm. I had also watched a baby being born on a junk we'd stopped in a Vietnam river to check for weapons smuggling. The sight made me sick!.

CHAPTER THREE

NOT SO VERY GOOD, BUCCANEER

Things slowed to a crawl as *Feliz Navadad* approached. Puerto Santa Cruz lamp posts and streets were decorated with huge, red bows and clusters of lights shaped into stars, bells and flowers. Americans and Spaniards were in a jolly holiday mood. Even the telecommunications world slowed as the fleet and ashore commands geared down for the holiday leave period. Christmas was in the air.

Things were going well at work. My administrative assistant squared away her gear locker and made a sincere effort to please me, even though her dislike remained obvious. If she had complained to her commander husband, he likely told her that master chief petty officers were not to be trifled with! Folks stopped bypassing me to see Commander Stoutmaster who was fresh and rested now that she was working normal shore duty hours. The XO has gone into sullen retreat since she started briefing him from my notes. He shifted his guns and was now heard bellowing at the female administrative officer in ship's office.

Patty and I received an invitation to visit from the lieutenant commander who was vacating the beach front cottage, for which we had already signed the leasing contract coordinated by the Naval Station Housing Office.   We jumped at his thoughtful gesture and drove the rented Seat to the house one cool, foggy evening.

Patty's breath drew in sharply when she saw the whitewashed, five-room cottage with black, filigreed, wrought iron grill work that both decorated and protected the windows and doors. "Oh, Clay-honey, fog is drifting from the sea through those flat-topped pine trees! I will never stay inside that house!"

Her comment shocked me all the way to my keel plates! The house didn't appear spooky and she wasn't afraid of ghosts. She had consorted with a flock of them at our farm on Berkeley's Knob in West Virginia, apparently discussing the need to get pregnant so the Berkeley Line would continue. (See Snug Harbor, Book I - The Launching.)

"What's wrong with it, Kitten? It's beautiful the way it sets so close to the water with trees all around.   Listen to the ocean roar as the waves curl up on the beach. Think what it will be like in warm weather when we're sipping a cool sangria under those trees while watching the sun set over the sea."

Patty gave me one of her impish grins. "I will never be inside the house because I will be spending *all* of my time on the patio, beneath the trees or on the beach! Stay inside? With scenery like that filling my eyes? Not bloody likely, Buccaneer, to use one of your phrases!

"Just think, dearest, the baby will be nearly three years old when we transfer from here.   He will be an accomplished swimmer by then!"

I reached and patted her belly, which had not, of course, started to show. "How do you know it will be a he?"

"Margaret Louise, your long-ago grandmother told me so."

I had gotten the impression from Hec that the occupant of the house was married. Not yet he wasn't, but there was a Spanish girl present who would have rated as a 'Nine' in the mind of a monk. Nati was obviously not a casual visitor and she surely had designs on his carcass. I knew that from having seen the same, strange looks from Patty when she was planning to bark my tree. It amused me to see that happening to another male and I could barely keep from snickering when she locked her flashing, green eyes on him.

The rooms in the cottage were small, but more than adequate for Patty, our future rug rat, our two pets and myself. The inside walls were painted a clean, sunny shade. Reddish tiles covered the floors. A cone-shaped fireplace, in which was burning a nut-smelling wood, filled one corner of the living room. It looked like a comfortable house.

I had a glass of wine with the lieutenant commander while Patty and his amour had a glass of sparkling water from a spring reputed to be located just below the ice-covered peaks of the northwestern mountains of Spain. The commander once served as weather guesser in *Forrestal*, but was aboard after my tour in her. After our chat, he took us to meet the neighbors on both sides of the house, one being our future landlord.

Both couples were middle-aged, prosperous looking folks who turned from friendly to delighted when Nati told them Patty was pregnant. The two women snapped onto Patty and led her and Nati into one of the houses. That left the lieutenant commander and me standing with the two Spanish men. One of them went into his house, broke out a jug of *Vino Riojo* and we drank that on his enclosed patio that had a fireplace in which was also burning a nut-smelling wood. When the wives returned, the Spaniards broke out some *tapas* and insisted we finish another bottle of vino.

It was quite late when we returned to our hotel.

Patty snuggled tightly against me and sighed.

"What's wrong, Kitten?"

"Nothing, dearest. It was a lovely evening. I like our neighbors so much! I suspect our son will have two additional grandmothers. It would be wonderful if Nati were staying here too. She is a very sweet person and I would like her for a girlfriend, or as you say, a running mate."

"She's leaving the area near-term?"

"Oh, did the commander not tell you? He is taking thirty days leave before he transfers to San Diego, California, so they can marry in her hometown of Bejar and take their honeymoon in the Canary Islands. His family is flying over for the wedding.

"Nati had even more difficulty getting him to marry than I had with you! After she convinced him to do so, there were serious objections. Her family was so angry she wanted to marry an American and a person of a different religion they talked of sending her to relatives in Argentina. Their objections ceased when they learned she was in the very early state of pregnancy. It works that way in Spain. Girls get pregnant – the sweethearts marry. Simple!

"Nati and I measured the windows. The Spanish women are going to assist in finding curtains. I will have to spend some money."

Damn! We'd been married three months and Patty still did not have a good grasp of our assets, which was mostly my fault

"Listen, Kitten, we aren't rich, but I most folks would think us wealthy. I'm not as well off as your dad, but we won't have to spend time standing in blood banks lines.

"I pulled a lot of liberty before I met you, but I never threw money away. I saved some of my pay and all the money inherited from my folks when they drown. I kept all of the two hundred thousand dollars from my folk's life insurance too. We own our home place as well as three other farms outright, the smallest about fifty-seven acres. We have something in excess of four hundred acres total, some with pretty fair timber. Coal is being deep mined on one of the farms, but the coal seams have not been touched on the other places and I have no idea how many acres of coal there are. We're getting royalties on a couple of natural gas wells. We, as you know, sell milk from about sixty cows and we raise a few head of beef cattle and a small flock of sheep. There are other small cats and dogs too.

"I've not paid attention to my affairs. I never had time, sailing the world as I did. Mister Pollard managed the farms as he has since before I was born. The sleazy lawyer who probated the estate takes care of the accounting, taxes and such. Honey, I really don't know how much we have in our savings account, or any other account, except checking. Bottom line is . . . I'm an idiot!"

"Henry Clay Berkeley! I have told and told you never to refer to yourself in such a manner! Your priorities are not always properly aligned, but you are extremely intelligent. Not to worry, dearest. You now have me. I will sort our finances as I once promised. I did not do that while we were at home because I was so busy teaching school."

"Kitten, stop fibbing!" I grinned at her. "The real reason you never got into our finances was because you were too engaged scheming to get naked and jump my bones. How you managed to remain a virgin for twenty-two years is beyond me!"

"Get naked? What a *tremendous* idea!" Patty exclaimed, pulling her nightgown over her head and heaved it toward the ceiling, flopped against me and clasp me tightly to her perky, little breasts. "Oh, I *love* such ideas!"

Just when I started believing I had a complete muster list and the keys to all the gear lockers, I heard a quiet sobbing in the commander's office. I milled about smartly for a couple of ticks, then said to hell with it and entered her office. "Something wrong, Commander?"

She raised her head from her arms folded upon her desk, jumped up, threw herself smack dab into my arms and commenced wetting down the military creases in my sharply pressed khaki shirt. I pulled free and held her at arm length. "What the hell's wrong?"

"The XO just chewed me terribly! I've never been so spoken to in my life!"

"For what?"

"Yesterday, only one of three emergency generators was working at the receiver site."

"Did you know? I sure didn't!"

"*No!*" she cried, bitterly.

"That situation was important enough for the division officer to have notified you directly. Fact is, he should have notified you as soon as he lost the first one. What in the hell was he thinking?"

"He is one of the XO's boys."

"Is that supposed to mean something?"

"The man you relieved must not have told you *anything*!"

I knew the connotation of 'Boy.' It did not mean a homosexual partner as a civilian might think. It meant that person was his superior's favorite subordinate and the senior acted as his rabbi -- his *'Sea Daddy.'*

She cut loose with another gusher and threw herself back into my arms. That was not in my billet description and had to stop!

I slid her down into her chair, walked back into my office and told Doris to go play with her cat, get her hair done, chase cars, whatever, just secure for the day and get the hell out of my eyes. I was certain she'd heard everything thus far and didn't need her spreading scuttlebutt. I got the commander a glass of cold water from our small reefer and re-entered her office.

"Obviously there are undercurrents I know nothing about. I realize the XO doesn't like you, but what does that have to do with the division officer being a moron?"

"There are two, maybe three, of my division officers and a couple of CPO's and some petty officers who reserve their loyalty for the XO, rather than me. They attend the same weird church in Cadiz. They are pure death on everything that involves human emotions of a lustful nature. They stick together. They tell the XO things they should tell me. This is the worst!

"We were required to submit a HAZCON message using immediate precedence to Commander, Naval Telecommunications Command because we were in a hazard condition so far as backup power was concerned. This we did not do! The XO told me I was incompetent and called me names."

"What sort of names did he call you?"

"He did not actually call me names. He is too smart for that, but he implied that I am a slut and a whore, or something close to one."

"You're a married woman!"

"No, Master Chief. I am not. Well, I am, but I'm not."

That statement caused my ship to run right into a rocky reef. "But, you're wearing a wedding ring!"

"One can wear anything, can't they?"

Ship still on the rocks . . .

"Maybe you had better lay a few groups on me."

"Master Chief, you certainly know of the prohibitions against officer-enlisted fraternization. Well, I did that . . . am doing that, I suppose. We are married . . . sort of."

"You mean, like at the present time? Like *here*, in Santa Cruz?"

"No. Everyone would know if I did such a thing in this small community."

"What, exactly, is your status?" I was some kind of confused. All my halyards were wrapped around the mast!

"I met a wonderful man in my last command. We later developed a relationship. He was, rather he is, a first class petty officer. I will be thrown out of the Navy if the XO learns what I did . . . am doing, actually."

"So why doesn't he just get out of the Navy when his time is up. You have the higher rank. That would make sense, I think. It happens."

"He shipped over for six years just before we . . . established our relationship."

"Oh."

This was a sticky wicket! There wasn't any possibility the petty officer could get out of the Navy until his enlistment was up, not unless he fouled up like a big dog, such as getting caught shacking up with a lieutenant commander! If that happened, both of them would be thrown overboard, stern first. She could, of course, resign . . . unless she owed years to the Navy for education, or some such.

Fraternization, once something to be winked at, was an absolute no-no in the New, Modern Navy. I, personally, seen nothing wrong with it, provided they were attached to different commands. I thought the military went overboard on prosecuting folks for falling in love -- or whatever they did to end in the same bed. God made 'em different for a reason and a mere Secretary of Defense wasn't going to change that!

"Commander, let me ask something in plain sailor talk. I can understand two people of different ranks being attracted to one another and I can understand them taking advantage of it. What I can't understand is why you just didn't continue to sleep together until the affair ended or his enlistment was up. Surely you could have kept it below decks and out of sight."

"I became pregnant!"

"An abortion was out, I assume?"

"We are practicing Catholics!" she cried and went back to pumping her tear tanks dry. "We married outside the Church -- by a justice of the peace. *That* is *not* married so far as we and the Church are concerned. Our child was born out of wedlock, according to the Church!"

"Oh."

I mulled that around in my head, while she continued to pump tear tanks. She had a *real* problem!

"Commander, what happened to the child, and how does the XO come into play?"

"I have a Spanish nanny for the baby, an eleven-month-old girl. I have no problem with the baby and will have no problems at all in four years, two months and three weeks when he accepts a discharge. Until then, it is sneak around, lie -- sneak around, lie. I just can't stand much more, not with the pressure the XO puts on me!"

"Your husband is in *Spain*?"

"He is aboard a fast frigate in Mayport, Florida, but he takes leave and flies here at every opportunity. His captain believes he has relatives who live in Spain and lets him take extended liberties when his ship is deployed to the Mediterranean and is in, or near, Spain."

"And the XO caught you?"

"Yes . . . no, not exactly. He somehow became aware of Paul staying in my apartment in Puerto Santa Cruz. I have no idea why he thinks my being with a man is strange, except that I have a child and my service record reflects that I am not married. That makes me a tramp in his eyes."

"And he believes you are shacking up with an enlisted guy?"

"He does not know about *that*! He knows only I have a child he believes to be a bastard and that I sometimes have a man in my quarters. I transferred here soon after the baby was old enough to travel. I spread a rumor that I had married a civilian who was killed in an accident just days after our marriage. Most of the people probably believe I am an unwed mother, but no one has said anything or treated me badly, except the XO. He is certain that I am in an immoral relationship and I fear he will learn the man who frequents my apartment is enlisted.

"I have a graduate degree in computer science. My husband has a degree in electrical engineering and is highly qualified in the electronic field. We could do well in the civilian world, but we want to stay in the Navy. I certainly do not want the disgrace of being *thrown* out of the Navy!"

"Commander, there must be something we can do to get the XO off your back about your kid and your love life. Let me think on it. Maybe I can come up with something."

"Oh, if only you could, Master Chief. I will be in your debt *forever*!"

"You wouldn't be in my debt. It doesn't work like that in my Navy. You're a shipmate, sort of, and I don't throw that word around lightly! Shipmates help shipmates. I'd like to discuss this with my wife. She is really smart and won't gossip. She gives me reliable answers when I didn't know she knew the question! She gives me answers when I didn't know I had a question!"

"Do as you believe best, Master Chief. It cannot get much worse!" she wailed, then gave me a crooked, little smile. "If you treat her as well as me, I can see why she married you!"

"I'm the lucky one, Commander. I believe I was a top performer professionally before I met her, but I wasn't worth powder and shot to blow me up otherwise. Flat down and out, lower than a fat pig's belly was what I was. I never knew that until she took me under tow.

"You will hear, if you haven't already, that I married a teenager. I didn't, but she is twelve years younger and she looks really, really young. It just sort of happened, much as happened to you, except she wasn't pregnant. I was never married before I met her and certainly didn't want to get married. Then one day, there I was, standing tall and shaky in front of the altar, supported by a giant Marine Gunny Sergeant who was as nervous as I was. So, here I am, married and happy as a hog in a big corn field. End of story!"

That got a big grin. "You and your wife *are* the talk of the community. Everybody believes you married a teenager. Some believe she barely meets that standard!"

Thanks, Commander. I really needed that.

I took Patty to a restaurant that evening where we dined on *Murluza*, a salted cod fish dish, and a dew fresh salad.

The restaurant, a fair piece out of Puerto Santa Cruz on the road to Puerto de Santa Maria, was a long, flat, single-story building that resembled a whitewashed milking shed. The sandy yard area around the restaurant had no grass at all and only one scraggly palm tree. It was, therefore, known among Puerto Santa Cruz sailors as: '*Chicken in the Dirt*.' All the proprietors had to offer was a clean restaurant with worn, cane furnishings, couple of stuffed animals for decoration and great food, their chicken highly praised by everyone who liked chicken. The establishment was always crowded.

After our meal, we stopped at a roadside tavern frequented mostly by vineyard laborers. Like the restaurant, it had its attractions. It was cheap, had excellent *tapas* and foreigners were not likely to meet anybody they knew. I ordered a sparkling water for Patty and a San Miguel for me. The beer arrived so cold the bottle's surface frosted when it was removed from the water cooler into the room's warm air, just as it had years before when I visited there with an evil warrant officer who had me under tow.

Patty was dabbing at her eyes with the corner of her dainty handkerchief by the time I finished explaining the commander's situation. The Spanish men in the bar had never before seen Patty, and sure as hell didn't know who I was, but they were staring at us and mumbling among themselves. There was something about Patty that made men want to protect her the moment they laid eyes on her tiny being. There was little doubt in my military mind that I was going to get taken to task some day because of that.

"Clay-honey, it was nice of you to comfort the commander. Is she pretty?"

I recognized that snake laying in the grass!

"Yeah, she's pretty. She's a mite overweight and a bit broad across the stern. She has ginger colored hair cut sorta short, bobbed or some such. She has a couple of crinkles beside her mouth, wrinkles, I suppose. She's somewhere in her 'thirties I would imagine. She's a nice woman. You'd like her."

I didn't mention the commander had heard that Patty was a teenager. Patty was sensitive about being so much younger than I was. Her fresh, clear skin did not need makeup, but she had started wearing some after she met me. I suspected she was trying to look older.

"I really do not know what you can do to alleviate their situation, Clay. They are in serious trouble if their marriage is found out. I do believe you should speak with your captain. You must do something!"

Patty read everything she could beg or borrow concerning the Navy, but she had not a clue as to how it actually worked or the relationships that had to exist within its framework. Discussing the commander's situation with the CO would place him in an impossible situation. Even if he were sympathetic, he could hardly ignore the commander's violation of a regulation that originated at the Secretary of Defense level.

CHAPTER FOUR

TEETH, HAIR AND EYEBALLS

The next morning, I told Doris Harris to contact the receiver site's chief and tell him his presence was expected in my office ASAP, if not sooner. I then told her to take a hike for an hour, or so.

The chief entered my office, threw his cap on the hat rack and seated himself before my desk. I had met him at my Friday meeting, but he was just a face in a gaggle of CPO's and I had not paid him any particular attention. He looked like what one would expect of a CPO. His shoes gleamed and the military creases in his khaki shirt would have cut a loaf of bread. He had only three ribbons above his left pocket: A Good Conduct ribbon with three stars signifying over sixteen years of undetected crime, a Meritorious Unit Citation and the National Defense ribbon. Not much in his background with only three ribbons to show for it, two of which were not earned by him, personally.

"Chief, I do not recall inviting you to sit!" I said, harshly, giving him my best nasty glare.

The chief leaped out of the chair and snapped his slightly pudgy body to his idea of attention. His idea of what constituted attention was not mine, and I wasn't all that military-minded myself.

"I didn't tell you to stand at attention, Chief, but if that's what you're trying to do, we attended different boot camps. Maybe that's what I should expect from a man who stabbed a nice woman in the back."

"What did I *do*?"

"You didn't tell me about those two emergency generators being INOP!"

"But . . . but, my division officer said he would pass the word? He didn't?"

"No, Chief, he didn't. You should have informed me."

"Master Chief, I roughed out the Hazardous Condition message and Mister Hinton left the building with it. The Seabees got both generators back on the line later. I thought no more about it."

"Who, might I ask is Mister Hinton?"

"Uh, he's a chief warrant officer, the receiver's officer."

"I've never met the man, but now that you mentioned his name, I do recall seeing it on the staff-line chart.

"Sit down, Chief. Grab a coffee and I'll explain a fact you obviously did not grasp during my lecture the other day. You'd damn well better ask questions in the future when you don't understand something I'm telling you!"

The chief's hand trembled as he was pouring his coffee. That was good. I had his complete and undivided attention. The Word would circulate in the CPO Lounge that very evening that my wants and wishes were not to be ignored. That would likely alleviate need for me treating another chief in such a manner. The bad was that I had to scare a chief I didn't even know.

"I told you all the other day I needed to know everything that happens of importance, so your division officer telling you he'd put the word out does not clear your deck. When something happens to your equipment or your people, you inform your division officer, then you inform me. I don't give two hoops in hell what your relationship is with him unless he abuses you, then I want to know ASAP, But, you had better damn well understand the relationship you have with me!

"I monitor the day-to-day workings of the operations department within the guidelines of Commander Stoutmaster. Your division officer's relationship with the commander is his affair, but I have to know what is going on too. And you have to tell me. Something bad wrong happened yesterday when the HAZCON fell through the cracks and the commander was not notified. She was embarrassed when taken to task for something she'd never heard about. I was embarrassed for her. I was embarrassed for me too because I didn't know and couldn't inform her.

"I'm not big on threats, but I tell you now, if this happens again, I will arrange to transfer you to the naval station master at arms force and you can check ID cards, ticket illegally parked cars and muster restricted men on the quarterdeck. You can guess what that billet description will look like to the selection board the next time you try for senior chief. Do you read?"

"Yes, Master Chief, I do, but Mister Hinton doesn't like things getting out of the site. He'll have my guts for garters if I call you."

"No, he won't. You tell him exactly what I told you. If he has questions, he can call me, speak with the commander, or who the hell he wants to. Understand?"

After the chief showed that he understood, I used the time proven technique a salty, old petty officer told me when I advanced to third class petty officer. He said when I was placed into a position where I had to eat stern, I should do the best possible job so I would not have to do a repeat. He said I should never let the person just admonished leave without saying something good to him, even if I had to dig deep to find something. He said the person might leave hating me, but he would respect me and likely make a sincere effort to never again cross my bow.

"Chief, your uniform appearance is impressive. You obviously understand that chief petty officers set the standard for the entire command. Good show, Chief!"

It was not long before my telephone rang and Mister Hinton started chewing on me. That was not in the Plan of the Day!

"I meant what I told the chief, Mister Hinton. If you don't like that, then you better have a talk with Commander Stoutmaster. Things have changed around here and they will change even more. Every piece of paper drafted in this department, except those drafted by the commander, such as *your* fitness report, will henceforth be reviewed by me and passed to her with my recommendations, corrections, comments, whatever. That includes request chits, annual evaluations, official correspondence, messages, everything. That is what the commander and I have decided and that is the way it is, until she tells me different.

"My main job is to keep the commander on an even keel by supporting her to the maximum. I will do that much better than you did yesterday when you took the HAZCON message directly to the executive officer. So, Mister Hinton, I would appreciate it if you do not attempt to lecture me on the chain-of-command when you, yourself, did not follow it. It behooves you to keep the commander informed. It is her responsibility to keep the XO and CO informed, not yours.

"I have no animosity toward you, Mister Hinton. I respect your rank. But you have to understand my position and while I hold this billet I am damn sure going to do my job!"

"I don't work for you, Master Chief. That is what you had better understand!"

"No, you don't work for me. You work for the commander and she deserves your loyalty. But, Mister Hinton, your people work for me -- indirectly, that is. Think just how miserable I can make your life from this chair simply by making their lives flat miserable!"

There was a slight click, then a dial tone in the phone receiver. The commander would receive a call next. Then, again, after the stunt he pulled and got caught, maybe she wouldn't. I went into her office and briefed her on what had just transpired. I then briefed her on a possible response to the XO in event he called her on the carpet, for my comments to Mister Hinton. Neither of them called.

What a day – teeth, hair and eyeballs all over the place!

Around 1600, a tall, rail-skinny, full lieutenant with a scarred face and a deck of four rows of ribbons on his chest came striding through my hatch, sort of leaned himself over my desk and held out his hand. "Allen Prince here, Master Chief. Welcome aboard!"

We had once spoken briefly on the telephone, regarding a request chit one of his electronic technicians had submitted for permission to marry a Spanish girl, but I'd never seen him except at a distance and barely knew who he was.

We, as is common between sailors who do not know each another, exchanged information on ships and commands in which we had served, found a couple of folks we both knew and basically felt one another out. When we finished, Lieutenant Prince asked, "Got time for a beer?"

"Well, it's not knock off time, but we can grab one. Where?"

"At Santa Cruz-Mar. That's a civilian housing complex maybe a mile from your hotel. They have a pretty fair little slop chute. Drinking and driving is *A Bad Thing To Do In Spain* and not just because of the Navy frowning on the subject. The Spanish cops don't go to pull drinkers over, but if you get into an accident after drinking, they will flat heave your navy blue stern right into the old grinder. That is why Santa Cruz-Mar is a good place to drink. And it's not far. from where either of us lives."

"Give me a tick to tell the commander I'm shoving off for the day."

"You're going to tell her?"

"Some reason I shouldn't?"

"She never knew from minute to minute where Seeley was. He never told her zip. He seemed to feel a master chief was above all that."

"She's a good officer and you never know when all hell will break loose. Even if it doesn't, she deserved a degree of respect."

"You think so?"

"Yeah, Lieutenant. I do!" I wondered if I had read the salty looking lieutenant with the Bronze Star on his chest wrong and he was actually one of the XO's Boys about to lecture me on my many failings. Good luck, Charlie Brown!

I told the commander I was taking off a mite early. She gave her blessing. I then told the lieutenant I needed tell my wife I'd be somewhat late.

"You have to tell her? You just got married, didn't you?"

"It's not a matter of having to do it. She's alone in the hotel and will worry if I don't muster in at a reasonable time." I said, then grinned at him. "However she sees fit to determine *reasonable time*."

"No different from my wife. Yeah, give her a call and ask her to wait about an hour, then come to Santa Cruz-Mar. It's straight up the road from your hotel. I'll call the wife and have her muster in too."

We each ordered a San Miguel at Santa Cruz-Mar and each took a lusty swig from our bottle. The lieutenant threw a pack of weeds on the bar between us and told me to help myself. I told him I'd quit smoking the damn things, except when it got down and dirty. I told him I liked a smoke with a beer, but when I did so I received Disappointed Look One thru Six from my wife and thought that odd, considering she didn't mind me smoking the occasional stogy. He then called to the bar keep and rattled off a quick stream of Spanish. That got us a couple of top-of-the-line

Cuban cigars that didn't cost much more than a set of new automobile tires.

When we had the Cubano's going to our satisfaction, along with a snifter of Spanish brandy, which goes better than beer with a cigar, he looked me straight in the eye and said, "Before we start throwing them down, let me tell you something. I'm so happy to have a regular, fleet master chief sitting in your chair I could damn near turn cartwheels! It has been a long, dry spell without one, I tell you that!"

"Hec Seeley was top drawer when I worked for him in *Frank E. Evans*, as good as chief as one would want."

"You two talk much before he left?"

"Very little. I got here one day. He left the next."

"Seeley was on the ROAD program, which if event you don't know, means 'Retired on Active Duty.' I doubt he put in a solid month of work during the entire three years he was here. Finding him at his desk was not a common occurrence when you needed him, not that he was of much help when you did. Things were SAT until the previous OPS boss transferred and Missus Stoutmaster arrived. The previous commander was an old sweat communicator that didn't need help from anybody, not even a master chief radioman. Things started falling apart after he left, mainly because Seeley didn't do squat -- and Lucy Stoutmaster didn't know squat."

"Lieutenant, I'd rather you didn't bad-mouth the commander."

"I'd be the last man in this command to bad-mouth her. She didn't get a lot of help from her people when she reported -- and she still doesn't, or didn't, until you arrived. I've sneaked in nights and did things I knew needed done, just to help her out. She's a computer whiz, not a communicator. She knew nothing about the fleet and not a hell of a lot about shore communications either. Still, her willingness to learn impressed me, so I took care of her pretty well for a while after she reported. Then she crossed the XO's path and it has been downhill since.

"Some officers and chiefs who are aligned with our stone-ass XO, back doored her, bad-mouthed her to her subordinates and stuff like that. I ripped off a couple of officer's heads, but that came back to bit me in the stern. My career now depends on what the CO does with my next fitness report. If he blesses what the XO will write, I can forget selection to lieutenant commander!

"I am, as you must know, a limited duty officer-electronics, just a standard old LDO. I busted my stern in my last destroyer *John Hancock*, to qualify as formation-steaming officer of the deck and to do all the stuff line officers do. I left that tin can with top marks on my fitness report. I came here and ran smack-dab into a bad situation with Lucy Stoutmaster. I hated to destroy my career, but I sure as hell wasn't going standby and let that nice lady get screwed, just to please the XO. I was ready to march into the captain's cabin and lay some groups on him about what the XO was doing when we received orders on you. I decided to make like a snake in the grass, keep my head up and see what happened.

"I called around and found some folks who know you, a chief or two, one captain and an admiral we both know. All said the same thing, pretty much. They said you knew your rating as well as one can in this constantly changing world, that you function well above the level expected, you are an excellent leader and manager, you are smart as hell and have a set of cojones the size of a Jersey bull. I didn't know about the Silver Star or the Purple Hearts until I seen them on your shirt, but that goes along with they all said about you.

"So, that said, today CWO Hinton came crying to his buddies at lunch time about how the new master chief ate him out like a boot seaman, but didn't say one disrespectful word that he could use to report him to the captain. He is some kind of upset, but he knows you flat put his goober stern in the chopper!

"I guess the bottom line of all this is that I'd like you to keep doing what you've been doing. I'll back you all I can, but I really would like to get a good FITREP next marking period."

"I think you underestimate Jiffy Jeff, Mister Prince. If he's the same captain as he was in *King,* the XO is not going to slide anything past him, let alone an unjustified fitness report

"I'm glad we had this talk, Lieutenant. I learned things I suspected

"I intend to get attention of the XO's group a little more. I'm going to ask the commander to rough out a FITREP on Mister Hinton, one that says, along with whatever else she might want, that he is a disloyal officer. Game plan is that she shows it to him, lets him believe that is going to be her input to the captain for the next report, then slip it into her safe and let it lay there and see what happens. My guess is he will tear her hatch down to support her after that. He's probably about to retire and I suspect he'd like to walk through the ranks of side boys when they pipe him over the side with his head in the air, not with a bad retirement FITREP shoved up his stern!"

"Admiral Grayson said you're crafty."

"Where did you know him?"

"He was my skipper in *William V. Pratt.* I made chief electronics technician working for him. He is one tough mother and sly as a fox. You learn that sly stuff from him?"

"Some of it, maybe. Strange as it might sound, I learned some of it from Seeley too. He was, as I said, a damn good man when I knew him. Guess he got old and tired."

"He got something. No one ever paid him any mind, almost like he wasn't here."

"One more thing, Lieutenant, before our wives get here. I hear the XO has a set of 'Boys' who take deep suction on him and attend the same weird church. Is that true?"

"The XO belongs to a church in Cadiz that has a hang-all-sinners preacher. He's a creepy looking Goon who looks like a witch burner who crawled out of Old Salem. The XO supposedly paid to bring that strange cat over here and set him up in a church. The XO's buddies started reporting for duty soon after that to fill various billets. I believe there are around of twenty of them, total.

Could be more. Could be less. Not all of them are in our department. My guess is they are spread throughout the command."

"What got the XO down on the commander, Lieutenant? She's not the type to prod a bull with a pitchfork."

"She's a female. She's got a child. She's likely never been married. Is that enough?"

I wasn't about to tell the lieutenant I knew the real story. "Where did you hear about her not being married? She wears a ring. I've been calling her 'Missus' since I got here and she's never said boo. You telling me she zigged when she oughta zagged and got a kid out of it?"

"So goes the rumor. I really don't know and I really don't care. I don't believe anybody cares, except the XO and his group of heretic burners. Having a kid out of marriage makes a harlot in their eyes."

"I picked up on the fact the XO doesn't like women. Is he light in the boondockers?"

"I doubt it. He has a wife who is as much a bitch as he is a bastard. She looks right through you, then sneers as if she suspects you of raping cats. She's a real piece of work! The naval station banned her from the chapel. She went hog wild one night and started screaming at folks about selling alcohol on base, showing movies with half-naked women in them at the outdoor movie theater by base housing, selling books in the bookstore that contained dirty words and a whole raft of other things. She then spouted about how people letting such things happen should be rounded up and incarcerated in stockades. She thought she was cussing out Protestants at a prayer meeting. They were Jews!"

Patty showed up, followed shortly by the lieutenant's wife, who he introduced as Becky. As seems standard practice among women, it took only minutes of chatting before they went to the head to powder their nose or some such. They picked up their drinks when they returned, sparkling water for Patty, white wine for Becky Prince. They then moved from the bar to a small table. That gave Allen Prince and me elbow room to talk, which we did. We refought a few battles and one war and learned we knew more people in common than we first thought. We ordered a meal of *bacadillos*, a Spanish sandwich made of a roll of crispy bread filled with ham, cheese, salami and other fillings -- a meal in itself. Then we all chucked it in for the night.

Patty stopped undressing, turned and asked, "What are you doing about the commander's problem, Clay-honey?"

"I'm not doing anything about it. I didn't take her to raise. She is nearly as old as I am, maybe older. She had to have known what she was letting herself in for. Legally, I should report her marriage."

"You would not do *that*!"

"No, I wouldn't. I never believed the Navy could keep folks from holding coupling drills. It is a stupid program with good intentions. Regardless, there is nothing I can do."

"You will think of something. You can do *anything*!"

Anything, except sleep, I thought as I watched her crinkle her lips in a sneaky, little smile, arch her cute rear into the air and wiggle her panties down her hips and free of her legs.

"Dearest, what would you have done had I been an officer?"

"What I would have done, Kitten, once I discovered you're such a minx that you'd conduct body exchange drills on top of Stonewall Jackson's statue, was pounce your pretty bones until your teeth rattled and your toes crossed. When we finished doing what comes naturally I'd tell the Navy to go bugger themselves!"

That statement raised a shocked hiss from Patty . . . and also got me more attention than I really needed after having sucked down some beers and a brandy.

CHAPTER FIVE

ENEMY IN SIGHT

I was reaching for my combination cap to tour the work centers in order to speak with the watch supervisors on a one-to-one basis and hobnob a mite with the watchstanders when the commander popped her head through the hatch. "I went to brief the XO, Master Chief. He did not want briefed today. He wants to see you!"

I knocked on the XO's hatch and stood straight-legged before his desk, but not at attention. If he was going to chew on me and wanted me at attention, by God, he was going to have to put me there!

"Have a seat, Master Chief. Cup of coffee?"

"No thanks, Commander. I've had my fill for the morning." No doubt in my military mind that he was a drinker of some sort of sissy coffee. I wondered about the sudden sea change in his manner.

"I had not studied your service jacket in detail when you reported, but I have since done so. There are some *remarkable* things in your record!"

Yeah, and some that weren't there, such as three days bread and water when I was a seaman, various misdeeds when I was a young sailor, and no mention of my having been fired from recruiting duty.

"Your record aside, you have been ranked in the top one percent of your peers since you made chief petty officer. That alone would be impressive, but your being awarded the Silver Star in Vietnam caps it all. All of your commanding officers stated your ability to lead is superb and your ability to grasp complex issues and plan accordingly is superior. You've been recommended for a commission a total of nine times, but no paperwork was ever submitted. That says you have no desire to be a commissioned officer."

OK, XO, let the other shoe drop!

"Master Chief, if you are really the superb individual several captains and one admiral believed you to be, why are you acting as you do here?"

"Afraid I don't understand the question, Commander. Things are going quite well so far as I am aware. There are a couple of items I'm still studying on, but those will, hopefully, work out. So, what is the question, or the problem?"

"Among others, you are supporting a woman of bad reputation, an incompetent woman, a woman who should be pushing paper aboard a destroyer tender instead of fouling up a command that supports important operations, for all the services. Why do you support her?"

"For several reasons. The major one being that's what the Navy sent me here to do. Had the Navy wanted me to do nothing, they would have ordered me to a do-nothing command. If the Navy wanted me to be the department head, they would have figured out a way to frock me to lieutenant commander. Since neither happened, I'm carrying out the billet of operations master chief as I understand it"

"That did not answer the question! Why would you want to support an incompetent female officer of no virtue? You obviously love the Navy."

"Commander, what we have on-going, I believe, is a failure to communicate. I really don't understand what you're talking about. I have no reason to believe Missus Stoutmaster is anything like incompetent. She is highly organized and has a darned good grasp on her job, considering she has previously held no such billet. I think she is impressive. I have no knowledge as to her virtue."

"She is not a 'Missus!' There is no record of her ever being married in her service jacket. Her child was born out of wedlock!"

"It is my understanding she was married to a civilian. They were not married long, weeks, maybe, before he was killed in an accident of some sort. I suspect she had not gotten around to updating her record. This is not uncommon No one thinks they or their spouse is going to die suddenly. I once heard a captain claim to have updated paperwork on a newly married man not yet chilled, so his widow would receive death benefits."

"You *really* believe that is true in her case?" the commander asked, in a snotty tone of voice.

"I see no reason not to believe it. She seems honest to me."

"If she is so perfect, why is she fornicating with men so soon after her husband passed away, assuming she had one? Can't you answer that?"

"First, I don't know she has. Second, there is no rule as to how long a wife must wear widow's weeds."

"She was seen leaving her apartment arm-in-arm with a male -- and not just one time."

Not so very bright, Lieutenant Commander Lucy Stoutmaster . . .

"Let's put this right up front, Commander. Folks do that sort of thing. It has happened on a regular basis since The Snake flogged apples to Eve."

The XO maintained, but he turned a little reddish, like he was about to lift safeties on his boilers. I hoped the ass would. That would give me an excuse to go off on him.

"Let me tell you about the *wonderful* woman you are so careful to address as commander when she is only a lieutenant commander. She used influence to obtain her current billet!"

"We all rub and purr to get the billet we want. I'm guilty."

"She did it in such a manner as to take transfer orders already cut on a fine officer. She used influence to soften her own nest and destroyed a career opportunity for a much better professional officer."

"What sort of influence did she use, Commander?"

"Her previous billet was flag secretary to a one-star admiral in Mayport, Florida. She should have gone to sea after that, now that the Navy is stupid enough to detail women aboard ship, but she didn't! Her initial orders to a destroyer tender were canceled. The officer from whom she stole orders to NAVCOMMSTA Santa Cruz went instead to Naval Communications Station Harold E. Holt in Australia, in a billet not nearly as career enhancing. She ruined a fine Christian officer's chances of early promotion. She used influence with her admiral to get her orders changed. One *does* wonder what *sort* of influence she used with *him*!"

The Snake had now poked his head from beneath the rock. No, he had slithered out and most of his body was showing.

"Commander, does the captain know your feelings about Missus Stoutmaster?"

"He could not but help to know I feel strongly that she should not be in the billet she holds. He seems to *like* her!"

"Commander, I'm uncomfortable discussing my boss. I'd rather not do that. Is there anything else you need?"

"Yes, there is. You may have been an important person in other commands and you could be an important person here. You will not though -- not if you fight with seniors and try to order them around. I strongly suggest you mimic the methods of your predecessor and keep your nose out of how this command is managed! That is all, Master Chief."

I bummed a weed from the officer of the deck as I passed the quarterdeck en route to my office. I got a cup of coffee, lit the butt and kicked back in my chair. It was time to exercise my brain cells, the few that I had.

I'd read a book when I was a kid that impressed me greatly, *The Tattooed Man*, by Howard Pease. The hero of the story was a heavily tattooed Merchant Marine captain who sometimes sailed undercover as a ship's cook in order to investigate crimes involving the shipping world. He believed that solving crimes or working through problems was similar to weaving a carpet. The task took a lot of threads, the proper colors and size threads, and those threads had to be woven in the proper order and direction. I now had a fair part of Missus Stoutmaster's and the XO's carpet completed.

The XO, who seemed to dislike women, at least Navy women in important jobs, had obtained a set of orders to Spain for one of his buddies, probably a staunch member of his church. His buddy lost his orders to Missus Stoutmaster and was ordered to Australia in a less important billet.

Missus Stoutmaster could not have served on a destroyer tender once she started to show she was carrying a baby. She'd have been transferred ashore at the sixth month of pregnancy, probably to a do-nothing job for at least a year. I strongly suspected her admiral liked her very much, knew she was pregnant and had her extended in her billet until the baby was born. He then obtained her a set of orders overseas in lieu of sea duty, so she could care for her baby.

Did she have anything to do with the process? Did it matter? I doubted she knew she had taken another officer's orders. I considered her lucky to have worked for a caring admiral. But it did make me wonder how much the admiral knew about her personal life. He probably knew a lot, considering how closely flag secretaries work with their admiral. The old devil might have known the entire unfortunate situation. He surely knew the sailor she married because he, too, was a member of the admiral's staff!

The mostly one-way conversation with the XO told me what had happened to Master Chief Seeley -- or maybe not. It did appear the XO put pressure on him to keep him from poking around and stirring up the XO's buddies in the operations department. I had no idea how the XO could have exerted such pressure on a master chief, but all things are possible. Seeley's lack of action in his area of responsibility was very strange for a man who had been a front runner when I worked for him. He had to have been a stellar performer throughout his career because less than one percent of the Navy can be master chiefs by congressional decree. The selection process is brutal and few of the very top performers are selected. Maybe the XO had something on him, or knew of something he wanted and exerted a little blackmail to keep him in line.

I needed improvement in my morale, so I telephoned *Playa de la Sol*, connected with Patty and asked her to take a taxi to the Sea Dragon Club for lunch. That made her bubble!

Patty wasn't all that impressed with endearments laid upon her, but she certainly liked to be petted and given little considerations, such as telephoning her for no reason, unexpectedly taking her for a beer or lunch, or simply walking up and kissing her. Kissing her, however, was not always a good idea. Kissing often caused her want to rub and purr and we'd end wrapped like snakes on the floor, couch, or whatever was close to hand, so as to speak . . .

Being twelve years older than hot-blooded little Patty didn't worry me. If the Berkeley genes ran true, making love with my wife would never be a problem. Berkeley males and females, while accomplished at holding Be Fruitful and Multiplying Drills, were not good at producing male children. One ancestor, an uncle, married a wealthy, thirty-two year old woman when he was nearing his 'sixties. They produced five daughters, the last when he was in his 'seventies. Old family journals hinted this uncle was something of a rake before and after he married.

Patty had a small steak with a salad and a glass of the weak Spanish lemonade, *Caserta*.

She had given up on caffeine laced drinks for the duration of her pregnancy. I wasn't all that hungry and had a hamburger, but didn't eat all of that. I wasn't worried for myself, but the entire Stoutmaster and XO problem was wearing at my brain.

"It is a pity he could not have been an officer or she enlisted." Patty whipped upon me.

"Who?"

"You know who!" Patty whispered, "The problem you are working on."

"How do you know what I'm working on, you little hussy?"

Patty reached across the table and stroked my cheek. "I *know* my husband and I *know* he will fix it. My husband is a *good* man!"

"I appreciate the confidence, but this one may not be fixable. I've never seen anything so snarled since several bales of coiled line and cans of paint fell from bosun's locker stowage during a major storm. She's an intelligent woman, but she's done some really stupid things. Lust will do that."

"Yes, dearest, it most certainly will! Only in many cases it is sheer love." Patty said, then lowered her voice as a blush crept up her cheeks. "In my case, it was both! Had I been an officer and you enlisted, one of us would have had to change rank!"

Bugger the bosun!

Why such a simple, possible solution to Missus Stoutmaster's problem didn't occur to me early-on boggled my mind. I wasn't going to say anything about my being dense. That always lit Patty off like a flare. But it had taken at least three hints before I caught on to what she had in mind about solving the commander's problem. And I was supposed to be the sly one! Patty was far too intelligent to let me know she was way, way ahead of me. For my part, there was no doubt in my military mind that she was head and shoulders above me in brain power.

Back at the NAVCOMMSTA, I obtained a thin, blue-backed manual and a copy of a recent Bureau of Naval Personnel Notice from ship's office and studied them carefully. I then called Allen Prince to request his presence in the commander's office, after giving him a heads-up as to what I had in mind. I then told the commander that there might be a way to solve her problem, but she should not get her hopes up. I reminded her that it was difficult enough to keep a secret between two people, let alone three, and she should not let the lieutenant know more than he needed. He seemed my kind of sailor, but one never knows when dealing with recent acquaintances -- and sometimes when dealing with familiars.

When we were all seated, the doors secured and Doris sent to search for a nonexistent message from the message center files, I started, "Commander, will you tell us something about your friend in Mayport. Professionally, I mean. What's his service jacket like?"

"His service record is perfect, I imagine. He was named *Ramey's* Sailor of the Year. He has been Sailor of the Month and Quarter in prior commands, such as the one in which we served together. He is currently leading petty officer of combat systems division, although he is not the senior first class in the division. It took him only five years to make first class petty officer."

That didn't compute. "Then he's a kid . . . er, somewhat younger than you?"

"He's a bit older. Why?"

"If he made first class in only five years, how old was he when he first enlisted?"

"Why, he must have been twenty . . . six. He completed college and worked for Lockheed, but he wanted a more exciting job. He's been in the Navy eight years. He tried for chief last year, but missed the cut-off score because he had so few years in the Navy."

"If he had a degree, why didn't he join as an officer? Is there something in his civilian record that prevented that?"

"Why all the questions about my hus . . . er, friend, Master Chief?"

"Hang with me, Commander. Why didn't he get a commission?"

"I don't know if he was offered one. He should have been what with a degree, shouldn't he?" she asked, concern in her voice.

"Having just left recruiting duty, I can think of reasons he might not have gotten a commission. He could have cut one hell of a score on the enlisted test and blown the officer test. He might have had poor grades in college and didn't make the cut. There is the possibility his recruiter didn't tell him about officer programs. Also, I hate to say it, but there might be dings in civilian life that kept him from being an officer. We all know enlisted with better educations than their officers, but aren't officers, for whatever reason.

"Commander, you need to call your friend at the earliest possible moment and ask if there is anything in his record that would prevent him from being commissioned -- mental, moral or medical. The three M's, as they say in recruiting. We need to know like . . . yesterday! If he has his shi . . . er stuff all in one sea bag, we're going to try to get him a commission, or least give it one hell of a try!"

I'd have liked to have been an artist then. I would have been instantly famous. I don't believe any painter has successfully painted such a look of sheer joy. Mona Lisa would have been sucking hind tit compared to a painting of the commander's facial features.

"Oh, Master Chief, if only you could!"

I held up the blue-backed manual and the BUPERS notice. "This manual tells everything needed to apply for warrant officer or limited duty officer. This BUPERS notice provides the date of the next selection board, which is near-term. He has to go for WO or LDO because he's too old to go to OCS. I think he should apply for both WO and LDO and hope he is selected for one. You've been down that road, Lieutenant. Will you write the application?"

"Do whales sing?" Allen Prince grinned. "You get the dope from your friend, Commander, and we'll start on the paperwork. Got to run. Got a scheduled meeting with my technicians like right now!"

"Hey, Lieutenant! Let's catch a beer at Santa Cruz-Mar around seventeen hundred. OK?"

"I'll be there!" Allen Prince yelled, hauling for the hatch.

"I'm good friends with the captain of Paul's ship." Missus Stoutmaster said, in a small, hesitant tone of voice. "Would a recommendation from him help?"

Here it comes,.

"How well do you know him?"

"We served on the same staff before he received command of *Ramey*."

"How *well*, Commander?"

"Quite well, really. He escorted me to the Navy Ball and we sometimes went to the officer's club for a drink after work. We liked each other, but something didn't click. Nothing serious happened. Not even a kiss. Then I met Paul."

"What does he know about your situation?"

"Nothing."

"Then we had better let this lay in the grass. He'd wonder why you are so interested in one of his men. He will have to write a recommendation and forward the application anyway."

"I'll ask the admiral for an recommendation too! He liked Paul."

"Commander, does the admiral know of this mess you got yourself into?"

There was a period of silence before she responded. "I'd rather not answer that, Master Chief. Please don't push me for a reply."

He did!

"It likely makes no difference what he knows, but an admiral's endorsement on an application can't but help. Well, I'm off to Santa Cruz-Mar in about an hour, unless you have something for me."

"Master Chief, you go where you want and I'll buy you all the beer you can drink, for an entire year, starting *right* now!"

"I'd like that, Commander, but we ought not be seen running together. It might trip the XO's trigger even more. I'm enlisted too. Remember?"

"We won't be by ourselves. Lieutenant Prince will be there."

Race, religion or creed, it makes no difference. It is impossible to lay logic on a female who has made up her mind!

"OK, but you have to first call your *friend*. You oughta do that right now, if you can get hold of him on the ship. It's not long before lunch time in Mayport."

"I can contact him. I told him to spread the word the female who keeps telephoning is a farm girl from Indiana."

Race, religion or creed. They are all sneaky too!

I whipped by the hotel and picked up Patty. I briefed her on the way to the slop chute and cautioned her to keep a tight lip. She told me I didn't have to tell her that!

Lieutenant and Madam Prince were at the bar when we arrived. He had already ordered drinks and purchased us Cuban cigars. He must have briefed his wife that he wanted to talk to me in private because she latched onto Patty and took her to a table across the room. That made sense because he was not aware that Patty knew more about the commander's situation than he did, let alone that the idea for getting the commander's main squeeze a commission originated with Patty

"Master Chief, what I wonder is why that ass didn't go for a commission as a line officer after he started rubbing belly buttons with her and you know that's what they have been doing!

"You would think she would have thought of trying to get him *some* kind of commission. She's so smart in some ways and so dumb in others that her head must hurt! Being ex-enlisted, I can understand a *line* officer not seeing the obvious, but one would think a sneaky, not to be trusted, *enlisted* man would have thought of getting some sort of gold stripe after he went and knocked up an officer, right in front of God and everybody!"

That statement caused my sails to flap! "What makes you think he's the father of her kid, Lieutenant?"

"Look, she shows up at NAVCOMMSTA Santa Cruz with a six-seven week old kid and a cockamamie sea story about her being a new widow and no sign of widow weeds Not long after she arrived, folks see her with a man more than once and it is always the same man. Then, today, I learn she has an enlisted *friend.* Pull the other one, Lucy Stoutmaster -- it has bells on it! We both know who impregnated her, don't we? The only thing that would surprise me now is to learn they aren't already married!"

"Uh, yeah, wonder who else thinks like you do?"

"Most folks around here think she's never had a husband, but there is no way anyone would guess the kid's daddy and maybe her *husband* is enlisted."

"I really like her, Lieutenant, but she's not the shiniest piece of bright work on the bridge, not when it comes to her personal life. She's done some really dumb things. I'm wondering just how worldly old Paul is."

"Those old glands will do it every time, Master Chief. Every time!"

The commander came zipping into the bar, smiling like an alley cat that found seven rotten fish and six in-heat female cats in the same dumpster. "A copy of Paul's service jacket will be shipped via DHL tonight."

"That's illegal, making a copy of a service record." I grinned at her.

She leaned over and whispered in my ear. "So is fraternization resulting in an officer becoming pregnant! It's a bit late to worry about *legal*."

Maybe she did have some common sense . . . when it didn't involve conducting body exchange drills.

"I checked, fellows, and Paul has taken the officer's test. His scores were so high they wanted him in Nuclear Power. He's leery of submarines. He likes to see the sun once in a while. When the Navy insisted he go nuclear power, he turned down a commission and enlisted. They still tried to put him into nuclear power field, but he slid out of that some way."

CHAPTER SIX

SOCIAL WORK

The next few days were spent reviewing watch bills and speaking with the wheels who ran divisions and watch sections. When I thought I had a good grasp on the unwed pregnancy situation, I laid course for the Family Service Center on the far side of the Naval Station.

Family Service Centers existed for years, but were originally staffed mainly with volunteers and operated, for the most part, with funds raised through raffles, bake sales and the like. The time expended by the volunteers was spent preparing layettes for babies of low-ranking personnel, providing limited financial and marriage counseling services, maintaining a list of rental housing for reporting families and a host of other functions.

The explosion of single-parents, marriage among young sailors with no financial sense, and a total sea change in how the Navy once viewed the family side of a sailor's life increased the functions and value of the FSC's many fold. The old Navy response to a sailor's family problems, '*If the Navy had wanted you to have a wife, they'd have issued one with your sea bag!*' was no longer heard.

Family Service Centers now had trained, paid employees augmented with volunteers and budgets sufficient to operate, among other things, day care centers for children. FSC's had, in fact, became a right arm for commanding officers and others in the chain-of-command who dealt with sailors' personal problems on a daily basis. *'My wife she . . . My dog it . . . My kids they . . .'* was heard in one way or another nearly every morning at divisional quarters when in home port.

After I introduced myself to the heavy, gray-haired FSC Director and we exchanged a few tidbits I said, "Missus Caulsen, I am in bad need of a hook-up."

"What sort of hook-up do you need, Master Chief." She was undoubtedly a long-time Navy wife who understood Navy lingo as well as I did.

"I just completed reviewing the status of female sailors at the NAVCOMMSTA. I have about fifty-three percent females in my department. That is a total of one hundred-eighteen women. Of those, thirty-six are pregnant. Of those pregnant, only eleven are married. I'm going to suffer huge holes in my watch bills over the next several months because of maternity leave and sick babies who have only one parent to care for them. Such shortages will continue, unless I can greatly reduce the rate of unwed pregnancies."

"You are in the wrong place, Master Chief. One obtains leg irons and chastity belts from the supply department." she snickered, a tough, old gal who had probably seen it all, heard it all and was shocked at nothing.

"That wouldn't solve my problem, probably make it worse. It would increase my pilferage rate drastically because of missing hacksaws, bolt cutters and jack hammers. No, I realize I can't change human nature, but I do have an idea I want to bounce off of you."

"Bounce away, Master Chief."

"I've spent most of my career at sea, but I'm not totally ignorant of what goes on in civilian life. I've read about the sexual revolution. What I read led me to believe civilian folks spent most of their time in bed. Men, since the time of Adam, have let the females worry about the possibility of pregnancy, which worked to some extent because the females were concerned about their reputations. That does not seen true in today's world -- neither males nor females worry about their reputation.

"What I learned about today's young people while on recruiting duty shocked me! Lots of them, male and female, hung around the recruiting offices after school and some of what I heard made my ears burn -- and me a sailor! According to them, male and female, they spent a fair portion of their time engaging in sex -- all sorts of sex! I believe they did too, most of them.

"I didn't review every enlistment kit, there were too many of them what with thirty odd recruiters generating kits. I reviewed only those who needed a waiver for marijuana usage, a minor juvenile record, or some such. Of all the kits I did review, and there were many, I never once seen a notation that a girl was a virgin on the medical examination form -- all were checked off as non-virgins. Based on what I'd heard from the teenagers that didn't surprise me. My female recruiters assured me that virgins had joined the Navy, but none of them had needed any sort of waiver. That tracks, I suppose. Girls with pristine reputations don't smoke dope and such . . . maybe.

"What tripped my trigger, eventually, was the number of girls who had enlisted into the delayed enlistment program, then could not ship out to boot camp because they had gotten pregnant between the time they enlisted and their shipping date. We lost several that way, which made me wonder just how much they really did know about sex. I made it a point to speak with as many male applicants as possible about what they knew and I tasked my female recruiters to try to determine just how knowledgeable about sex their female applicants actually were. What I ultimately learned is that today's kids do engage in all sorts of sex as a matter of routine, but they are still as green as I was when I joined the Navy in many areas. Some are flat, right down, a-number-one-ditty-bag ignorant! Some, male and female, didn't know even the basics of preventing pregnancy.

"I brain stormed the problem with my recruiters and we came up with a plan.

"What I did was to have a female recruiter sit every female enlistee down and conduct a one-on-one. The recruiter told the female enlistee how one got pregnant, or rather why one got pregnant, how much it hurt to give birth, the sleepless nights she'd experience caring for the urchin, how she would lose her friends because she couldn't tote her kid to places she now frequented and the lifetime financial consequences of raising a child. The intention of the recruiter was to scare hell out of her.

"I had a similar thing done to the males with the intention of scaring the boot topping off of them. They were told the financial aspects of having to pay for their child's upkeep, the hell their girlfriend would cause them every time the kid coughed, the medical expenses, the problems they would have with any man their girlfriend might eventually marry, and the shame his parents would feel when they learned he had impregnated a girl. They were told if they married a girl because of pregnancy, they would not be just playing musical beds, particularly with a kid bawling for attention.

"The minority males were also told, in no uncertain terms, by a black recruiter that fathering a child out of wedlock was not a mucho act, but an act of stupidity that anybody with a stiff . . . er, natural equipment could do. My top recruiter, a black female, cut me in on that one. It seems that fathering a kid enhances a fellow's standing among his peers in the minority community, so she said. She also said it is difficult to get child support from most minority males because they feel no responsibility toward the children they father. I ensured all females were told that."

"We lost not *one* applicant after that because of pregnancy! And I know in my military mind that The Snake continued flogging apples to the girls and boys who had enlisted."

"Ah, The Snake does get around! Do you wish to establish that program here?"

"Not here, exactly. I want to establish it in my department. If you want to use it for the naval station and tenant commands, you're welcome to do so. I can't patent it!"

"I'm certainly going to review your results. Unwed and single mothers are a heavy drain on our resources. We have a few single fathers who are as huge a problem as the females. What I don't understand is what you want from me."

"I want you to find me a couple of women who are not shy and are willing to explain the facts of life to young female sailors in my department. It is not necessary that they be single moms or have had an illegitimate child, but they need to have given birth so they can explain the procedure in graphic terms. I'll take any women able to get the idea across to the girls."

"Why don't you use the women in your department?"

"I think my recruiters were effective with the civilian girls because they were still in awe of a female sailor. Not so now. The young females already had some sort of lecture about sex in boot camp that didn't stick. A civilian woman would be better.

"I'll sic a tough petty officer on the males. Male sailors do not relate to civilian males very well, not like females relate."

"I see your point. I assume this will be an unpaid position?"

"Unfortunately, it is. I can get them an office where they can counsel the girls. I can round up enough money from the chiefs and officers who are fighting the problem to take them to dinner every so often. Maybe a few other perks we can dream up, certainly a framed letter of appreciation signed by the CO."

Missus Clausen stood and stuck out a hand near the size of a kid's baseball glove. "We need more thinkers like you, Master Chief. How come you're not in a command master chief billet?"

I grinned at her. "My parents were married -- to each other!"

"Ah! One of the few who understand that some command master chiefs fill the billet only for the prestige and perks of the job."

"Partly. I don't enjoy playing politics, even when necessary, and CMC's do a lot of that. Some CMC's are more interested in themselves than their troops. There are many fine ones though, enough that the CMC program is doing a lot of good."

"Yes, there are fine ones. My husband is one of them."

"Who is your husband, Ma'am?"

"He transferred from being CMC of Naval Air Station Santa Cruz to CMC aboard *Nimitz*. He'll have one more tour after the current one before retirement upon completion of thirty years of service. We hope he can do his twilight tour here."

"Well, if he doesn't have the hook-ups to get transferred back here for his final tour, I expect you have the contacts and pull to get that accomplished, what with contacts from this job."

"Yes, Master Chief. I suppose you could say that." She gave me another of her sly grins. "In fact, I'm certain you can say that!"

Navy Wives -- God bless them, each and every one!

It being Christmas Eve with almost no one except watch standers working, I checked a few things after I returned to the office, started to weave some words, then said to hell with it.

I did one other thing before I left the office. I called the female senior chief who had asked why the commander couldn't come in on days when I didn't. I gave her the duty of reading the messages and making a quick, daily round of our work centers until I returned -- whenever I determined that would be. I then went to the hotel and told Patty to pack a bag for two-three days and we set out for Gibraltar.

I completed telling Patty of my plan to reduce the pregnancy rate just as we started climbing into the jagged mountains above the sea near the town of Tarifa.

"I will brief the girls, Clay-honey. I would love to do that!"

Salvation Army Officers were hard-nosed women-of-the-world. Experienced social workers were hard-nosed women-of-the-world. Red Cross Officers were hard-nosed women-of-the-world. Patty Lane ranked with Snow White!

"Kitten, I'd rather you not do that. You really don't have the background for it."

"Why not? I *am* experienced in how one becomes pregnant and I will have been experienced at giving birth in July. Why should I not assist my husband?"

"Honey, some of the girls, the ones from the slums, in particular, has experienced hurts you could not even imagine. That is what causes some of the problems. A male finally treated them nice, so they laid down and spread their legs, thinking he loved them. You really would not know how to talk to such girls."

"I am not unworldly! I have been to Washington, Baltimore and Philadelphia. I traveled all the way to Spain. I taught school for . . . well, a few weeks. I knew some nasty girls in college. I *know* how one gets pregnant. I *am* pregnant. Remember?"

Logic -- don't fail me now!

"Patty-honey, some years ago, a senator was lollygagging in his office, eating a bag of popcorn, chewing the nubs off pens, telling sea stories with his running mates, whatever, when an aide told him the President intended to appoint his wife as Secretary of Transportation, or some such.

"He flat tore off the Hill, up Pennsylvania Avenue and steamed right into the oval office where he told his old buddy, the President, that he oughta not do that to him. The President, thinking he had done his friend a favor by appointing his wife to a job, for which she was highly qualified, was stunned. He was totally adrift, so he asked the senator as to why he should not appoint her to that post.

"The senator said: 'Mister President, you will place me into an untenable position! If she becomes Secretary of Transportation or anything else, I will have to vote on bills concerning her department. If I vote *for* a bill she favors, folks will say I voted for it because she is my wife. If I vote *against* the bill . . . I've got to go home that night!'"

"So, Kitten, if I agree with you on something, folks will say I am showing favoritism to my wife. If I take you to task for something, I have to go home."

"Oh."

Two *Guardia Civil*, a sergeant and a private, pulled us over at a roadblock just before La Linea. The road check did not surprise me. There had been a bombing the previous night by the Basque separatist group, ETA, in a town not far from the Gibraltar border. The Sergeant checked my ID card, but waved away the passport Patty extended toward him. "*No necessitio, Nina.*" he said, smiled at her, gave me a sort of funny look, then waved us on our way.

"Clay-honey, did I correctly understand his connotation of '*Nina*' means he believed me to be a little girl?"

"That's what he said." There was no doubt in my military mind that the *sarjento* meant exactly what he had said. He'd called her a little girl and had given me a look that meant he thought I was a dirty, old man.

"Why did not he call me '*senora*,' or even '*senorita*' if he did not notice my wedding ring."

"Beats me, honey." I really did not want to discuss it!

We crossed the causeway between *La Linea de la Fronteri*a and Gibraltar with no problems from the Spanish border guards, but the immigration police on the Gibraltar side took a hard look at my ID. They did not check Patty's passport. I decided I could probably rent her out to a terrorist group as a courier if I ever got hard up for money,

I circled the parade ground bordering the only runway in Gibraltar, then worked my way up Main Street until I turned to zig-zag up The Rock. A few twisting turns and we pulled in front of the Rock Hotel, which clung to the mountain side about one-half way up the northern facing slope.

Patty jumped from the car, gushing about the view, the ships in the harbor, the ships sailing past The Rock, how far she could see into Spain, and the beautiful Alameda Gardens just below us. She ran to me, rose on her tippy-toes and kissed me. "Clay-honey, last year I would not have even *dreamed* I would stand in a place so beautiful. Thank you, dearest."

No, thank you, Patty.

I never dreamed, last year, that I would be so happy and satisfied with life. I decided, right there, that if I lived long enough I was going to show my perky, little wife the entire world. Then a really bad thought came into my head. What was I going to do if I ever lost her? I shivered when I thought of the forthcoming birth.

"Are you catching a chill, dearest? You must be. It is very warm!" Patty asked, concern in her voice.

"I just shivered for some reason."

We took a short nap, a somewhat delayed one when Patty's snuggling turned into something else, after which we toured the top of The Rock. The rock apes entranced Patty until a couple of them decided to engage in obvious foreplay and a third ape decided to abuse himself. "Oh, how nasty! Clay, do you *believe* that they are doing?"

Yeah, I believed it. The apes had been doing it for hundreds of years and nosy tourists were not going to change their lifestyle. And they didn't even need The Snake to egg them on!

"Those guys have quite a history, Patty. There is a legend that if the apes ever leave Gibraltar, the British will lose it. Winston Churchill believed that so strongly he sent a destroyer to North Africa during the height of World War Two to capture and bring back apes when those on Gibraltar caught some sort of virus and started dying off. He felt the morale of England would suffer if it became known the apes had disappeared from The Rock.

"There is a funny legend too. The apes steal everything they can get their hands on! They yank windshield wipers from cars and rip off radio antennas and grab gas tank caps. Supposedly, the apes have a deal with garages. They get a cut of the price of the replacement items sold!"

I knew the Rock Hotel put on quite a spread for their evening meal, but that meal was hours off and I was hungry. I took Patty down the hill to a small alley just off Main Street and knocked on a sliding panel in the side of the building. The odor of hot grease poured out into the alley when the panel slid open. I paid for my order and handed Patty one of the large cones of newspaper. "Hang on to this, Patty. We'll eat it on the promenade overlooking the harbor. We'll get something to drink on the way."

Patty poked into her cone. "Why, these are *French* fries?"

"French fries *and* regulation English fish and chips! That cubbyhole has been there since the Royal Navy started anchoring in the harbor. Sailors come ashore, tear up the bars, then buy a mess of fish and chips rolled in newspaper to eat on the way back to their ships. The fish and chips supposedly sober them up. I've had fish and chips in England, Singapore, Sri Lanka and other places. These are the best!"

Patty gave me a sly smile. "Did you do that, Clay? Tear up bars, I mean?"

"Gunny tore a couple near to the ground! I got run over one night just up that street when a bar full of fighting Limeys and Yanks, including Gunny, spilled out into the street. I was just walking along, not bothering anybody." I told Patty, referring to my long-time running mate with whom I'd once served aboard an amphibious ship, an '*AMPIG*' cruising the Mediterranean We had been stationed near each in other areas a couple of times since, most recently both on recruiting duty in my home town of Big Otter, West Virginia. Gunny Thorton, USMC, was my best friend.

"Oh, I *certainly* believe that big fib!" Patty exclaimed. "I can just imagine you and Gunny back-to-back, fighting your way out of a bar!"

She really could read minds.

"Speaking of Gunny, this is the fifth day of their honeymoon. Let us compute the time zone in Saint Croix and call them real late at night as Gunny and Elizabeth did to us when we were honeymooning in Elkins and interrupt . . . *whatever* they are doing. Clay-honey, I will tease Elizabeth silly!"

I wasn't sad that I'd gotten fired from recruiting, not with now being able to steam around Spain with my sweet, pixie wife. I felt bad, though, that I had not been unable to function as Gunny's best man, as he had for me.

"You're turning mean, do you know that, Patty Lane?"

Patty exhibited an impish grin. "Pay back is one sweet Mother . . . Oh, my Lord! You are corrupting me totally! I nearly used that evil *sailor* word. I have never used *that* word in my entire life!"

Nobody could make me laugh like Patty, particularly when she blurted something she did not mean to say and went Condition Red, or when she tried to copy my sailor slang and messed it up. Patty Lane was a trip!

We spent the remainder of the afternoon running the shops. Patty bought several small items she needed to decorate our new house and about eleventy-eleven yards of various colors of silk material, for her mother and other women in West Virginia. The Indian merchant who sold her the material was initially very obliging, but his demeanor deteriorated as the bargaining progressed. Patty was no slouch when it came to dickering, having learned the art from watching her father trade livestock, coal, timber and such. She had practical experience too; she traded livestock she had raised herself since the age of ten.

I was trying to balance all the stuff she had bought as I puffed up the steep hill toward the hotel when Patty, who had been looking puzzled as we walked along said, "Do you think I received a good price, Clay-honey?"

"Like I told you earlier, regulation Indians from India could beat old Satan out of his pitchfork. Then too, most tourists are confused about the value of the local money and pay what is asked without any great effort on a shopkeeper's part. You can bet they make a huge profit. That fellow didn't make much off of you. I wouldn't be surprised to see him shuttering his shop next time he sees you coming!"

We attended evening services at a church, then engaged in something approaching an English Christmas Eve by touring pubs and participating in sing-song evolutions, which occur in establishments inhabited by Limeys. Patty knew a lot more of the songs that I did who knew almost none, so I mainly sucked up on the good English beer and let her have at it. I couldn't carry a tune in a sea bag anyway!

Virtually everything was closed on Christmas Day, so we walked about Alameda Gardens, inspected historical sites and, in general, had a grand old time. We left The Rock early on Boxing Day and returned to Puerto Santa Cruz.

My game plan in keeping Patty busy over Christmas was to prevent her from thinking about her folks in West Virginia and feeling sad on her first Christmas away. She seemed quite happy after she telephoned her parents from the hotel, but I wondered if I had made the right decision when we arrived back in our hotel room because Patty looked wan. Actually, she looked quite beat down.

"Do you feel okay, Patty?"

"I am a bit tired and my feet are killing me!"

"Why don't you take a nice, hot bath and get some rest? I'm going to run to the station and check things out." I said, partly out of the door.

"Will you please stay here, Clay-honey?" Patty requested, in a small voice.

"I won't be gone more than maybe an hour."

"I want you to stay, dearest. I do not feel well."

I closed the door and caught her in my arms. "Where don't you feel well, Kitten?"

"No place in particular. I just feel ill. Let me take a hot bath. I really would like you to remain here with me."

Not a problem. Ask for my soul. You'll get it.

I dozed throughout the night, but woke each time Patty started tossing and turning. Her not sleeping soundly worried me. I frequently felt her forehead. She did not seem overly hot, but she did not look at all well. Her skin did not have its usual fresh glow and her lips looked dry. She looked pale too.

I inspected her carefully when she came from the bathroom early the next morning. I did not like what I was seeing. "Get dressed, honey. I'm taking you too sick bay."

"No, dearest. I am okay. I just feel tired and worn. I suspect I do not feel well because of the different foods I ate. The cigarette smoke in those British bars was terrible too."

"Get your clothes on! We're going to sick bay!"

"But, I --"

"Get 'em on, or I'll put 'em on you!"

She gave me one rapid flash of her broad-toothed smile. "*That* would be *quite* different!"

I whipped the Seat into the parking spot nearest the front entrance of the Naval Hospital, zipped around the car and opened the door for Patty. She worked her way out of her seat and stood in a wobbly manner. I caught her, lifted her in my arms, and headed for the door.

"Put me down, Clay!" She yelled, kicking her legs and pushing against my chest.

"You sure?" I asked, slipping her down on the pavement feet first, but still holding her against me.

"Yes, I can walk. I am not ill, really."

I steered her through the double glass doors and with my arm around her we headed for the check-in counter. We were not far across the lobby when she gave a little cry and sagged toward the deck!

CHAPTER SEVEN

DISASTER

"Mister Patterson, first, let me tell you Patty is going to be fine. Second, she had a miscarriage and is in the naval hospital in Santa Cruz." I choked into the electronic path reaching from Naval Station Santa Cruz telephone exchange into the white, two-story farm house on Jessie's Run, West Virginia. What I received in return for my statement was a period of silence.

"Clay, we didn't know she was pregnant. You sure she is a-goin' to be okay?"

"I just spoke with the commanding officer of the hospital, Mister Patterson. He assured me she is going to be fine. On the other thing . . . you remember how Patty carried on just before we left for Spain about how you and your wife had to come over here in July? Well, that was because she had just learned she was pregnant and due in July. I didn't know she was pregnant, not until just before we landed in Puerto Santa Cruz.

"I asked Patty when she called you on Christmas Day why she didn't tell you folks she was pregnant. She said she wanted to see the look on your faces when you stepped off the airplane in July. You know how Patty is. There is no way of changing her mind when she has steerage way on. I'm sorry, Sir. You have no idea how sorry I am."

I heard Mister Patterson's voice in the background, followed by Missus Patterson's scream. It was several minutes before he came back on the telephone. I could hear Patty's mother crying in the background.

"Call me back in thirty-forty minutes, Clay. I'll let you know when our plane will arrive."

"Patty is going to be alright, Mister Patterson. You two don't need to come way over here and . . . well, maybe you should. She really wanted that baby. Yeah, it'd be really good if you came over, like tomorrow, if you can."

"Clay -- is she conscious?"

"Mister Patterson, maybe you ought not tell your wife until she calms down, but Patty had some sort of complicated tubular pregnancy. She was operated on a couple of hours ago. I tell you, Sir, the doctor says she is going to be fine!"

"Son," Mister Patterson said, when I called him back. "We can't go direct to Puerto Santa Cruz. We got a flight from Big Otter to Washington this evening and then on a Spanish plane called Iberia to Madrid and then on another plane to a place called Jerez. I couldn't get an arrival time in Jerez -- just tomorrow sometime because the plane from Madrid is a local plane, probably like the puddle-jumpers we have a-flying into Big Otter. The gal on the phone said Jerez is the closest we can fly to Puerto Santa Cruz. Is that right?"

"Yeah, Mister Patterson. Jerez is the closest airport, only a few miles away. I'll keep contact with the airport to keep abreast of your exact arrival time. I'll meet you when the plane lands. Get a pencil and paper and I'll give you the phone number of the hotel and hospital in case we miss each other at the plane. "

"You certain my girl Patty is okay, Son?"

"The commanding officer has been a Navy doctor for maybe thirty years and he's personally taking care of her. Now, try not to worry."

"You sound awful, Clay! Don't you go a-havin' a breakdown, or some such. She'll need you real bad now."

"Not even a speck as bad as I need her, Sir!"

The Word was out. Captain Keene, Missus Stoutmaster, Lieutenant Prince and his wife, Missus Caulsen and the senior chaplain had mustered in the lobby of the hospital while I was at the telephone exchange. I spoke and was walking around them when Allen Prince caught me by the arm, pulled me back and started to speak, only to be interrupted by Captain Keene.

"Your wife is still asleep. The doctor was just out here speaking with us. He said she would not know much until tomorrow morning. She's doing fine. Here, sit down!"

"I have to go to her, Captain."

A heavy hand grabbed me and pushed me down in a blue, plastic chair. "He said, 'Sit down!' Here, take a swig. You need it. Doctor Church said you're already half out of your mind, or will be, if you keep running around worrying. Now drink!"

It was either drink from the flask Missus Caulsen pushed at me, or suffocate from the huge woman levered against me, holding me in the chair. I drank.

"Now, you calm down, Master Chief." Missus Caulsen ordered, sternly. "It wouldn't do for you to go in her room all excited. She probably won't know you are there, but supposedly people sense things after an operation, so it can't do her good if you go in there carrying on. Everyone has taken very good care of her and they still are!"

I took another pull on her brandy flask. "Yes, Ma'am, I did act nuts this morning, I suppose. I shouldn't have done that. I'll have to apologize to Captain Church."

"He's not upset at you going off center on him. He said your wife acted the same way the day you passed out on the airplane. He says it must have something to do with you two being hillbillies."

That caused a weak smile on my part. "It may have, Missus Caulsen. We got a terrible bad rep!"

A hand touched my back and Missis Stoutmaster whispered, "No matter what you or Patty need, if it is in my power, you have it! We're shipmates. Remember?"

I got myself back on an even keel, then went to see Patty. She looked so tiny laying on the white bed. She has a tube in her nose, one in each arm and a couple that disappeared beneath the white sheets. I almost lost it! I moved toward the bed, extended my hand, then drew it back.

"Touch her, if you want, Master Chief. It won't hurt her. She might sense you are here."

I stroked Patty's cheek and brow. "Thanks, Captain. I'm sorry I popped off at you this morning. You didn't deserve that."

"People get excited when something happens to a loved one. Remember how your wife poked at me when I was trying to check you out a few weeks ago? She informed me, rather bluntly, that the first couple in your family line was married for eighty-one years and she intended that you two last at least that long! My wife like to wet her skivvies laughing when I told her the things your wife said to me.

"Lieutenant Prince said you two have been married only a few months. That's awfully soon for something like this to happen, but you both will weather it. Master Chief, I see all sorts of relationships in my business. I thought I'd seen it all, but your wife started worrying about you as soon as we threw you out of the room and she was still chattering about you when we put her under. Master Chief, she was more worried about you than herself!

"Lieutenant Prince tells me you are an up-front sort of fellow. I'm an up-front fellow too, so I hope you take what I'm going to tell you as me being just that. I know of doctors who try to hide things from their patients and their spouses. I'm not one of them.

"Patty is in excellent health. But she could never have given birth to a child. Her reproduction system was far from normal. Therefore, the operation was not at all simple. She should not have gotten pregnant, but then there was no way she could have known."

"I knew. I knew she is too tiny!"

"No, she isn't. Her insides were not conducive to carrying a fetus. She is lucky the problem surfaced when it did. The baby could not have possibly matured past the third or fourth month, after which we would have had to terminate the baby to protect her life. It would have been much more difficult for her, mentally, had she carried the baby to where she felt it moving about, then lost it. I'm likely wrong about that because I doubt the fetus would have ever moved inside her. She is, in a way, lucky, as I said."

"Do you have to tell Patty this?"

"I do. Otherwise, she would keep trying to become pregnant and worrying when pregnancy did not occur. Yes, I have to tell her and I hate to do it. She is one sweet, impressive, little lady. She knows her mind, that kid!"

"Can you hold off a while, Captain? She is going to take the loss of the baby badly to begin with. She really wanted children."

"I suppose so. She will have to make follow-up visits after I release her from the hospital. Her's was not a simple procedure. It will take a while before she is totally healed inside. I can hold off until then."

About eight in the evening, the medical staff chased out the group who had shown up that morning and then mustered and re-mustered throughout the day and evening. That left me with nothing but my thoughts -- none of them good. I spent the night in a chair beside Patty's bed. No one tried to talk me out of that. First, I was a master chief, USN. Second, I was a hillbilly!

I dozed during the night, but tried not to sleep. I had the terrible feeling that something would happen to Patty if I did not keep a close eye on her.

Patty spoke a few words the next morning, but they were so soft I could barely hear her voice. I leaned close to hear what she was saying and seen two little tears trickle from beneath partially closed eyelids. She then returned to sleep, leaving me to wonder what she had tried to say.

Mister and Missus Patterson looked old and worn as they walked slowly across the tarmac at the Jerez airport. I remembered that Patty once told me they had married young, but she had not been born until they were in their 'thirties. That made them pushing sixty and they both looked it today.

I tried to get them to wait until the next morning before going to the hospital. I lost that one before I started.

Patty tried to sit up and hug her Mother when she opened her eyes and seen her standing there. Her mother bent over, kissed her and hugged her across the shoulders. She stayed in that position for a long while, whispering into Patty's ear. Mister Patterson went through essentially the same motions. I did not hear any response from Patty. That worried me greatly.

The Patterson's went into closed-door session with the doctor while I went outside to smoke a weed from what was left in the package I'd bought only the morning before. Visiting hours were over when the Patterson's finished their session with the doctor and I almost had to pry them out of Patty's room. I had gratis to visit the room whenever I wanted, but I did not think the staff would let them, not unless they went into their hillbilly mode.

I intended to take them to the hotel restaurant after we returned to their room, but they were not hungry. I was about to return to the hospital when Mister Patterson caught me by the arm and said, "You never seen me drink, Clay. I need one now."

Missus Patterson gave him a pretty hard look, so I asked her if she wanted to accompany us to the bar. She said she'd like an iced tea or soda delivered to the room. I walked across the room, pulled open the door of the small reefer and stood back.

"Goodness gracious! Would you look at that, Charlie? There are all sorts of food and drink in there!"

I told her she was welcome to any of it. I had already made up my mind to pay for their trip, so a few more bucks on the tab for items taken from the reefer wouldn't break me. I knew the Patterson's had scads of Yankee Green Dollars, but since I'd participated in causing the disaster, I thought paying for their trip fitting and proper.

"Charlie, have you ever seen anything like this room? I haven't!"

Mister Patterson hugged his wife. "Unless you've been a-steppin' out on me, you've only been in one other hotel in your life. I hope you remember *that* one!"

"*Charles!*" she cried, turning red.

When we were seated in the bar, Mister Patterson said he no longer drank whiskey but wanted something stronger than beer. I ordered him a brandy and coffee.

"Am I supposed to pour this stuff into the coffee, or what?"

"You can drink it either way, Mister Patterson. The Spanish do."

"I want her straight!" he said, throwing the small glass of brandy down his throat. He immediately snatched his coffee and threw that down after the brandy. "That stuff has got character!" he gasp. "It's a lot smoother than stump juice though."

"Yeah, *Carlos Mendoza* is good stuff. That bottle is likely ten years old, which makes it pretty smooth. You got to watch it though -- it has a real kick!"

"The stuff I drank when I was young never seen ten days old! Get me another, Son."

Mister Patterson was a quick learner. He didn't try to drown the insides of his feet with the second brandy, he only sipped it. "They sell Cuban cigars over here?"

"They do. I get you one right now, Sir." I said, signaling to the waiter I required his assistance.

"You never did see me drink anything, Clay, except that bubbly wine at Patty's wedding. That stuff wuz not really drinkin'. It wuz like soda pop. Bet you didn't know I drank, did you?"

"No, Sir, but I then I never thought about it."

"Well, now, I used to be a rounder! I could stick with the best of 'em -- drink stump juice all damn night and work all damn day! I had to stop that after I married my Virginia. She put the clamps on me!

"Oh, she put up with it for a while, but I come home pretty tanked up one night with a truckload of calves I'd bought at the Elkins stockyard. Matter of fact, your dad wuz one of the fellows a-buyin' stock that day. We all had us a jug and we took turns a-samplin' each other's brew. It wuz all good stuff. Lord, all of it wuz good in them times when I wuz young

"Anyhow, I come a-tearin' down out of them mountains, just a-hellin' down the road in that big, ole International truck. I got home and swung toward my stock pen and backed her smack-dad right into the corner of my pole barn! I knocked the side of the barn plumb-off, run my truck into my tractor and like to ruined a new manure spreader. Didn't hurt myself or none of the calves.

"My Virginia came a-runnin' out of the house and when she seen I wuz alright it wuz flat cryin' time. She screamed and yelled and cussed me out. I didn't even know she knowed words like that! End of the story wuz that I quit the booze, or she wuz a-goin' to quit me! I didn't see no choice, so I stopped the hard stuff right there. Got so I didn't much want even a beer, 'cept maybe on a real hot day. I believe tonight is the first drink of hard stuff I've had since way, way before Patty wuz born."

"Your daughter put the clamps on me in more ways than one. You know something? I'm happy she did!"

"Yeah, it goes like that. It is said man ain't really moved too far from being an animal, so he needs a woman to keep him cinched down. But, you know, Clay, they ain't nothin' you can do for them sometimes. Like right now. I know my Virginia is a-layin' across the bed, a-cryin' and I can't do nothin' about it. Fact is, she don't want me in the room 'til she gets done with her cryin."

"I understand, Sir."

"I'm a-gittin' awful tired of hearin' that 'Sir' and 'Mister Patterson' stuff! You ain't got no daddy no more. We never had no son 'till Patty drug you home. Now we got one, so you call me Pa, or some such."

That comment brought tears to my eyes. "Yes, Si . . . er, Pa."

"Son, you oughta noticed how close me and my Virginia is. We're tighter'n the bark on a apple tree! Patty is our only child. You ever wonder why?"

"No, Si . . . er, Pa. Lots of folks choose to have only one child."

"We didn't! We wanted kids somethin' awful, but it never happened until we wuz up in years. We'd been married a-goin' on sixteen years when Patty wuz born.

"She wuz our first and our last. My Virginia had a terrible time with having that baby. She stayed sick and in bed most of six months. Patty wuz born in the seventh month. She weighed only a mite over three pounds. The doctor said she wuz probably a-goin' to die, but an old granny lady, Granny Dawson, took over and started a-pourin' catnip tea down her, one teaspoon at a time. Two-three days later, Patty wuz a-tryin' to hold her little head up! But, Clay, I always wondered if maybe that's why Patty stayed so darned little. Oh, she wuz never sick, or nothin'. She just didn't grow much!

"It hurt like the dickens when the doctor said my Virginia shouldn't have more kids. Oh, it hurt us somethin' terrible! But, we did have Patty and she's been our blessing her whole life.

"Now, that Navy doctor told us Patty can't ever have a baby. Son, did God curse us, or what?"

I had to think about that one for a mite.

"I know you are a religious man and so is your wife. Patty too. I certainly believe in God. I've seen too much not to. But I don't believe He has time to pay attention to me, personally. I just can't fathom Him worrying about a person as insignificant as I am. No, this just happened. I don't believe He caused it."

"Me neither, Clay. I wuz just a-spoutin' off. But you're wrong about Him not a-carin' about you. It says in the Good Book that He cares about the sparrows a-fallin to the earth and He counts the very hairs on your head. I believe that, Son. I really do. What I don't understand is why somethin' awful like this happens to a good girl like Patty. It flat don't make no sense!"

It damn sure didn't!

Patty slept through the night and woke hungry. Doctor Church directed a nurse to remove the tube from her nose and feed her. Patty ate everything on her plate and wanted more. She gobbled away, but kept laying her fork down, reaching over and touching me on the cheek. She didn't seem interested in carrying on a conversation.

Her parents came charging into the room around eight-thirty. That was much earlier than the start of visiting hours, but nothing was said. Except for meals in the cafeteria, they stayed until eight o'clock that night, Missus Patterson kept a steady stream of chatter toward Patty, but Patty didn't say much. I wondered if her throat hurt because of the tube that had been in her nose and questioned the doctor.

"She had only an oxygen tube connected to her nostrils. I'm not going into medical terms you wouldn't understand, but what is happening is she is sort of in shock at what happened to her. That is the best way I can put it. She'll likely come around by tomorrow.

"That will raise a problem. We could let her go home in two-three days, but Lieutenant Prince tells me your house won't be available for a while. I don't want her in an off-station hotel, no matter how nice, and she won't want to stay in the hospital. What are you going to do?"

Damn good question.

I beat feet to the housing office to see if they had any furnished, temporary quarters on the base we could use. There were none. I then checked in with the Navy Lodge, but there were no quarters available there either. I then did what any right thinking sailor would do when the world was closing around him. I went to see The Man, the Command Master Chief of Naval Station Santa Cruz. I hoped he would turn out to be a regulation sea-going type and not a shore puke.

"We have VIP quarters for fleet and command master chiefs who visit Santa Cruz on business on as regular basis, but we try not to let them stay vacant. We put local or transit master chiefs in them with the understanding that they move to a regular master chief room if the VIP who 'owns' the room shows up. Two VIP rooms are currently empty and there are no master chiefs to put in them. How about I give you two rooms until she can move into her own house? They are right next to each other, but they don't connect with a door. You can stay in one, she can stay in the other? Those rooms are plush! Old Man Trump would feel at home."

"That'd be great, Master Chief." I told the old boatswain's mate with a wide, weathered face and a body like a huge block of cement. "I have another problem, but not a big one. Her parents are here from West Virginia. They are not the most worldly folks running loose. I really don't like leaving them in a hotel by themselves. Any idea where I can put them on base?"

"I don't have any more open quarters, but is there some reason you couldn't give one of the two rooms to them and you sleep in the hotel by yourself? Or you could sleep on the couch in your wife's room. I can fix them up with a temporary base pass and get them limited authorization so they can buy health and comfort items at the commissary and Navy Exchange. Will that work?"

"Damn sure will, Master Chief. I appreciate the hook-up."

"Least I can do. I been meaning to call you, but never got around to it. I know you aren't assigned as the NAVCOMMSTA command master chief, but I like to keep in touch with master chiefs in tenant commands, of which they are not many. Which reminds me . . . you haven't met the NAVCOMMSTA CMC. He's been at a do-nothing, something or other, study group in Norfolk since you got here. You heard anything about him?"

"I found he was absent when I was checking into the command. His office was locked and has stayed locked. I finally quit trying to check in with him."

The old master chief spit a stream of tobacco juice in a lined trash can. "He's slimy!"

"*Slimy?*"

"He is that. He's a photo-intelligence specialist. Wouldn't know a damn ship if he run off a pier in his car and landed on one! Spent his career moving from command to command in Maryland and Dee Cee. I've pulled chestnuts out of the fire for a few NAVCOMMSTA folks, for things he oughta squared away himself. If you get the feeling I don't like him, I don't!"

I would have never guessed.

Patty shifted back to near-normal Patty mode late that afternoon. She jabbered about how nice the hospital staff was and how they couldn't seem to do enough for her. She didn't think highly hospital chow. It was bland and the portions were small. She spent the evening hours with her mother, planning the move to our new house and catching up on the gossip from West Virginia. She made no mention of the baby.

I moved her parents into the VIP quarters the next afternoon. They sure weren't poor folks, but the fine Spanish furnishings and layout of the room astonished them. Missus Patterson was quite taken with the glass-fronted cabinet filled with *Lladros*, the porcelain figurines of Spain. She particularly liked the shepherd boy blowing on a flute while his dog listened at his feet. I made note to take her to the *Lladro* factory before they left Spain and get her a few of the figurines. I then guided them through the commissary and Navy Exchange. I cautioned them they did not rate full privileges, but their authorization would permit them to purchase health and comfort items needed for their stay aboard the naval station. I also showed them the location of various other facilities, such as the theater, after which I took them to the Sea Dragon Club for supper,

The waiter flourished a bottle of pretty good *Rioja* wine, then poured a bit into my glass. I tasted it and nodded my head in approval at which time he upended the other glasses and filled them. Then, I remembered.

"I'm sorry, Missus Patterson. I'll get you something else to drink. What would you like?"

"Is this wine?" she asked, holding up her glass and inspecting the contents.

"It is. Just sit it down. The waiter will take it away. What would you like to drink?"

"May I sip this?"

"Sure, it's yours, but Patty said you never touch alcohol of any sort."

"I don't, but I noticed the Spanish people drinking wine in the hotel, men, women and their *children*! I've seen none of them making a fool out of themselves . . . like some I know." she explained, casting a coy look at her husband.

She took a tentative sip, and then a couple more, each larger than the previous one. "Why, this is delicious! Clay, I had a taste of wine a long, long time ago. It was nasty! Sour and bitter. This has a wonderful flavor."

"It's a pretty fair wine, but it will make a person drunk. Most folks over here don't drink wine to get drunk. They view it as a food. They drink it with every meal, just like we drink water or some other beverage."

"I can see why!" Missus Patterson said, taking another sip from her glass.

We all had a nice steak, a baked potato and a green salad, followed by a selection of pastries brought by the waiter on a small cart. I then took them into the tiny CPO Lounge area.

Mister Patterson hauled out one of the Cuban stogies I had gotten him that morning, ordered a *brandi-cortado* and a glass of wine for his wife. Missus Patterson did not object.

"I didn't get you one of these brandy drinks, Mother, even if you have turned into a wine swiller. You ain't ready for this! It is pure, smooth fire."

Missus Patterson turned a light pink, but she didn't say anything. She just picked up her glass of wine and had at it!

"Clay, was that steak from Spain, or America?"

"Here, I suspect. The Navy tries to buy local stuff, Pa."

"Well, by God, I never raised better!"

"Charlie, you stop swearing. That happens every time you drink!"

Patty had a gaggle of visitors in her room when we returned. Missus Prince, Missus Caulsen and six Spanish ladies who were our future neighbors were going at it full bore in low-grade Spanglish. I grasp the Spanish ladies had shown up at the main gate to the NATO base demanding entry from the gate guard, a Spanish Marine. When denied access, they threatened to tell the

Marine's mother that he would not allow them to go to the naval hospital. No male Spaniard, regardless of age, would think of getting his mama down on him, so the ladies were granted instant, illegal access. The Spanish *senoras* had visited a *pasteleria* en route and bought enough pastry to fill a Seat automobile. Some florist had a good day too.

Patty was sitting up in bed, chatting with the best of them, probably not understanding one-quarter of the conversation. She waved me to her and gave me a big smooch, then kissed her mother, jerked her head up and locked eyes with me. I gave her the arms out, palms up, signal that meant: "Yeah, you smell booze on your mother's breath, but I didn't cause it."

I received those looks throughout the evening, probably because Missus Patterson thought everything was funny! She probably didn't understand any of the Spanglish tossed around, but she carried her own. Patty bumbled along with her high school Spanish. Probably nobody understood anybody, but it seemed to make no difference. Patty's father went to sleep in one of the chairs.

We moved Patty to the VIP quarters two days later. The naval station CMC and Missus CMC showed up to supervise. I had worried how I was going to tweak Patty into the tiny Seat automobile, but the commanding officer of the hospital had foreseen that problem and ordered an ambulance to transport her. The hospital CO accompanied Patty in the ambulance, which surprised me greatly. It seemed uncommon for a high-ranking doctor to take such personal interest in a single patient.

The CO inspected the quarters and pronounced them SAT, then told me to get my stern to the Navy Exchange and procure a soft pad, or some sort of soft, thick blanket because he considered the leather lounge chair too hard for Patty. He wanted her walking around on a very limited basis, but mostly he wanted her in the chair or on the bed. He threatened to draw and quarter me if she wasn't four-oh in the next few days. He checked her position in the lounge chair two-three times, told her he would return the following day, then bent and kissed her on top of her wavy-curly hair.

Everyone loved Patty.

After the doctor and other assorted individuals departed, Missus Patterson called me aside and quietly asked me to remove all hard booze from the liquor cabinet in their room. I thought it significant that she made no mention of removing the wine.

I had intended to return at night to the hotel the Navy was paying for, but Patty vetoed that idea. She wanted me to sleep alongside her. I vetoed that. We compromised and I agreed to sleep on the leather couch, which was almost as wide as a single-person bed. She wanted me to pull the couch alongside her king-sized bed so she could touch me at night, but I would have needed a working party to move the monster, so that didn't happen. The Navy was somewhat less than efficient at not having seen foreseen the current situation, according to Patty. No doubt about it, Patty was becoming four-oh.

The situation stabilized. Patty and her mother spent their time crocheting, knitting and planning the move to the cottage. Mister Patterson, being at loose ends, nosed around the naval station and fell in with an aged Spanish landscaper.

The landscaper started taking Mister Patterson to farms and ranches on a near-daily basis. When they were not steaming around such places, Mister Patterson helped the old man cut grass and trim shrubbery around the base, after which they went fishing from the fueling pier.

I have no idea how they communicated, neither spoke more than a few words of the other's language. They had a couple of things in common, other than fishing. Mister Patterson supplied the Cuban cigars the old landscaper could never have afforded and the landscaper supplied a local stump juice. Missus Patterson never caught on, or if she did, she said nothing. Mister Patterson never stumbled or slurred his speech, but he looked pretty happy when he returned from fishing in late evenings.

Missus Patterson continued her wine drinking. She had a glass with every meal and one before bed. She liked red wine, but made no preference as to what brand, so long as it was Spanish. She was probably going to have to get off her wine kick when she returned to West Virginia. There was no Spanish wines available in Big Otter County so far as I knew. I wondered about her reaction when she had her first sip of Golden Pheasant or Mad-Dog Twenty-Twenty!

Our furniture shipment and Patty's little Chevette arrived on the same ship. Spanish movers, under contract to the Navy, moved our furnishings into the house the day after the previous tenants vacated the premises. Patty was less than happy when the doctor would not permit her to go to the cottage to supervise, so she sent her mother who harassed the movers mightily, not caring that the movers did not speak English. Mister Patterson was a shrewd old bird. He went to inspect a ranch that raised fighting bulls on the far side of *Puerto de Santa Maria*.

Missus Patterson hooked up with the neighbors, one of whom was our landlady. They set out, en mass, to *El Corte Ingles*, *Pryca* and other department stores to purchase curtains, rugs and other household necessities. A lack of a common language seemed not a barrier. After a long day of non-stop shopping, during which they likely inspected every article for sale in Southern Spain, they decided they had done enough damage to my wallet and started squaring the cottage away.

The Spanish ladies became agitated when Missus Patterson pitched in to help the girls they had hired to perform these tasks. They were even more agitated when they learned a woman of Missus Patterson's means did not have even one maid in the United States. It took some doing, but the *senoras* finally convinced Missus Patterson that ladies of her income level did not clean, lay carpets, hang curtains and such. My wallet wasn't the only one that would be hurting if Missus Patterson started liking the life style enjoyed by upper middle class Spanish women and insisted on a maid when she returned home.

When the ladies were totally satisfied with their efforts, we vacated the VIP quarters and shifted to our new home. Although Patty was mobile, the doctor insisted she not ride in her little Chevette that had, by then, cleared customs. He and his wife, who had previously entered the picture as a shopper of some expertise, transported her in his Navy sedan. That action told me the doctor was a hard shell only on the exterior, despite the fruit salad on his chest that showed he had served tours curing the ills of the Fleet Marine Force in combat.

With Patty sleeping in the gigantic, four-poster bed from our house in West Virginia and the Patterson sleeping in the second bedroom, I again ended on a couch not nearly as plush as the one in the VIP quarters. Patty complained mightily and at length about this arrangement, insisting her incision was not even sore. When I told her she was fibbing, she puffed out her lower lip and called me cold and unfeeling, for making her sleep alone.

Puffed out lip or no pulled out lip, I stuck to my guns. There was no doubt in my military mind what would happen if I surrendered to her wishes, even if I placed a pillow between us as she wanted. Patty was prone to wrapping me like a snake climbing a sapling when she slept. The pillow would end on the floor and the dressing from her incision would probably get torn off when she went into her snuggling mode. We didn't need that!

Patty's parents learned of an open-air ballroom in Cadiz that catered to the old style dances, mainly for English, German and Spanish tourists. Her parents suited up and headed out with our neighbors. They could barely communicate, but seemed to have a lot in common. I'd never seen the Patterson's dance, didn't even know that they could, but I had seen lots of aged tourists tearing up dance floors in Spanish cities. Most were flat good.

"Clay, may I have a beer, please?"

"I don't know, Kitten. What did Captain Church say about you drinking alcohol?" Patty liked her beer, but her tiny size prevented her drinking much. One beer: OK. Two: she got frisky. Three: she got *really* frisky. Four: no idea and didn't want to find out.

"I did not *exactly* ask him, but it is not on the list of prohibited items. I am *sure* it is okay."

I wasn't, but I noticed the puffed out lower lip. "Let's compromise. I'll pour you half a glass and I'll drink the other half."

The lip puffed further out. "You are treating me *mean*, Master Chief!"

Patty had taken up addressing me as 'Master Chief' when I did something she really liked, or something she didn't. I questioned the reason for addressing me as such and was told I was a master chief when we married and would always be a master chief in her mind. I really didn't understand her reasoning.

"Mean old Master Chief, that's me." I said, getting a San Miguel from the reefer. "Sure you won't drink something else?"

"I do not want a glass of water, or that awful orange juice Mommy bought. I want a beer -- the entire bottle!" No note of a receding puffed lip. It was puffed out further if anything, a really bad sign.

God knows one cannot argue with a head as hard as the sides of a battle wagon, so I started to pour the beer into a glass.

"No, I want to drink from the bottle. The entire bottle."

"OK, OK, hold on a minute! But if you get sick, fall down or something, Captain Church is going to draw and quarter me."

"Good! You need the occasional drawing and quartering."

Patty sometimes disagreed with me, or took something I'd said wrong and got her dander up, but she never picked a fight. It appeared she wanted one this time.

"Are you mad at me? If you are, you should tell me why."

"*You* hid something from me!" Patty cried, taking a lusty swig from her bottle.

"I never!" Wasn't no way in hell I could hide anything from the female version of Sir Winston Churchill.

"You did too!"

"If I did, I have no idea what it was."

"*You* did not tell me I could not have children."

"Well, no . . . but we did discuss it, my thinking you were too tiny."

"Not then. Now!"

My halyards snapped and all my flags and pennants were flapping in the breeze.

"*You* were told I can never bear children. *You* did not tell me!"

Rats! That darn doctor told her way before he said he would.

"Well, er, Kitten, I intended to tell you when you got on your feet. I didn't think I should, not just now, you being ill and all. What did the doctor tell you?"

"*He* is worse than *you*! He kept putting me off. Mommy told me! I know you were only trying to protect me, but did you really believe I wanted to wait to learn that?"

"That's exactly what I thought. The doctor thought so too, sort of."

"What are we going to do, Clay-honey?"

"About me not telling you?"

"No, about us not being able to have children. We must, you know."

"How . . . Why . . . I mean, uh, I don't understand."

"We cannot let the Berkeley Line terminate. We must have a male child!"

"Patty, maybe you had better discuss this with the doctor."

"Henry Clay Berkeley! Do not *hide* things from me! I *know* I can never give birth. Acquiring a male child by whatever means is the question!"

"Patty Lane, I don't often tell you no, but we are not going to discuss this right now. When you get full up and four-oh, we'll hash it out."

"I *knew* you would say that!"

Patty finished her beer, placed the bottle on the table beside her chair, stood and walked toward me with small, halting steps. That told me her incision was still sore and that she had fibbed about it. She bent down, probably with difficulty, and kissed me, long and hard. "Clay, you are a wonderful man and you are the most intelligent man I know. But sometimes, dearest, you can be so *dumb*!"

Whatever in the hell that meant.

"Listen, dearest, you have read the old Berkeley journals, but I suspect you paid attention only to the parts about Indians and the spicy portions. You did not seem to have learned much else from them."

"You can't know that, Patty! You couldn't have had time to read them all, not with teaching school, reading Mom's diaries, those Navy books, and that illustrated marriage manual that got you doing things that you'd never before dreamed of doing."

"Oh, but I did read every one of them. Carefully too. I took them home before we married. You surely do not believe I would marry a man and not know about his family, do you?"

What I thought was that once she decided to marry me, she would have done so even if I had a graveyard full of skeletons in my closet. The gates of hell would not have stopped her!

"So you sneaked them out of the house, right in front of me, but you had to do that over several nights. There has to be at least seventy-five pounds of the things."

"You do not need to know how I got them, but I will tell you. It was partly *your* doing." Patty said, turning bright pink.

"Even though we never so much as held hands in front of your housekeeper, Missus Jenkins knew we were doing *It*. She could not help but notice the mess we made, the sheets torn off the bed, my perfume in the bed clothing, everything. That was *your* fault because after I went home, you no doubt went to sleep and left the bed in total shambles when you went to work, leaving the mess for her to find."

Patty crinkled her lips and turned even redder. "If the bed clothing and perfume were not enough, there was the evening when it got so late I had to rush home and I forgot my bra on the floor in the library! At least that is where I suspect I left it. That was your fault too. I was so late starting home it was a wonder I put on my panties. I did not even think about the bra until I unbuttoned my blouse and discovered my teacups were bare. I am certain she found the bra the very next morning, although nothing was ever said. Where *is* that bra, I wonder?

"Missus Jenkins pulled me aside one evening when we were waiting for her to leave so we could . . . you *know*, and asked when I expected to *move* into the house *permanently* and did I understand what I was currently doing was a sin. She is a friend of Mommy and it would have been very bad had she told Mommy was I was doing with you. Mommy would have had a fit! Daddy would have blacksnaked you! I gave her a sad little smile and told her that after you first seduced me, I had no choice but keep doing *It* until I could get you in front of the minister, otherwise, you might leave me!"

It wasn't enough that Patty destroyed my love life in two places, West Virginia and Kentucky, after we started dating, first by telling everyone I had gotten a girl pregnant and later I had married the young girl. No, that wasn't enough. She had to ruin my relationship with my housekeeper too, a woman who had known me since I was born. No wonder Missus Jenkins turned cool toward me!

"Clay, you might have noticed she started acting much nicer to me than when I first started visiting your house. So, I took advantage of the old lady by going alone to your house one evening before meeting you at your office. I chatted with her for a few minutes, had a cup of tea and thanked her for not telling Mommy. I then marched right into the library, opened the old chest and carried all of the journals right past her, just like I owned them. It took five trips to carry them to my car! I did not say a word. She did not say a word. Not to worry, I had a fib ready."

No doubt the sneaky, little hussy did have a fib hanging fire. I wondered how many other fibs she had whipped on people while running me to ground.

"There is much in those journals significant to where you came from and where we are going. I say 'we' because you are no longer an 'I' or a 'me.' We presently have no future, or rather our name has no future.

"The journals record that the Berkeley's first arrived in Western Virginia in 1709. The Patterson's came with two or three other families in 1712. Unfortunately, my ancestors were not as literate as the Berkeley's and did not keep a record of their endeavors.

"Clay, your family might not have descended from the Berkeley's in England. Yes, that is what your first American ancestor wrote in his journal, but he may not have been an out-of-wedlock off-spring of the great Berkeley family. Why? Well, his grandson suspected his grandfather had misrepresented who his father was. He did not record why he thought that. Did he meet someone from England during the Revolutionary War who had known his grandfather in England, or did he meet someone from the Berkeley family who simply wanted to deny it? No one will ever know.

"No one will ever know the name of Henry Clay Berkeley's mother. Was she a Berkeley maid, a village girl, a blue-blood girl, or what? .We will never know her name because Henry Clay Berkeley failed to record who she was or where she lived in England She could have been anybody, but she was likely unmarried when she gave birth"

"What are you telling me, Patty? That I am the end product of a horse thief and an indentured servant who both might have crawled out of the gutter? Yeah, Kitten, I read about him swiping a horse from the Berkeley he said was his father and hauling stern to Bristol, England. And I read he married an indentured servant by jumping over a stick in Norfolk, Virginia. That doesn't bother me. I'm not name proud. I'd be just as happy being a Jones or a Smith, provided I could still be married to you!"

"Oh you! You can be proud of your family even if he stole his name from the town beggar! But let we assume that his father was a Berkeley. That option is as good as not.

"Regardless of who they were, Henry Clay Berkeley and Margaret Louise Tinny came here with essentially nothing. They ended with many acres of land, a six-room log house, which was a really fine house in that era and location, and they produced thirteen children in their eighty-one years of marriage.

"If that is not enough for you, grandsons of Henry Clay Berkeley fought in the Revolutionary War. They were members of the group of men George Washington, himself, recruited from Western Virginia. They worked their way from a muster point near Winchester, Virginia to Boston! Those men. the ones who survived, fought throughout the war. General Washington praised those men as his best and most reliable soldiers. He said: 'Their word is good -- and they don't run!' That is a really good thing to say about any person. Are you not proud? I am! I am very proud to have married a Berkeley, valid name, or no. I *will* be a participant in furthering the name!

"One Berkeley, the journal does not say exactly how he was related, was recommended for the Medal of Honor in the Civil War, but there is no record of him ever having received the award. Numerous Berkeley men died in wars. I would be surprised to learn any family in the entire United States contributed so much to her defense.

"There was limited opportunity for females until the nineteen-hundreds, but women in your family managed to contribute. They doctored the ill. Two served as nurses in the Civil War. I cannot tell if they were official nurses, but they did nurse soldiers throughout much of the war. They volunteered to do that after their brother died from battle wounds on Rich Mountain. Several of your female ancestors taught school. One was a tax assessor. One was even a Justice of the Peace, then an important post -- much like a judge.

"Your father earned field promotions during World War Two from sergeant to captain. He also earned several medals for valor.

"Look at what you did! You wear the Silver Star and two Purple Hearts!

"Clay, my dear, dear husband, we are not going to let a family of such statue die out, simply because you are the last male Berkeley and I am so useless! Not bloody likely, Buccaneer, as you are so fond of saying. We will do *something*!

"Patty, Honey, You're the best wife a man could possibly have. You are good at everything. I cannot think of one damn thing you can't do well. So, Kitten, I never, ever want to hear you say anything about you being useless. Not ever again, Patty Lane! You are the woman I love and I love you as a partner, not as a brood mare!"

I kissed Patty as much as I dared, considering her physical condition, but there was nothing else to say. Patty could not have children. The Henry Clay Berkeley – Margaret Louise Tinny line was at its end.

CHAPTER EIGHT

TURNING AND BURNING

Patty became increasingly touchy and belligerent as she became more mobile. She didn't want to watch Spanish or Armed Forces TV, she didn't want to sew, she didn't want to play cards, or anything else we could come up with. What she wanted was to leap smack dab into arranging her new house, prowling the beach, visiting stores, eating Spanish food in restaurants and running the streets while she experienced Spain, all evolutions for which she was not yet fit.

Patty flat had us all climbing bulkheads! Missus Patterson hung out on the patio, when she couldn't escape with neighbor women. Mister Patterson helped the landscaper clip hedges. I put up with Patty's puffed out lip for two more days, then held a change-of-command ceremony with her parents and shifted my Flag back to my office.

There was not one single sailor of the 225 assigned who could have kept me in the state of tension Patty generated, not if all 225 went off-plumb at the same time. It was A-number-one-ditty-bag enjoyable to sit at my desk solving problems of the world and not have to listen to: "Why cannot I have a beer?" "'Why cannot I go down to the beach, it is only a short distant?" "Why do I have to stay inside, it is a very warm day?" "Why do I have to eat this bland stuff?" "Daddy, I hope you brought your gun. I want you to shoot Clay. He is being *mean* to me!"

The CO of the hospital had apparently taken Patty as his Number One Patient. He showed regularly to check her out. He, too, came beneath her guns. Same questions. Same complaints. Plus, he had to listen to: "I am not an invalid! I can walk fine. I could walk all the way to the naval station right now!" "What is wrong with me going out on the beach?" "Shopping would not tax me!" and "Nothing is sore!" The doctor solved his problem when he heard that one. He poked gently at her belly with his forefinger and Patty let out a yelp. He smiled at her, finished his glass of wine, patted her wavy-curly head and left. Patty sulked the rest of the day and evening. *Everybody* was being *mean* to her!

The doctor finally granted her a certain amount of freedom. She was allowed to walk the streets, shop and generally hell about the town, but she was not to lift anything or do any sort of physical labor. I found her the very next evening, happily clipping away at the bougainvillea vines that climbed the front of the house, sweat running down her smudged face and dirt all the way to her elbows.

"Patty Lane! What in the *hell* are you doing? The doctor said *no* physical labor and he damn well meant *no* physical labor. Quit that right now!"

Patty jerked around and let go with a major blush. "I am just *trimming* these flowers a tiny bit. I have not been *working*!"

"You call it what you want, but quit doing it. Folks who can afford it don't take care of such things in Spain. They hire a gardener."

"I will care for my own yard!"

"Look. Many gardeners in Spain are old folks who live on small pensions and they need the extra money. You are taking bread and wine from their mouths by doing your own work."

Patty gave me a long look. "I wish Jarhead were here. I would have him bite you!"

"Maybe you can get that accomplished near term. They are being shipped day after tomorrow." I grinned, informing her that our English bulldog, Jarhead, and Persian cat, Blue Suit, would soon join us in Spain.

Patty let out a whoop, then sashayed back and forth across the small front yard until I grabbed her by the shoulders and made her stop. She squeezed tightly against me and probably shocked any passing Spanish by throwing a lip lock on me that would have excited an eunuch. "Oh, I will be so happy to see my animals!"

My animals? They were *my* animals, or had been until Patty mustered in. They shifted their affections to her the very day she first visited my house. They totally abandoned my ship after Patty and I married. I went from Prime Owner to Excess Gear before Patty got halfway through the door after our honeymoon.

Patty could barely stop walking, let alone sit, without Jarhead flopping his big, ugly head across her feet and slobbering on her. Even the barflies in Moe's slop chute where we hung out, started referring to the hell-raising, beer drinking Jarhead as 'Patty's Dog.'

Blue Suit rarely purred before Patty arrived on the scene, but became so happy at having a soft lap to curl on, he took up running his sawmill as a full-time occupation. He continued watching TV newscasts from his perch on the back of the couch, as always, but did not seem to worry so much. Still, wrinkles on his forehead occasionally reappeared, probably when he worried about hail, rainstorms, pestilence, bugs, the Middle East and the horror of hair balls. Blue Suit was a pessimist and a wimp!

Blue Suit lay flat in his cage, worry lines crossing his forehead, as his shipping cage circled the luggage carousal at the Jerez airport. Jarhead stood bowlegged in his cage, chest pushed out, just waiting to chop down on the first person who said 'Boo' to him.

Their papers had cleared customs in Madrid, so we opened the cages and let them out. Blue Suit slipped between Patty's legs and cut in the steam line to his sawmill. Jarhead flopped his head across her feet, let out his characteristic moan, grunt, grumble, whatever, and slobbered on her shoes.

Patty dropped to her knees and tried to scoop eighty pounds of animals into her arms. I put a stop to that! She petted on them and jabbered at them with total disregard of passengers trying to get past her to collect their luggage, probably wondering what in the hell was going on with the crazy American *Senora*.

I had warned my neighbors about Jarhead, whose main occupation was impregnating any gyp, large, small or middle-sized, that crossed his bow. He wasn't into associating with other males, except for kicking hell out of them on a regular basis. I intended to keep him inside the house until I got a high fence built, but I knew what a loser that was even before it started. Jarhead was an accomplished escape artist and I suspected Blue Suit guilty of aiding and abetting.

The evening they arrived, we went to the tiny bar where Mister Patterson had taken up card and domino playing with the Spanish landscaper and his running mates. We invited Blue Suit to accompany us, but he wasn't about to venture outside, not when he didn't understand the language. Jarhead was ready for anything!

Everyone had a San Miguel, except Missus Patterson who asked for red wine. Patty whipped a small bowl from her shoulder bag, filled it with beer and set it on the floor. Jarhead sniffed it a couple of times and looked up at her, then me. *'What in the hell is this stuff?'*

"Drink it, Jarhead. You are in Spain now. They have no Rolling Rock beer. That is all you are going to get, so drink it!" Patty ordered.

Jarhead gave it a couple more sniffs, then lapped at it if he wasn't certain what it would taste like. He looked up, beer dripping from his chin, sort of grinned, then stuck his ugly head right into the bowl and started lapping it out.

Playing cards and dominoes went flying across the room as Spanish men came boiling out of their chairs. *"El Perro esta bebiendo cerveza*!" (The dog is drinking beer!)

Jarhead paid no mind to the chattering crowd milling around him. He finished his beer, licked the bowl shiny and looked up at Patty with hope and love in his eyes. She refilled his bowl and said, "That is all you get, Jarhead. You act weird when you drink to excess."

"Que perro! El un perro muy fuerte!" Mister Patterson's running mate exclaimed. *"Que perro*!" (What a dog! He is a very strong dog. What a dog!) That comment lit them off with each trying to outdo the other with descriptions of Jarhead's strength and attributes.

Jarhead wouldn't be so popular, or so admired, once he climbed their fences, knocked up their gyps, ate their flowers, tore their shrubs out of the ground and whipped up on their male dogs!

"Missus Post told me Jarhead drank beer, but I had difficulty believing it." Missus Patterson said, speaking of the Head Spook of the *Big Otter Quilting Circle and Gossip Society*. Nothing got past Missus Post, my nearest neighbor and a wonderful woman who had watched out for me after my folks drown when I was sixteen. Rumor had it the CIA and the KGB solicited her advice.

"Yeah, but he is not very good at it." I told her. "He prefers Rolling Rock, but he can't drink but two of the little bottles before he wants to act up, or go to sleep. I don't know what this Spanish beer will do to him."

Jarhead soon answered that. He started nosing around the floor looking for a bit of food. Jarhead liked a snack with his beer. A Spanish man, who obviously understood dogs, slipped him a slice of *chorizo*, a hard, roughly ground sausage. Jarhead gulped it down and looked up at the man. When no further food was forthcoming, he found a nice smelling pair of feet belonging to a card player and went to sleep on the man's feet. That action tickled the Spaniards immensely and lit off another round of conversation.

"*El perro esta borracho!*" (The dog is drunk!)

"*Si, el esta muy borracho!*" (Yes, he is very drunk.)

With Jarhead asleep on the man's feet and nothing of interest happening, Patty and her mother went to the far end of the bar and started throwing pesetas into fruit machines, which were similar to slot machines. In my years of running Spanish cities, I had never seen a person win. Still, the Spanish played them with great gusto, yelling when the fruits almost matched in the windows and groaning when the fruits failed to match. I suspected they played them for the bells, the ching-ching noise and the gurgling sound.

"Clay, did I tell you I had a run in with Curtis not long after you left America?"

"No, Pa, you didn't. What sort of run in?"

Curtis P. Longly, a Navy chief journalist and Patty's first cousin on her mother's side of the family, was my enemy, though I never understood why. He had hated me since I was in the first grade and he was in the third. We were paddled in school any number of times for fighting. Sometimes I won. Sometimes Curtis won. He, being older, joined the Navy and was already seaman when I joined. I passed him after the second class petty officer level and was now two ranks senior to him.

We were twice stationed in the same location and each time he made a sincere effort to do me dirt. He finally succeeded when he released the rough draft of an interview Patty and I conducted for her college newspaper the day we met. What I said about the Vietnam War and how we recruited minorities was for her ears only and not intended for publication. Patty, the paper's editor, had blue penciled the interview, then passed it to Curtis' girlfriend for final typing. The girlfriend gave it to Curtis who gave it to a bunch of newspapers and the rest is history. I was fired from recruiting and transferred to NAVCOMMSTA Santa Cruz.

Curtis would have likely done that anyway, but my thumping on him at our wedding reception after he made off-color remarks about my innocent bride didn't improve his attitude toward me. Curtis wasn't at all happy at me stuffing a towel into a commode and flushing it a few times while he lay unconscious on the tile floor. Cracking two of his teeth didn't help either.

"I went over to your farm, Clay, to see if your manager needed anything and found Curtis a-sittin' in his car just past the Post place. He sorta ducked down when he seen my truck a-comin' up the lane. I figured that right odd, like he intended to do a meanness, so I pulled over and asked what he wuz a-doin' there.

"He got right upset. Said that me bein' his uncle didn't give me no right to follow him around. I told him I didn't follow him, that I wuz there to see my friend, Dana Pollard, who managed your farms. I asked him what he wuz a-doin' around my son-in-law and my daughter's place where he didn't have no business a-tall.

"He might have been a-drinkin', or he might have been in one of his crazy moods, for he came a-boilin' out of his car and sorta swung at me.

"I jumped flat on him and cussed him out. Told him I wuz a-goin' to call his daddy and tell him he needed to lock him up before he went plumb nuts and hurt someone. He started a-goin on 'bout me a-likin' you better'n my own kin. Then he made his real bad mistake and started sayin' stuff 'bout what Patty had been a-doin' with you a-fore you two got married. I ain't a-goin' to repeat what he said. It wuz flat mean!

"Well, now -- I broke a trace chain while a-plowin' the garden with my old mule that I like to work once in a while so she thinks I need her. It'd been a-layin' on the truck seat 'cause I wuz a-goin' to get it welded first chance I got. I grabbed that trace chain and I flat laid into him! I wrapped it around his big neck and yanked him near off the ground. I told him if he ever did say anything bad again 'bout Patty I wuz a-going to shoot him to flinders!"

"I expect part of his acting that way was because things haven't been going good for Curtis since he got me fired from recruiting."

"How so?"

"My recruiters were some kind of mad when I got fired, so they evened the score with the folks who did me in. They learned of illegal stuff the commodore was doing and turned him into the Navy Department for fraud and abuse. He was fined at Admiral's Mast, which is sort of a Navy court of law, and told to retire. A Sicilian girl, wife of one of my recruiters, sic'd Mafia types on Curtis and scared him into requesting a transfer. When he did, a senior chief called a buddy in Washington and got Curtis orders to an aircraft carrier in Japan. Curtis doesn't like ships. He's never served in one. So, he requested to transfer to the Fleet Reserve, which is, really, the same as retirement. I heard he's now working for the *Star-Journal* in Big Otter now and don't much like it."

"I knowed he was out of the Navy, but didn't know why.

"You know, Son, he's my own nephew, but I do believe he's got a loose strap or two on his harness. He done some awful things when he wuz a boy. He shot one of my cats and two-three of my chickens. Seems like he liked killing things, not to hunt them, just to kill them. He wuz flat mean to animals and people.

"He tried to push little Patty off that loading chute at the cattle barn when she wuz six. I seen him do it. I took him home and watched his maw and pa bawl him out, but they never whipped him like they oughta done. That's part of his problem. He wuz born mean to start with and they never did give him no discipline. He wuz such a pretty baby that folks bragged on him and his folks took up for him, no matter what he done.

"He done something terrible bad to Patty once, but that stubborn girl never would tell me what he done. All I seen, when I walked out of the milk barn, wuz her a-trying to stick him with a pitchfork! She like to got him too! Well, I couldn't have my daughter a-stickin' folks with a pitchfork, not when I didn't know why. So, when she wouldn't tell me, I turned her over my knee and warmed her little butt! I give her one hell of a lecture too. I told her she had a daddy to protect her and I expected her to let me do that. She wuz flat mad at me for a good week. I don't blame her. She wuz sixteen, 'most grown. She never had but maybe one spankin' in her whole life and I tell you she flat didn't like it even a little bit!

"After I got done cussin' Curtis, I took him home and told his daddy that he know'd damn well Patty weren't mean and didn't hurt nobody, but Curtis done something so bad she tried to stick him with a pitchfork. I told him to keep Curtis off'n my place and away from Patty when he was home from the Navy!

"I think he's flat crazy, Clay. Dangerous too!"

I didn't believe he was necessarily dangerous, but I went along with the crazy part.

The Patterson's returned to West Virginia a couple of days after the doctor pronounced Patty totally fit and proper. Patty began doing all the things she wanted. Our life together continued pretty much as it had before her operation, except the doctor cautioned us no hanky-panky drills were to be executed, not until he gave the okay. Patty complained bitterly about that!

Patty's return to a healthy state freed me to get on full-time with the business of the NAVCOMMSTA. I was doing just that when a yeoman striker with huge ears and thick, black-rimmed eyeglasses stuck his head into my office and announced, "The Command Master Chief wants you!"

I'd seen that sailor walking past my office a time or two. I knew nothing about him except that he was a yeoman striker. His announcement and the way he slouched against my door casing sort of tripped my trigger, as did the surly tone of his voice.

"That may be, Pens, but I don't believe that was how you were taught to relay a message."

"The Command Master Chief wants to see you ASAP."

"I got that part, but unless you're Paul Revere, you get your butt in here and make that announcement in the proper manner!"

He came to my desk, stood at something approaching attention and said, "The Command Master Chief would like to see you as soon as possible, Master Chief."

I stood and petted him on the shoulder. "That was a lot better. Do things in a courteous manner and you'll likely never get yelled at. Give the master chief my regards and tell him I'll be there as soon as I receive a telephone call that's hanging fire."

"He said right now, Master Chief."

"Don't concern yourself. I'll be there when I get there."

"Did my yeoman tell you I wanted to see you ASAP?" That was my introduction to the long-absent Command Master Chief when I showed up ten-fifteen minutes later.

"He did." I replied, holding out my hand. "I'm Clay Berkeley, as I am sure you know. And you are Ken Bryan, I suppose."

He took my hand, but didn't reach out and grab it with any great degree of excitement. "Yes, I am, but I am addressed as 'Master Chief.'"

"Then you can address me the same. We're of equal rank. I don't know who is senior."

"You are senior in grade, but I hold positional authority by virtue of my position. I trust you understand that!"

We were really hitting it off! Sort of like the Greeks and the Turks. He seemed to have an idea that his billet placed him at the Right Hand of God. I had held the command master chief billet in a cruiser-destroyer group and understood exactly what he did for a living. His authority, other than that derived from being a master chief, was confined by the desires of his commanding officer to whom he directly reported.

"Is there something you need, or is this your standard welcome to newly reported sailors?"

"I thought it proper we meet."

"We've done that."

"Er, yes, we have."

114

A little off balance there, Fellow. .

I inspected him carefully. He was recruiting poster sharp. There wasn't a wrinkle anywhere. His brass gleamed and his graying hair was clipped less than one inch long. He was almost as pretty as Chief Journalist Curtis P. Longly and had the same overbearing 'I'm a superior individual and I'll keep you aware of that fact' attitude. The five ribbons on his chest showed his travels in the Navy were sparse. He had no 'Hey, I was there too!' campaign ribbons. His two senior ribbons were a Joint Service Commendation Medal and a Navy Achievement Medal.

"I trust your wife is recovered?"

"Yes, she is. She's in Seville today, trying to seduce some unsuspecting Spaniards."

The dazed look on the CMC's face told me I had got him again. I laughed, then said, "Her Spanish neighbors are teaching her how to bargain and haggle with the locals. They took her to Seville for her final test. She is already competent in the art, so some poor man or woman is going home tonight, wondering what happened to their coin purse, three-quarters of their wares and maybe their first-born child."

"Uh, yes."

"Anything else, Master Chief. Duty calls and all that rot, you know."

"Well, actually there is. I understand you have experienced problems with various individuals since you reported."

"Such as?"

"Chief Warrant Officer Hardin, for one."

"I don't see our conversation as a problem. He didn't seem to understand how the chain-of-command works. Strange a man of his time and seniority in the Navy didn't understand that."

"You believe it proper to correct a senior?"

"One of the reasons for creating the master chief rank was so there would be a person who could work across departmental lines and smooth out wrinkles. I didn't feel that I was correcting him. I simply reminded him of how things are supposed to work. I'd do that to a person of any level. Have done so, in fact."

"Well, yes, I suppose I can understand that view, but you have expressed no desire to work with the executive officer either."

"I don't work for the XO. I work for the operations officer."

"He is second in command!"

"Yeah, he is -- according to the staff-line chart, but executive officers usually limit their effort to ensuring the command's organization is functioning properly. About the only time XO's generally get involved in operational matters is when they are at general quarters filling their battle billet. Or, in small ships where they are double-hatted, as both XO and navigator. Oh, there is one other time. That is when the command has a weak CO. Jiffy Jeff is not a weak CO, so that does not apply here."

"*Jiffy Jeff?* You refer to the *commanding officer* as *Jiffy Jeff?*"

"That's what we nicknamed him in *King.* Seagoing skippers always get a nickname, good or bad. He was one hell of a fine destroyer skipper, so he got a good nickname."

"You served with the commanding officer? Before, I mean?"

"We're old shipmates."

Bite on that Command Master Chief. Here's another for you. . . .

"I've heard quite a number of complaints about the crew's paperwork getting lost, or not processed. That is your bailiwick best I remember the billet from when I had it for an admiral, ensuring that the troops are treated fairly and that they get what they need. Some complaints involve their missing out on rating examinations and promotion. I don't need to spend time answering a letter to some congressional creep about how we mistreated a constituent's children. We need to get that squared away."

"I've heard nothing of the sort!"

"I'll see if I can get you some names, but bear in mind they happened before I got here and before you went to the States for that study group. If you have nothing further, I must toddle on my way." I stood, then noticed the CMC's eyes lock on my middle section.

"Master Chief, surely you do not consider that belt buckle suitable for wear?"

"What's wrong with it?"

"It has an insignia of a ship on it. It is not regulation."

"I beg to differ. My wife, who has turned into a resident expert on uniform regulations, and most everything else related to the Navy, took me to task last fall for a non-regulation tie clasp. She reminded me that certain small insignia on a belt buckle, cuff links or a tie clasp are authorized, provided they are of a personal, sentimental, or historical nature. My belt buckle meets at least two of those requirements, maybe all three."

"Uh, yes, I do believe that is true. But that buckle is in terrible condition. It is nicked, scratched and no longer carries a decent shine. It is disgraceful!"

That lit my boiler.

"*Frank E. Evans* was cut in half by the Australian aircraft carrier *Melbourne* in the South China Sea during the Vietnam War. She lost sixty-eight men that night. Evans was an old, World War Two destroyer with a tight crew. I personally knew those killed, even though I had transferred to *Forrestal* shortly before the disaster.

"This belt buckle carries the silhouette and name of that ship. It relates to the men who died. I think of them every time I buckle or unbuckle my trousers. It also reminds me of other Navy men and women who went to sea or to battle and lost their lives for their country. If you want this buckle off me, then I strongly suggest you round up the master-at-arms force and muster a working party, because that is the only way you will stop me from wearing it!"

The CMC was sitting frozen-faced behind his desk with one hand partially raised in the air when I turned and left his office. I suspected that would be the last time we would speak. The CMC of the Naval Station was correct. He was a non-seagoing, nit picking Slimy Creature!

That afternoon, the captain hailed me as I was walking from my car toward the NAVCOMMSTA building as I returned from lunch. "Is that the same belt buckle you wore in *King*, Master Chief? The one from *Frank E. Evans*?"

Uh, Oh, I thought. That slimy CMC went crying to the captain. Now, I'm between the deep, dark sea and an ocean of kimchee.

"Yes, Sir, it is. It's still hard to believe what happened to that ship."

"We must keep the memory of those brave men, Master Chief. I, too, like to remember things of a significant nature." He pointed to his belt. "I went home to lunch and got my old buckle from *King*. It is in marginally better condition than yours."

"It is a pity, Captain, that so few of us see fit to keep the past alive."

"It certainly is, Master Chief. Say, I don't believe I have a nickname here. Do you see your way clear to spread the Jiffy Jeff nickname around? I did so enjoy hearing the watches refer to me as such when I slipped around the dark decks at night. My nickname was far superior to what we dubbed the captain of *Lang*, my first ship. He was Mouse Marvin the Mean."

Missus Clausen mustered in late January with two fairly young women under tow. "Ladies, this is Master Chief Berkeley, Patty's husband . . . her burden to bear. Master Chief, this is Lisa Merkling and Helen Elliott. They volunteered to assist with your campaign to reduce the spread of unwanted cracker snatchers. Both have two children and both are married to first class petty officers."

I got the women a cup of coffee and a sticky bun and we adjourned to the conference room. Missus Caulsen had already briefed them, but I expounded on the subject, telling them I didn't want them to hold pleasant conversations with my female sailors. I wanted it scary and dirty. They said they had no problem with that. I showed them the location of the office they would use. I told them I would like all the females to have had the briefing ASAP. They seen no problem, but wanted to conduct the first few briefings together until they could get a feel for how it would go. I had no problem with that.

Missus Caulsen and Missus Merkling went to powder their nose before leaving the building, but Missus Elliott declined to go. She seemed nervous, so I asked if something was wrong.

"Do you know who I am, or rather who I was, Master Chief?" she asked, timidly.

"No, I don't. Should I?"

"Not unless there are old records around. Master Chief, I reported to this command eight years ago, directly from radio school. I was here eleven months before they discharged me for pregnancy, which was then the procedure. I will not say the man involved was totally at fault, but I didn't know anything about anything, except I was in *love*. He completed his enlistment and returned to the States before I learned I was pregnant and I never again heard from him. I took my discharge in Norfolk and found a job. I was too ashamed to return home to Pennsylvania.

"What we are doing is wonderful! I wish something like this would have been available when I was eighteen years old. Oh, I love my husband and I love both children, but I loved the Navy too, what little of it I experienced before discharge. I love my life as it is now, but I cannot but wonder what it would have been had I not gotten pregnant. I intended to get a degree and apply for an officer program. Instead, I fell for a man who didn't really care for me as a person, just as a *thing*. Master Chief, if we prevent only one unmarried pregnancy we will have succeeded. You can count on me to give my total effort. I *know*!"

"You didn't need to tell me that, Missus Elliott. The Navy doesn't keep sensitive records like yours at command level. The only record of your time in the Navy is locked down in Saint Louis and there it will stay, unless you request a copy. No one will ever know."

"I am no longer ashamed of what I did, but I will never forget the terror of being pregnant and alone. Luckily, I wasn't alone so awfully long. I met my husband weeks before the baby was born. We later dated, fell in love and married. I told him the entire story on our third date. He loves both our children equally and has adopted the first. He is a good man, Master Chief."

"Yeah, he sounds like it. And you're a fine woman, Missus Elliott."

"Thank you, Master Chief. Oh, here come the ladies. I'll see you tomorrow!"

Missus Elliott had not mentioned where her husband was stationed and I didn't know of him. I checked the watch bills to see if he was a NAVCOMMSTA sailor. There he was: T. J. Elliott, Watch Supervisor of Delta Section in the Anti-submarine Warfare Operations Center, one of my own people, but in a division distant from the headquarters building. I suspected I had seen him around, but had not spoken to him or to many other sailors who stood rotating watches. There simply wasn't enough hours in a day to do all the things I wanted to do and even some that I needed to do.

I went to ship's office, pulled his service jacket, returned to my office and read it. He was a top sailor in any man's Navy, but he had not made chief radioman after three attempts. His evaluations were numerically perfect, but the narrative portion was weak; not a single command has taken the time to fully justify the numerical grade given in each trait. He was likely a quiet man who did not blow his own horn; hence, no one else did either. He appeared as fine a man as his wife believed.

I was going to need an administrative assistant near term as I did not intend to renew Doris Harris in her temporary position. If, after I interviewed him, he looked as good as his jacket suggested, it would be of no difficulty to transfer him to headquarters. I would re-title his billet prior to writing his next evaluation to say, *Assistant to the Operations Department Master Chief.* It never hurt for a good man or woman to have a sea daddy!

The briefings began as scheduled. I kept my eye on the passageway as individual female sailors left their briefing given by Missus Elliott and/or Missus Merkling. Some faces showed shock, some disgust, some looked ill, and some showed nothing at all. Would the tough love work? Time would tell.

I located a not-so-old chief who had a gator freighter full of ex-wife and ex-girlfriend troubles and a bale of financial problems caused mainly by the child support he was paying. If anyone was ever a walkin' talkin' billboard advertising the need for a man to fire no live rounds during sexual encounter, it was he! Again, time would tell if he was able to get the attention of the young, male sailors he would brief.

The executive officer eventually got wind of the program, probably some girl complained to the CMC. The XO pounced upon the commander about the harsh treatment the young females were receiving at the hands of the two briefing ladies. He did not mention the same thing happening to the young male sailors. The commander trained her batteries and laid a round right between his eyes by asking if he had ever been *knocked up*, rather than using the socially acceptable term, *pregnant.* When he got through stumbling past that one, she told him she could think of little worse than being pregnant and alone without the support of a husband and that she would see the captain immediately if he interfered with the program. She reminded him that he had directed *her* master chief, the very day he reported, to fix the pregnancy problem and that was exactly what was happening. The XO lowered his Flag and sailed away in defeat.

The CO heard about the program, probably after the XO repaired his damaged vessel and sailed into the CO's cabin with crying towel in hand. The captain called the commander to his office and asked her to explain the program. She must have done well because the CO told her to continue on course and if the program proved successful, he wanted me to get with the ladies involved and see if they would expand the briefings to include every young female in the command. The commander told him there could be no concrete determination of results near term, like for three or four months -- maybe longer.

The commander reported to me that the captain laughed and said "I'm not an understudy to the village idiot, Missus Stoutmaster. I've never married, but I *know* how a woman gets pregnant and that it can sometimes happen despite precautions. I realize a few pregnancies will likely occur no matter what we do.

I walked into the commander's office just as she arrived at work and announced, with a very serious look on my face. "Commander, you better take a look at *this* message!"

She took the message from my hand, looked at it, screamed, dropped her head on her arms and sobbed. Then she leaped from her chair and started kissing on me. "Oh, Master Chief, this is the most fantastic thing! Oh, thank you so much!"

"Yeah, Commander, that third line really is quite significant. *Paul D. Hunycutt appointed to the grade of Ensign, Limited Duty Officer for Electronics.* I'd appreciate it though, if you'd stop kissing on me. Patty doesn't approve of such carryings on. You can go to work on Lieutenant Prince when he gets here. I called his attention to the message a tick ago."

"Master Chief, You are wonderful! Your reporting to this command changed my life! I will never, ever, be able to repay you!"

"That's your opinion, Commander. There are others who would disagree strongly. You owe me nothing. We're sorta shipmates."

"They can go fu . . . er, uh, well, fiddle with themselves!"

Allen Prince strolled through the hatch and received much the same treatment as I had. She then realized what time it was and dashed out the hatch. I wondered what the XO thought when she showed up for his morning briefing with wet spots on her blouse and her lipstick smeared. It would probably confirm his belief that she was a slut.

The commander returned from the brief a total twitter. She said the XO chewed on her several times because she couldn't lock on to anything he asked her, didn't remember to read the notes on the messages I'd given her, then drifted totally away at the CO's morning briefing. She seemed to think that funny!

She drifted around all day. She simply could not sit still. She would peek through the window between our offices and give me a big grin and a thumbs up what seemed like every few minutes. I called Lieutenant Prince around 1600 after she started tearing up and down the passageway like a mad woman. I told him we'd better get her out of there before she went off-plumb and told someone what was going on. She didn't act like she had one lick of sense!

We bundled her into Mister Prince's car, her being too flustered to be trusted in Spanish traffic. We then made like a gator and hauled sterns to the Santa Cruz-Mar where we bought her a brandy and made her drink it. Patty mustered in shortly after I called her. She had her buddy, Jarhead, in tow. I ordered both of them a beer.

Patty had barely gotten seated at the bar, when the commander like to ruined my week. "Patty, I kissed your husband today."

I could see a Patty explosion on the horizon. She was jealous at any time, certain all women lusted after me as much as she did. That had gotten worse since we were prohibited by the doctor from making love and she started giving me hard looks every time I even glanced at a Spanish woman on the street. She outwardly cautioned me that if I got my hands on a Navy girl, regardless of degree of contact, she was going to save the Navy some money. She qualified that by saying the Navy would not have to worry about finding an escort for my body because there would be nothing left to ship to my Home of Record when she finished with me.

When I told her no woman who worked for me had ever shown an interest in me, she said, "How about your Big Isaac recruiter, Barbara Randolph, who begged you to visit her station every week?"

I protested that Barbara had no designs on me. She was just an eager, hard-working recruiter who occasionally did need help in her remote, one-person station. Patty's answer to that was, "Could I interest you in purchasing some flat land in West Virginia, Master Chief Berkeley?"

Missus Stoutmaster seen the Patty explosion coming too. "He fixed it so Paul and I can really marry. Paul is getting a commission! So, I kissed him. I kissed Allen too."

Patty and Missus Stoutmaster grabbed on to one another and started wetting down the terrain. Missus Prince showed up, asked what the hell was going on, and she too joined the party. It eventually got around to the idea that Paul's applying for a commission had originated with Patty and that generated a further session of hugging, kissing and crying. The Spanish barkeep looked like he was about to abandon ship. He had a gaggle of female maniacs in his bar, all crazy Yankees!

Allen Prince got them under control by telling them they'd better shut up before an outsider came in. Commissioning or no commissioning, Lucy Stoutmaster, an officer in the United States Navy, had shacked up with an enlisted man in the United States Navy and gotten herself more than a little pregnant. Some secrets had to remain just that. Secret.

"Patty, guess who is going to give me away?" the Commander asked, after she glanced suspiciously about the room.

"Why, your father, I suppose."

"I don't have a father. I am an orphan. The Catholic Church raised me. I couldn't relate to girls in college who had parents, not after having spent my entire life surrounded by Catholic nuns and orphan girls. Heck, I couldn't relate to *anybody*. That is one reason why I joined the Navy. I was accustomed to a cloistered society."

"So, Lucy, who is giving you away?" Patty asked.

"The Master Chief! And you and Becky are going to be my maids of honor. Allen will be best man. We will have the wedding in the base chapel."

"Uh, Commander, I don't think that is a good idea -- terrible actually. Maybe you should take leave and marry in the States. It is just a drill anyway, considering you're already legally married. Me, giving you away is *not* in The Plan of the Day!"

"Why in heavens not? None of this would have been possible were it not for you. Neither Paul nor I consider ourselves really married because we married outside the Church. I want a military wedding by a Catholic priest. Paul will want the same."

Paul-baby probably wouldn't have a choice!

"Look, Commander. I've never heard of a chief giving an officer away. Actually, I've never attended a female officer's wedding. Why can't Lieutenant Prince do it?"

"Because . . . I've never been close to a single person, not really, except Paul. I feel very close to you, who didn't really give me a choice. You simply appeared and acted as though you'd known me forever. I feel comfortable with most of the people in Santa Cruz, maybe because it is a small community and people help each other, so I want to marry here. I really want you to give me away. Please do not turn me down!"

"It'd make more sense if the Lieutenant gave you away and I acted as Paul's best man, him being ex-enlisted. Get that admiral you know to give you away. You were close to him, I think."

She caught me by the arm and clutched it tight. "Clay, I think highly of the admiral, but he is retired and traveling the world with his wife. Allen is really high on my list of Good Guys. I never knew until recently what he did for me, but I was sinking fast until you arrived and solved every standing problem I had. I want to point to my wedding picture someday and tell my children, 'That man saved my career and made my marriage to your daddy possible.' Clay, you are like a brother, or maybe like a father to me. Please give me away!"

Bugger the Bosun! Now I was a father figure to a woman around my own age. That, coupled with being married to a woman most suspected of being a teenager, made me think it might be time to turn in my sea bag. I didn't like my boss calling me by my first name either. I surely wasn't going to start calling her Lucy. Life was strange!

The ladies shifted to a table so they could plan a wedding without interference from mere males, so Mister Prince and I had another cup of tea, so as to speak. Things were on my mind.

"Folks are going to talk when she marries an ensign, and she does it the first time he puts on his dinner dress uniform. Having a CPO give her away will make it worse. Lieutenant, do you get the feeling she don't give two whoops in hell if she advances to full commander?"

"Maybe she knows she is not in running for selection to commander. A flag secretary job for an admiral would normally be career enhancing, but the one she had is likely not. The command her admiral held it is a tombstone slot for a one-star admiral. His signature on her FITREP won't carry the weight one would from an admiral in a hot-running command. Unless she has held some top billets, she'll probably not make the slate when the selection board for commander meets, even if the admiral wrote her a walk-on water FITREP.

"We both know that lieutenant commander is the grade where officers usually die on the vine. Lieutenants are separated from the service if they twice fail selection to the next grade. Lieutenant commanders are safe to serve a full twenty years and retire, even if they don't promote to the next rank. That doesn't apply to me. I am an LDO. I'll get my twenty regardless."

"Even if she doesn't select for commander, Mister Prince, she will still have one or two billets more before she retires. Her enlisted shack job will get his commission after he attends Knife and Fork School in Pensacola, but there is no telling where they'll send him for duty. They might not be able to live together for years. He has about twelve years to go before he gets his twenty and she's got seven or eight, or more."

"She just wants to get married and stop sneaking around. Things might work out so that they get stationed in the same location. She can only pray, Master Chief."

"Regardless of her feelings about promotion, and whose trigger she might trip, I wish you would talk to her and explain that she really should have you give her away. You know how folks are. There is a big dividing line between chiefs and officers, even if chiefs do carry some of them on their backs. Folks will talk! What chiefs do as you know, having been a CPO, is function inside a sort of shadow chain-of-command and work around roadblocks, be that a bureaucratic rule or an officer. There are officers and there are chiefs. They nearly always work well together, but they ought not mingle. It is frowned upon. Let's get her back on the straight and narrow!"

"I don't believe we can, Master Chief. She's got the bit in her teeth. Yeah, she realizes I did a lot for her before you reported, but she also knows that was an officer helping another in a professional sense. You pulled every single chestnut burning her pink fingers out of the fire. She was in trouble before you reported, both professionally and personally. Her life was some kind of screwed up! The way I see it is you are something like Moses to her." the Lieutenant snickered and followed that with a short giggle. "You came down out of the mountains carrying The Word on a couple of flat river rocks, and then you blessed her and saved her soul! Sorry, Master Chief, you'll have to give her away!"

"I'll sic Patty Lane on her. She can square this away"

"Patty doesn't care about the dividing line between officers and chiefs. She doesn't see anybody as junior to you. She believes you rank a level or two above the Chief of Naval Operations, so she tells my wife and everybody else. You're stuck, Big Guy!".

CHAPTER NINE

ROCKS AND SHOALS AND TRANQUIL WATERS

Missus Clausen, Elliott and Merkling and I reviewed the pregnancy rate among our unmarried female sailors at the end of February. Only one pregnancy had occurred since the program started. That proved nothing. Based on a woman's body cycle and the date she last engaged in body exchange drills, there could be dozens of pregnant sailors running loose who did not yet know they were pregnant. That, of course, could occur during any review of the program, no matter when conducted. Still, the pregnancy situation looked good, for now.

Things coasted along rather smoothly until the captain took leave to Germany. Hail, rainstorm and pestilence descended about our heads and shoulders the very day the executive officer took over as acting commanding officer.

The XO immediately scheduled a formal, white-glove one-day notice material inspection of every space in the command, including open areas around the buildings. The command was so short of radiomen and cryptology technicians that the communicators were standing a three-section watch bill with limited time off and had been doing so for weeks. That left not enough people in any given watch section to perform their normal duties while holding a full-blown field day to spit-shine the spaces, so off-duty watch standers were pulled in to conduct a major field day.

That caused a gaggle of wives, who saw little of their husbands in a three-section watch bill situation, crying to the chaplain and a host of angry sailors of both sexes complaining to the chain-of-command and threatening to request transfer. The CMC, seeing a cluster of unhappy sailors milling about out outside his office, slid into the XO's cabin and, I suppose, tucked himself safely beneath the XO's sheltering arm. Supervisory and management personnel, also angry at the burden imposed on the watch standers, stayed with their troops and helped with watch standing duties and cleaning. That was good leadership.

The inspection was a cluster-seduction! The XO crawled beneath tables, climbed on top of equipment and ran his hand over every surface, peered under equipment and poked beneath them with a damp cloth on the end of a metal ruler. He did not like it when told that sticking a wet or metal object beneath electronic equipment was not in keeping with electrical safety regulations.

A salty-dog chief warrant electrician from plans and public works department took me to task, "Keep your chow chute shut, Master Chief. Let the ass electrocute himself!" I later heard the warrant officer threatened to retire after the XO ordered him to install a grounding strap on a workbench in the air conditioning room. The fact that it was a wooden workbench, which could not possibly conduct electricity, did not impress the XO. The Book said work benches were to have a grounding strap connected between the bench and a grounding point and, by God, it was going to have a grounding strap!

He then scheduled a personnel inspection for the entire command, including off-duty watch standers, for Saturday morning. When asked why Saturday, he said it was "Old Navy." He initially wanted first class petty officers and below to lay out the contents of their sea bags in front of them as they stood in ranks. That got stop-gaped when the administrative officer 'lost' the manual that provided a listing of uniform items a sailor needed to maintain a 'full' sea bag. I had not seen a sea bag inspection conducted in years. It was one of the old, demeaning practices best lost in time.

I had stood a personnel inspection as a young sailor beneath the age-dimmed eyes of an elderly admiral suited out in a pre-World War Two dress blue uniform that had turned greenish, but I never seen anything like the XO.

His body was crammed into an extremely tight set of dress blues adorned with six medals of no real significance and wearing a sword that sagged from waist to shoe top. His idea of military bearing left something to be desired as he shambled proudly through the ranks behind the chief master-at-arms. Following behind was the CMC who nit-picked the sailors every step of the way, a yeoman with a pad on which to record uniform discrepancies and a hospital corpsman carrying a bottle of alcohol and a towel, for use in event the XO needed to clean his hands after touching an enlisted puke.

It was the rare sailor with whom they found no fault. If they could not find anything else, they made male sailors lift their trouser legs to inspect for proper stenciling on their socks. The females jumped pretty well slick in that area. The inspection party did not inspect the upper legs of females for runs in their nylons, but did take a hard look at the heels of their black pumps for nicks and scratches.

The XO experienced a problem when he stepped in front of an extra-tall sailor God's People Fitters had blessed with a magnificent superstructure and found himself eyeball to nipple with her. He turned beet color and stepped awkwardly sideways to inspect the next sailor. He tripped over his sword and would have fallen to the tarmac had the chief master at arms not grabbed him. That earned the CMAA, a well-liked man, the instant enmity of the crew.

"That prick couldn't possibly rate that yellow medal with the red stripes, unless he served with Dewey in the Spanish-American War or some such! I don't know what it is and I never seen a post-World War Two medal I couldn't identify!" growled the beat-up chief warrant electrician as the XO passed by the chief and officer ranks without looking at us.

"Could have gotten it in Sea Scouts, or maybe he bought it in a pawn shop because the color matches his skin so well." I whispered out of the corner of my mouth. That generated a stifled laugh from a couple-three chiefs and officers, which caused the XO to whirl around and again trip over his sword. The CMAA caught him again!

The instant the inspection secured, the crew adjourned directly to the Sea Dragon Club and All Hands commenced to bitch, moan and throw down booze.

Patty had accompanied some Navy wives to a canopied seating area, provided for guests by the supply department, in order to observe her first formal military function. I was waiting for her to show up at the club when the chief warrant electrician, armed with a drink in each hand, slide beside me and said, "Master Chief, you've seen Indian fakers climb ropes, hookers give it away, bar girls refuse a drink, strange sightings at sea and goats screw in the marketplace of Tangiers, but I doubt you've seen anything like this son-of-a-bitch! He's acting CO for a week and he thinks he's Admiral Nimitz!"

"You want something to worry about, Sir? Think what would happen if the next selection board goes totally bananas and promotes him to captain. He could be our next CO!"

"I'll retire and take up selling pigs to Arabs before I serve with him as skipper!"

The XO held a recall alert drill on Sunday and called everybody back to the command to check the accuracy of the Emergency Recall Bill. Monday, he hit us with a series of fire drills and bomb threats and a repel boarders exercise, for which there were no personnel assigned and no defensive weapons except two .45 pistols.

There was hardly a period throughout the week when he did not spring something on us. There was no general announcing system installed, so he wore the CMAA to a frazzle by running him up and down the passageways to announce: *'Fire in the message center!' 'Bomb in technical control!' 'Riot on the quarterdeck!' 'Intruders making way across the parking lot!'* and a gaggle of other drills and exercises. When he finished terrorizing one building, he went to another and started all over.

When he was not conducting drills, he organized us. He shifted officers and chiefs among divisions like pegs on a pinochle board, with 'His Boys' moving into prime billets. He wrote 'Special Evaluations' on everybody who had ever crossed his bow, which was a considerable number of people. The senior chief yeoman had the bad evaluations typed and signed as ordered, but stashed them in his safe instead of mailing them to the Bureau of Naval Personnel.

Morale was a low ebb throughout the command. Every machine capable of preparing a typed document had a sailor in front of it writing their congressperson. The XO threw Missus Stoutmaster and the Head Spook in charge of the Naval Security Group out of his office when they dared complain about his treatment of their personnel. I then caught him in the passageway and laid similar groups on him. He told me he would relieve me for cause and send me to the naval station awaiting orders. I told him to do it!

Two admirals in command of battle groups at sea and captains of eight ships sent messages querying why important messages had not reached their destinations in a timely manner. The delays were due, of course, to the XO's drills that required on-watch communicators to evacuate their working spaces instead of processing messages. Delay or non-delivery of message, is *A Real Bad Thing*, but the XO gaffed me off when I tried to explain the havoc he was causing.

Mister Prince and the chief warrant electrician were standing tall on the quarterdeck at the exact moment the captain returned from leave. They had beaten me to that location by a tick of the clock!

Minutes later the Captain called the XO into his cabin and serious yelling, laced with words usually heard only at sea and in sailor bars, echoed down the passageway. Fifteen minutes after that, the CMC, who had aided and abetted the XO, was called into the presence of the Captain and again, sailor-type yelling was heard.

The Captain was waiting for me when I hit the quarterdeck at 0600 the next morning. "Come into my cabin, Master Chief. Get a cup of coffee and take a seat."

I couldn't think of anything I had done to aid the XO in totally screwing up the reputation of the command and the morale of the sailors that would, in turn, cause nasty letters to flow from congresspersons within a couple of weeks.

"Master Chief Berkeley, as of 0800 this morning, you will relieve Master Chief Bryan, who has left the command, as Command Master Chief. Your letter of appointment will be forthcoming. It will outline your responsibilities to me and the enlisted men and women of this command. Questions?"

"Uh, Captain, you might be jumping a little too fast here. Nothing that happened was Master Chief Bryan's fault. He is really big on how a junior acts toward a senior. Captain, in his mind, the XO *was* the commanding officer and had every right to do what he wanted. The fact that the XO was only acting as commanding officer while you were on leave and the things he did were screwed up as a three-decker soup sandwich was not a consideration so far as Master Chief Bryan was concerned. I think you oughta give him some slack, Sir."

"You do not want the billet, do you?"

"No, Sir. I don't. But even if I did, I'd want to be fair to the incumbent."

"Do you know anything about Master Chief Bryan?"

"I've only met him once, Sir."

"There is a term that applies to what you just said, Master Chief. It comes out of a bull's rectum! Tell me what I already know."

"Well, Captain, he has no sea time and does not relate to sea sailors. He nit picks in enforcing regulations and lets difficult issues under his cognizance slid. He understands how to impress a senior a whole lot better than he understands loyalty to the people he is supposed to look out for. If you are asking if I like and respect him, the answer is no

"That said, he is one hell of an impressive looking master chief and his knowledge of rules and regulations is lots better than mine. He is probably damn good in his professional field, considering he made master chief in a rating that has only two or three master chiefs. It may behoove you to sit him down and explain how the Navy outside of Washington operates."

"If we have to start training *master chiefs* this Navy is in serious trouble!

"He is a politician who believed volunteering for the CMC program would get him into a relaxing job. He should have never been detailed to a CMC billet, but since there is no selection board for that billet, commands are going to get the occasional CMC with narrow views who cannot do the job. He should have made an effort to influence the XO and prevent the chaos that occurred. Instead, he aided the XO in his stupidity! I considered relieving him months ago. I did not do so. I was wrong and my sailors paid the price.

"Master Chief Bryan is gone. You have the billet. I do not wish to discuss it further."

"We have to discuss it further, Captain. Who is going to relieve me in my billet? I have a bunch of stuff hanging fire."

"I will assign Warrant Holt of the earth satellite station to the billet until a master chief is ordered in to replace you."

"Operations department is darned short of folks with heavy fleet experience. It might be better to assign his senior chief to that job. He has a better background, a broader one. He reported from a billet as communications officer for Destroyer Squadron Seventeen. I believe Mister Holt spent a large part of the enlisted portion of his career in airdale commands flying patrols out of Sicily, Iceland and Japan."

The captain leaned back in his chair and clasp his hands behind his head. "That would be a better choice, considering Mister Holt has had no sea duty to speak of and the operations officer has none. Let's go with that. That way Missus Stoutmaster can continue improving her knowledge of operational communications. No doubt you will ensure Senior Chief Meyers will whisper guidance into her little pink ear and hold her lily white hand to comfort her as you have done."

"Captain, you and I both know females get detailed to billets that require knowledge of the entire Navy, including the fleet, even when they don't have the background She's good and getting better, regardless of what the XO might think."

"Well, if Senior Chief Meyers can't keep her in trim, I suppose the lieutenant will resume his efforts."

"Lieutenant?"

"Yes, Master Chief. The Machiavellian Prince, the sly mind behind every throne, mine included, I suspect. The best overall officer in my command . . . which, of course, you know."

His statement proved an old Navy adage. Seagoing captains really do know everything going on from keel plates to mast head!

"One final question, Captain. You fired the CMC. What are you going to do with the person who actually caused the rumpus? The sailors will want to know."

"Ah, the XO! I have not entirely made up my mind. Court martial him . . . for what? Incompetence? Stupidity? I do not yet know. Let us just say that he is no longer involved in anything remotely related to operational functions. He will continue to perform his administrative duties until I decide his future. Recent events suggest he has a mental problem.

"Oh, Master Chief!" the Captain called as I was heading for the hatch. "Take a few days straddling both jobs until the senior chief has it totally under control. And present my compliments to your commissioned striker and tell her she will no longer attend briefings at the XO's pleasure. He will conduct no further briefings!

"It is just as well this happened. Fleet Admiral King, himself, would not have been able to handle Missus Stoutmaster after you and Prince tweaked on her for a couple of years!"

The commander went totally off-center when I told her I was leaving her department. "Take you away from me? Oh, no he is not! I don't care if he is the commanding officer! I'll be right back, Master Chief."

I caught her by the arm as she zipped toward the passageway hatch with meanness flashing from both eyes and a really tough set to her lips. "Hang loose, Commander. Don't make waves over something you won't be able to change. It a done deal. I fought against taking the billet – and lost Big Time! The man replacing me has a fine background in sea communications. He'll do as well as I ever did."

"No one will *ever* do for me what you did! No one could! Damn it!"

"And the good news is the XO is out of your life so far as briefings and the operational aspects of your job are concerned. He is restricted to pushing paper."

"First, you strike me with a club, then you shower me with rose petals. Is that another thing master chiefs do?"

"I just told you what the captain told me. He didn't do it to make your life easier. Well, maybe he did. Regardless, the XO is near history."

She clutched my arm. "You are still going to give me away, aren't you?"

"Did I say that I would? I said it was a bad idea. I did say that, didn't I?"

"Well, yes, you did, but I never believed that you would not."

"I thought you would think it through and have Mister Prince do it."

"Patty said you *would* do it!"

I wasn't but half bright, but I knew when I lost a battle.

"Can I wear my monkey jacket with the pretty little medals?" I teased.

"You can wear dress skivvies so long as you give me away!"

"Consider it done, Commander. On a bright morning at a date to be determined, I will walk you down the aisle, so long as you don't dream up one of those crazy wedding marches with the halting steps. I never could march worth beans."

"Just walk me down the aisle in a sober state. That is all I ask . . . Shipmate."

"Commander, we agreed that Doris would not be retained in her position. I'd like Petty Officer T. J. Elliott assigned and the billet title changed to better reflect what he will actually do, as opposed to what Doris does, which is essentially nothing. I strongly recommend you assign him as Assistant to the Operations Department Master Chief."

"Oh, you found yet *another* crippled kitty to care for!"

"He's never been a crippled kitty in his life! Let's say I am paying back for something that happened to another person years ago. Something that should not have happened."

"Oh, one of *those*!" she exclaimed, with a heavy question mark in her voice.

"Yes, Commander. One of those."

Directly after the CO swapped personnel back to the billet they held before the XO moved them, my first task as CMC was to pass the word that the 'Special Evaluations' would not take effect. Evaluations would stand as submitted during the previous marking period. I then linked up with the senior chief yeoman and we ran the ones the XO had prepared through the crosscut shredder. That they no longer existed did not make them dead. They would provide our young sailors a good sea story about an off-the-wall XO when they wished to entertain shipmates in a CPO mess or wardroom on some future night at sea.

My second task was to draft, smooth and put a memo into the guard mail. The memo solicited inputs from sailors missing request chits, who had not received a reply to a document they had submitted, or who had unresolved issues. That done, I started through the file cabinets to get a handle on past happenings of the command. There was almost nothing on file. I called in my yeoman striker.

"Are you going to fire me, Master Chief?"

I looked up at the big-eared kid who had crossed my bow when he informed me in a surly manner that the CMC wanted to see me. "Have you done something I don't know about, Seaman Grosnick?"

"No, Sir, but you yelled at me a while back. I guess you don't like me."

"I did not yell at you. I corrected you. If folks got fired every time they get corrected, we wouldn't have a Navy left. I would not have lasted past my first year. No, you'll be here for a while, but it's not fair to keep you in this job. You won't learn much about your rating doing light typing, filing and running stuff around for me. You need to get back into ship's office before long -- let's say another couple of months in this job. I'll need your corporate memory for a while, like right now. Where do you keep the CMC files? I find almost nothing in the cabinets. And, as a matter of possible interest, I have no reason at all to dislike you."

"That is all the files we have, Master Chief. I don't know of any other files."

"What did the past CMC do with his stuff? He must have kept some things."

"If he did, he didn't allow me to see them. I filed everything he gave me."

"What did you do for him?"

"Mostly, I took telephone messages. People were always looking for him and they would get angry when I didn't know where he was. He *didn't* like me. I didn't like him either!"

"We'll start from ground zero, Pens. I'll let you know what paperwork I want to keep as we go along. First thing we're going to do is move my furnishings into the rear room of this office and you into the front space. I can live without the amount of space of the front room, but I do need privacy.

"I also don't need those three shelves of notices, instructions and publications, not with ship's office having the same set next door. It's one hell of a waste of time and money to keep them updated. Take them to ship's office. If they don't want them, try the technical library. It they don't want them, put them in the mulcher room for destruction.

"Who you will grant access to me, and when, will vary. Distraught sailors and all division chiefs will be given instant access. Missus Caulsen, Elliott and Merkling will have access to me at any time as does Chief Ricks. These four folks brief sailors on the hazards of pregnancy in case you didn't know. I'll see anybody else when they show up, if I am not otherwise engaged. If I am busy, or with somebody, give them an appointment and keep me abreast of who is on the list, and for what. Try to determine their watch schedule and make the appointment at a time best suited to their needs.

"Try to judge telephone calls as to their importance before you patch them to me. If you can't, or the person is nasty to you, patch them through. I'll take a call from the CO, any department head, the CMAA, or CMC's from other commands whenever they call. The handling of officers below department head level is a greasy pig! Such officers often believe the CMC exists only to pull their chestnuts out of the fire. They can be a real pain in the stern! Ask division officers if what they want to discuss is hot. If they say it is, patch them through. Otherwise, take their name and number and I'll return their call when I can. If in doubt, patch the call. Think you can handle that?"

"I'll handle it, Master Chief."

Nothing of major significance happened over the next week. My days were spent sorting out wives and husbands terrorizing each another, sailors with credit cards and not a glimmer that they ultimately had to pay for their use in a timely manner, working through personnel problems, conferring with the captain on proper punishment, or non-punishment, of people who crossed the wrong bow and listening to a host of: 'My wife, she . . . My dog , it . . . My kids, they . . . ' stories. In my spare time I kept an eye on Senior Chief Meyers and the commander.

I had just completed a telephonic scuttlebutt session with my counterpart aboard the naval station when I heard somebody yell, "Bomb in ship's office! Clear the spaces!" I grabbed my yeoman and we made like long-legged alligators and dragged stern through the alarmed rear hatch. This was not the only alarm that sounded. Alarms could be heard from every emergency exit in the building.

By the time we had zipped around the corner of the huge building, the parking lot was filled with sailors. A few were still streaming from emergency exits that opened out of top secret spaces. Goat Rope Number Whatever was in effect and I didn't know why! I leaped into the mass of sailors and started pushing and shoving on them. "Get behind the supply building! Take cover!" The chief master-at-arms was doing the same thing at the main entrance to the building. I then noticed the XO milling about smartly, yelling at people. That tripped my trigger.

"Sheriff," I yelled at the CMAA, "Where's the skipper?"

"He's on the Spanish side of the base, for a luncheon!"

I was making my way to the XO when I was almost run down by a white panel truck with flashing red and blue lights. It slid to a stop ahead of me and six men in camouflage clothing and web gear leaped out and yelled, "Where's the bomb?"

"Not certain there is one, but one was reported in ship's office." the CMAA yelled to the Explosive Ordnance Demolition Technicians who were grabbing stuff out of the back of their van. "Ship's office is inside the second door from the quarterdeck."

One of the EOD technicians gingerly entered the main double doors and disappeared from sight, followed at a distance by two others. I went looking for the XO and found him inside a clump of sailors against the far bulkhead of the supply building. "Commander, is this a drill?"

"This justifies the drills I held!" he screamed, slinking tightly against the concrete bulkhead.

Bugger the Bosun! He's bombed the building!

Eventually the EOD techs appeared in the main doorway, carrying a long, slender, cardboard box. They crossed the tarmac and laid it beside a row of hedges. They milled around the box, held a short discussion, then one reached in and lifted the contents.

It was a dildo! It wasn't just any old dildo either. It was a double-ended, triple-expansion, three-ringed dildo, or some such, and it was buzzing like a nest of rattlesnakes. The thing looked eighteen inches long!

The XO let out a war whoop and dashed toward the EOD folks. They started to grab him, then seen he was a full commander. I couldn't hear the conversation, but the XO turned and screamed for the CMAA, who trotted across the tarmac toward him. They held what looked like an argument, then the CMAA turned with a disgusted look on his face and ordered, "Seaman Everett! Front and Center!"

A small, very slender brunette, not much taller than Patty, ran across the parking lot, stopped in front of the XO and saluted. The XO started screaming at her. It was time for me to enter the picture, regardless of what was going on.

141

"Any woman who would order such filth --"

"What is going on, Commander?" I broke in.

"*This*!" he screamed, blowing spit and waving the still buzzing dildo in the air. "She ordered this . . . this *thing*. It is addressed to her. I'm going to *hang* her!"

"Sheriff, leap in a car and find the captain!" I ordered.

"We don't need the captain! I'm throwing her in the brig! I'm processing her for discharge!" the XO screamed in my face again.

I pushed him gently away. I felt sorry for him. "We need the captain, Sir. You need to go to your office and wait for him. I'll handle this."

"Don't you dare give me orders! I am a commander. You are a master chief!"

I leaned toward him and whispered, "I'm not giving you orders. I'm trying to keep you from embarrassing yourself in front of a large part of this command."

The XO stared at me, then his face totally relaxed. He turned and walked stiff-legged toward the main entrance of the building. I motioned to a group of officers and chiefs standing a few feet away and when they approached, I said. "I strongly recommend whoever is senior detail a couple of khaki to keep an eye on the XO. He might slit his wrists!"

The old chief warrant electrician shoved a warrant officer and a chief toward the building, turned to me and asked, "What the hell happened? I was in the telephone exchange across the street and missed the whole damn thing!"

"I believe, Chief Warrant Officer Hawkins, that we were attacked by a dildo!"

The little sailor was, by then, sobbing, shifting around, scared out of her wits and, in general, about to fall apart. I put my arm around her and said, "Calm down! We'll get this squared away."

"I'm going to the brig! My parents will die!"

"No one can send anybody to the brig, for something like this. You ordered nothing illegal. Nothing will happen to you."

"I didn't order it!" she cried and let loose with a loud cry of anguish.

I tucked her beneath my arm and led her through the still open rear door of the building and into my office. I told my yeoman, who tagged along behind, to get me a paper cup, then get lost.

I went to my safe, removed a bottle of brandy, filled the paper cup and handed it to the girl. "Don't think I sit around here sucking up on booze because I don't. Having had this job before, I knew someone would need a stiffener some day. That is what it's for. You need it. Drink it!"

The little girl didn't even raise her lowered head. Her shoulders heaved in rhythm with her deep, rasping sobs.

"Drink it!"

"Sir, I don't drink!"

"You do now. Drink it!"

She took a couple of tiny sips, made a face and set down the paper cup.

"Tastes like medicine, huh? It is medicine, for the purpose we're using it. Drink it all!"

She made a sincere effort, but I could tell she had never before tasted brandy and didn't like it one bit. When she calmed down to a random, jerking sob, I explained there was nothing wrong with what she had done and nothing was going to happen to her. Again, she protested she had not ordered the dildo. I then asked how it came to be addressed to her.

"I didn't order it, Master Chief. This is the first one I've ever seen! How could you believe I would even want something like *that*?"

For the same reason other women wanted them, I supposed, but I didn't say that. "Do you have any idea how it came to be addressed and mailed to you? And for what reason?"

"No, Sir, but I was once teased about a . . . one of those things. The girls in storekeeper's school were giggling over a silly magazine one evening. I didn't understand why, so they showed me the picture. Stupid me! I didn't even know what we were looking at. They started pestering me about my ignorance about men and such things, so like a fool, I told them I'd never . . . I'm a virgin! Is that so bad?"

"No, maybe a bit uncommon, but certainly not bad.

"Pens!" I called at the top of my voice, suspecting he was standing by in ship's office. When he trotted through the door, I told him to go and get the dildo and the box it came in from the supply officer who, for lack of anybody better, had picked it up and taken it with him.

I held a mostly one-way chat with her while we awaited the return of my yeoman. I learned her first name was Alice and that she was not yet nineteen years old. She was from the wheat fields of North Dakota and had joined the Navy because of few employment opportunities in that area for a girl just out of high school.

She wasn't a pretty girl, darned plain, actually, but she had a fresh look about her. I suspect her school years had not been filled with fun, frolic and dates. She looked the sort who would be a flute player in the school band, a member of the glee club and, surely, a member of the *Homemaker's Club*. She would not have been a cheerleader.

"Can I get a transfer, Master Chief?"

"You just told me you got here a few weeks ago. The Navy is not going to transfer you that quick!"

"I need a transfer!"

"Are you being badly treated in the supply department?"

"No, Sir, I'm not. But I will be!"

"Why so?"

"Because of this stupid . . . dildo thing! I will be teased and teased. I will never get a date!"

I surely understood her concern. No sailor would want to date a girl who could use such a monster. In her case, though, I didn't believe she would have had many dates, even if this had not happened. She was less than pretty. The male sailors weren't going to fall down before her and chew rocks, not when they were reapers in a field of plenty. Females in the Puerto Santa Cruz area, counting Navy women, Spanish girls and dependent daughters probably outnumbered male sailors.

Still, she seemed a nice girl and something about her, looks aside, told me she would be quite a handful given the chance and desire. My own wife had endured a somewhat similar situation in high school and college because of her moralistic leanings. That aside, there was a huge difference between Patty and Alice. Patty was ravishing compared to Alice. Patty was well built, considering all her parts had been issued in miniature. Alice was flat on both sides.

I suddenly thought of another plain person, probably also a virgin, and filed that away

Grosnick charged through my hatch carrying the box. I took it from him and sent him on his way, then inspected the mailing labels and the shipping documents. Seaman Everett averted her eyes and shuddered.

"This package was forwarded to you from Storekeeper's School in Meridian, Mississippi. Assuming you took the full two weeks leave before you reported overseas and I'm sure you did, someone other than you ordered it. You surely would not have ordered something mailed to a place you knew you were leaving. Whoever ordered this didn't know your future address in Santa Cruz, but knew it would be forwarded.

"Somebody played a joke on you, Seaman Everett. They probably did it to shock you. It did, but not the way they expected.

I suspect it started buzzing when a yeoman dropped it or banged it against something while taking it out of the mail bag."

"It is not a nice joke, Master Chief. I will be teased and teased. I am so tired of teasing!"

"Look, Kid. Listen to your friendly neighborhood master chief. I tell you that you will not be teased. If you are, hell is going to descend around the head and shoulders of those who do tease you!"

"Now, you're upset and I don't want you to work the rest of the day. I don't want you brooding in the barracks either. What I want you to do is go out into Puerto Santa Cruz and look around the town. Maybe get a meal at a Spanish restaurant and enjoy yourself."

"But I have never been off the naval station. I can't speak Spanish!"

"You don't need to speak Spanish to survive around here. Most locals speak some English. Anyway, so you won't be lonely, brood and feel sorry for yourself, I'm sending my yeoman with you, just to keep you company. Is that okay?"

"Why, yes, I suppose. What is his name?"

"His name is Darrell Grosnick. Wait a minute and I'll go get him. Now, this is not a date. He is just going to escort you around and show you the sights. I don't want you telling people I pushed anybody on you. You got that?"

Alice gave me a timid little smile that slowly broadened. "Got it, Master Chief!"

I pulled Grosnick from ship' office into the passageway, told him what had happened to her, then laid a few, fatherly rudder orders on him. I told him if he treated her badly, tried to jump her bones, or otherwise acted an ass, he was a piece of dead meat that I was going to transfer to the dirtiest ship in the entire United States Navy . . . after I killed him. I then slipped him a couple of twenties in case neither of them had money.

I called the division chiefs and told them an unknown person had played a trick on Seaman Everett and that she had not ordered the dildo and knew nothing about it. I told them to spread the word that no one in the command was to mention the dildo to her, or tease Seaman Everett in any way. I further told them that Alice Everett seemed a quiet, shy girl and if anybody really wanted to experience mean, all they had to do was violate my order! I told the senior chief yeoman to mark the box "**REFUSED**" and mail the dildo back to the company that sent it. I then went to see the skipper.

The captain leaned back in his chair after I completed my spiel and said, "We're men of the world, Master Chief. We've seen the souks of Egypt, we've seen the Green Flash, we've seen Saint Elmo's fire playing in the rigging, we've heard whales sing and the sun rise over remote islands, but we don't know how females relate to one another and we don't know how terrible they can be among themselves, do we?"

"We're not alone, Captain. No male understands them."

"Speaking of females . . . There is no longer need to keep your hand loosely on the tiller of the operations department. It is under total and complete control. Lieutenant Prince has the conn."

I had to restrain from leaping from my chair. "What did you do with Missus Stoutmaster, Captain?"

"She is the officer next senior to me in this command. I appointed her acting executive officer. I believe her administrative background and the fact that the crew likes her will allow her to do quite well. It is impossible she could do worse than the previous one, a man I should have relieved when I became aware of his shortcomings, but didn't for various reasons."

I almost split my face grinning. "Where is the previous one, Sir?"

"At Naval Hospital Santa Cruz. I suspect he will be medically retired. The man has a severe case of ulcers, a nervous condition and a mental problem best left to headshrinkers to diagnosis. I gave him slack because of his physical condition, but I did not realize until very recently that he has another problem. He is, in layman terms, **A Flaming Nut!**"

The captain would get no argument from me on that statement.

CHAPTER TEN

FORMATION STEAMING

Things proceeded quite smoothly with Missus Stoutmaster behind the XO's desk. She was doing one hell of a fine job. I noticed the captain was absent more than when the previous XO heated the chair. Rumor had it that the captain was helping the captain of the Spanish aircraft carrier tear up the turf on the golf course.

I had been asked to be guest speaker at the forthcoming graduation at the Petty Officer's Academy, which was not an academy at all, but a two-week training course for seamen advancing to petty officer third class. Consequently, I was preparing my speech when the XO called me to her office.

There was no one behind her yeoman's desk, so I knocked on her door and entered.

"Lock the door, Clay. I don't want anybody to hear this."

Calling me by my first name meant she wanted to discuss something of a personal nature.

Not so very good, Buccaneer.

"Paul just graduated at the top of his class in the officers' familiarization course."

"That's good, Commander. There were a couple dozen selected for warrant officer and LDO."

"They gave him a presentation sword for that accomplishment."

"That'll save you some Yankee Green Dollars." I said, waiting for the shoe to drop.

"He received orders."

"I trust he got something good."

"He's transferring to Santa Cruz!" she squealed, hugging herself.

Not so very good, Buccaneer.

"I don't believe a man and a wife can serve at the same command if one is senior and supervises the other. I hate to pis . . . er, wet down your parade, but one of you will be transferred once you get married. You better nose around and see exactly what current regulations say."

She hugged herself again.   "He's going to Ground Electronics at the Naval Air Station. We will not be in the same command!"

"Well, I'm happy for you." I was, but would be happier when they were living in conjugal bliss in a Navy recognized fashion and her problem stopped being my problem.

"We will marry Friday." she said, quietly.

"*Friday*? That's three days away! What's the rush?"

She radiated a perplexed look, then said, "*Surely* you don't intend for us to *shack up*, waiting for everything to fall into place, do you?"

I didn't see why not. That was what they had been doing when he knocked her up while an enlisted man. "I can understand you wanting to make it legal Navy-wise and church-wise, but you need to wait a couple of weeks, at least. He's an officer now. No one will say anything if he comes out of your place on a regular basis until you tie the knot."

"That, Master Chief, constitutes *shacking up*." she said, primly. "It has nothing to do with our both being officers. I *will* be a bride on Friday!"

I wondered if she had been taking lessons from Patty as to what did, and what did not, constitute shacking up. She was spouting the same logic, or nearly so. Patty's logic went that whatever we did before we married was null and void from Day One because we intended to marry. Therefore, we were married from Day One and nothing we had done constituted unmarried sex -- and certainly not plain, old shacking up. Heaven forbid!

I was no expert on the female mind, but marriage to Patty had given me some slight insight. One should never frustrate one's self trying to talk a female out of anything, no matter how wacky, once she gets the bit in her teeth. Lucy Stoutmaster not only had the bit in her teeth, she had run off, broken the trace chains and busted up the wagon! Still, I had to try.

"Commander, does the captain know you are getting married and intend to take leave?"

"Why, no. He doesn't."

"When, may I ask, do you intend to tell him?"

"Thursday. That will be of such short notice he could not possibly turn down my urgent request for leave." She leaped from her chair. "*Could* he?"

"He *could* do damn near anything he wants! Look, Commander. I never steered you wrong, so will you please listen to a little logic?"

Her head bobbing up and down indicated she was willing to listen. Whether she would do what I advised was a totally different kitty cat.

"Commander, there are things at stake here, leave being the most unimportant and yo --"

"I must have leave! We cannot honeymoon without leave. Therefore, I must have leave!"

"Right. I got that. I understand that. What you do not seem to understand is the captain and God-World is going to wonder where you, a senior lieutenant commander in the Navy, suddenly grabbed this brand spanking new LDO ensign **WHO WAS ENLISTED UNTIL HE WAS COMMISSIONED ONLY THE FRIDAY BEFORE THE WEDDING!**"

"Oh. Yes, I see your point."

"I should hope so. Look, just tell your hubby-to-be to check into the naval air station, get a room at the BOQ, you two can meet that evening in the officer's lounge, have a smashing romance and rush madly to the altar in a week or two and make it all legal."

"We are getting married Friday."

I looked at the overhead and mentally said a short prayer.

"Lord, I know I've been a bad boy, but can you see your way clear to cut me some slack in just this one situation. Please give me a little help here, Lord."

Rudder orders were not forthcoming from the Big Admiral in the Sky.

"Commander, think! You are going to tell the captain you are getting married on Friday and want leave. He will surely ask who the lucky man is and you will say he is an LDO ensign. That will trip the captain's trigger and he will ask where he is stationed. You will say he just graduated from Knife and Fork School and is reporting to Naval Air Station Santa Cruz. Big trigger trip on the part of the captain who will ask where and when you met him. You will say, 'Oh, in Mayport, Florida, when he was an enlisted clod who got me pregnant while we were engaged in a little friendly fraternization. But it's okay, Captain -- he's an officer now!'"

"We're getting married Friday."

The Big Admiral in the Sky was not going to help and I couldn't think of any possible way to turn her off, so I said, "Commander, if you are going through with this, you better come up with one hell of a lie! Tell the captain you seen Paul's picture in the *Navy Times* and fell madly in love, wrote him a letter and now he is some sort of mail order groom. Tell him you engaged in phone sex while he was in Knife and Fork School and now you want to experience the real thing. Tell him . . . Oh, Hell! Think of your *own* lie!"

"You are becoming perturbed, Master Chief. That is not good for your blood pressure."

I checked my sea bag for proper stenciling and counted the keys to the gear lockers.

"Commander, what are you going to *tell* the captain?"

"Oh, I just thought of a plausible story! We didn't know the other was in the Navy when we met. When we learned I was an officer and he enlisted, we ceased dating because of fraternization regulations. He pined and pined for me until he thought of a solution to his misery and applied for a commission. After he was selected for a commission, he contacted me via telephone. We talked and talked, on and off, before he proposed and I accepted. Is that so unlikely, Clay?"

No . . . not if she intended to sell the plot for a tear-jerking show on Japanese television. I am not a suspicious person, but damned if I believed she dreamed that tale up on the spot!

"OK, Commander, I'll break out my dinner dress uniform, knowing in my military mind that nothing short of a deluge from heaven is going to stop you having this wedding on Friday. Not the captain, not a bad FITREP, not an earthquake, not Moses himself. You better hope the captain will buy your crazy story!"

"Oh, he will. He is a very understanding man!"

Maybe so, but he was not a non-graduate from Idiot's School.

"Clay, we must get busy."

All back full, Master Chief!

"Doing what?"

"Why, preparing for my wedding. We must find a space for the reception, arrange with the chaplain to marry us in the chapel, have my dinner dress uniform tailored -- I have not worn it for a while, order flowers, decorate the chapel, rent a nice car for transportation between the chapel and the reception. There are so many things we must do!"

"Let us forget this 'we' stuff. I agreed to give you away and I'm proud to do that, even if I do think it is a bad idea. I want you to read my lips, Commander. I don't arrange weddings! I don't know anything about arranging weddings! I don't have time to arrange a wedding! Bottom line: All I am going to do is suit up in my dinner dress uniform, walk you up the aisle, hand you over to the quaking soul waiting for you at the altar, throw flowers and rice at you, dance with my wife at the reception and generally get catawampus on Champagne, which is something long overdue. What I'm *not* going to do is arrange a wedding!"

"Patty said you would help!" she wailed.

I headed for my office and the telephone, but first I whipped into the operations office.

"She's going to tell him **WHAAAT**?"

"Lieutenant Prince, this can go two ways. She can tell that tale so truthfully, while doing her blubbering, sniffing, 'I'm so happy!' female act, that she'll have our salty dog captain dabbing at his eyes with the bitter end of his necktie and begging her to take leave. The alternate is that he sends her to the fuel farm awaiting orders.

"Look, she can tell him she met Paul-baby while riding a unicycle naked down Atlantic Boulevard in Jacksonville, Florida, for all I care. But now she thinks I have a direct responsibility to arrange her wedding. Either that, or . . . Oh, hell. Who knows what she thinks!

"I'm going to call Patty Lane Berkeley and tell her in sailor English that I'm arranging no wedding, I'm participating in no labor to prepare spaces for the wedding and if her and her running mates want to do it, have at it. Me, myself and I, am out of the commander business. She is a grown woman with the common sense of a teenager who just experienced her first session of pipe fitting.

"If I read this right, she is now an initiated, card-carrying associate of the bunch of wives she recently met, two of whom control our destiny. That 's not good, Buccaneer. You better head for the tall corn because I strongly suspect you are next on her list!"

"Got you, Master Chief. Thanks!" Mister Prince said, grabbing his cap.

The commander caught him as he was crossing the quarterdeck en route his automobile.

I called Patty and laid down the law!

Lieutenant Prince and I, along with sailors we press ganged by promising them beer, decorated the chapel Thursday evening. This was after a hard afternoon of lugging tables, chairs and flowers around the reception room at the Spanish officer's club, washing the captain's white Navy sedan he insisted the commander use for her wedding and a few dozen other odd tasks. We were supervised mightily by various female buddies the commander had acquired since she met Patty and Missus Prince shortly after she had sprung: 'I've been shacking up with an enlisted clod' situation on me. The lieutenant and I also met Paul-baby when he arrived at the air station around ten that night and checked him into the BOQ, pre-marriage bone jumping not currently in her script. We then proceeded, badly used , beat down and worn out, to Santa Cruz-Mar, sans wives, and got plastered.

Friday morning we held muster and got the key players into their proper position while various chiefs and officers seated the guests. I had a few minutes of ease while waiting for the commander to come out of the room where the women were holding a husband control training session, fixing the bride's hair,

155

painting her toe nails, dressing her, whatever, so I idly scanned the packed church.

I'd have been a wealthy man had I been able to get my hands on the gold braid assembled there. The Spanish admiral who commanded both the NATO base and the Spanish fleet was present, accompanied by his staff and what looked like the captains and senior officers of every one of his ships;. the CO of the NAVCOMMSTA; CO of the naval station; CO of the naval air station; CO's of tenant commands and a horde of commanders and other lesser beings, many of whom brought their wives or girlfriends. A goodly number of the NAVCOMMSTA crew with wives and girlfriends mustered in too. I pondered why so many high-ranking brass attended, then realized what had happened. Jiffy Jeff wanted his XO, now a waif he had dragged in out of the snow *if* he bought her story of a resurrected romance, to have a memorable wedding and invited everyone worthy of note.

I wondered if the captain and I should hold a change-of-command ceremony to pass control of the personal life of one Lieutenant Commander Stoutmaster, soon to be Lieutenant Commander Stoutmaster-Hunycutt. I really liked her, loved her like a sister, in fact, but by the name of John Paul Jones, the captain was more than welcome to her. I feared her having a husband was not going to improve her common sense level when it came to matters of a personal nature. Initial impressions were that Ensign Hunycutt would not act a great deal more worldly than she!

I noticed my big-eared yeoman striker sitting hip to thigh with the little storekeeper striker. Alice had her hand resting on top of his and was laying the same smile on him that Patty had laid on me when she was plotting my demise as a single sailor. They were, to some extent, crippled kitties, but even crippled kitties can have baby kittens.

I made mental note to ensure both were graduates of the *Rug Rat Prevention School*, as sailors were now calling the prevention of pregnancy counseling sessions. It was not beyond the realm of possibility the two inexperienced kids had already figured out what males and females do for recreation. The possibility of their increasing the pregnancy rate aside, I was happy the never popular, outside the circle kids found each other . . . just the way I planned it on a near moment's notice.

Legend has it that all brides are beautiful and Lucy Stoutmaster certainly was that day. She glowed! The fact that she had lots more gold on her arms than her husband did not generate catty or ill comments that I heard.

I could have floated The Ark with the tears falling to the deck by the time they walked down the aisle and passed through the honor guard who crossed swords into an arch above the proudly marching couple. I helped cheer the happy bride and groom into the rear seat of the captain's sedan and watched as it pulled slowly away from the curb. I was quite pleased with myself. I was out of the marriage business!

"I hear you and Prince stashed the ensign in the BOQ last night." the captain said softly in my left ear. "I guess he didn't see his daughter yet."

"Far as I know, Captain, he has yet to see his new daughter."

"What are we doing here? Rearranging history?"

"I don't understand, Captain."

"The baby, the child, the kid, her daughter! Or better yet, *their* daughter."

I did what any right thinking CPO would have done. I evaded the issue. "Well, it's their daughter now."

"*Is*, Master Chief -- like in it always has been *their* daughter. I will kiss your stern on the quarterdeck and give you fifteen minutes to draw a crowd if she was ever married to another man. Better yet, I'll do the same if you come up with another man in her life -- *ever*!"

"What are we saying here, Captain?"

"What we are saying is that Lucy Stoutmaster, now Hunycutt, has led us, or rather me, down the primrose path! What they do tonight will not, in the truest sense, consummate their marriage. They consummated their union a good while back, unless that child is the product of Immaculate Conception. Further, I don't know which of you -- her, you or Prince, dreamed up that sea story about a long-ago relationship . . . hell, I don't even *want* to know!"

"Are you mad at her, Captain?"

"Mad? No, I'm not mad. What is done is done. This would make one hell of a sea story, except no one would ever believe it. Carry on, Master Chief!"

"Aye, Aye, Captain!" I barked and saluted him smartly.

The skipper returned the salute in the manner it was given, but with a big grin.

I didn't get an opportunity to get catawampus on Champagne as I had told the commander I intended because Patty started bugging me to return home. I figured she had worn herself out over the past three days, so I bid the groom well, kissed the bride and we left. I barely had hung my uniform in the closet when Patty grabbed onto me and started climbing over me like a wildcat scampering up a tree.

"Uh, Patty, let's not get carried away. We can't do anything."

"Why not, dearest?" she murmured, running her lips up and down my neck.

"Because of your . . . operation. That's why not!"

"Oh, but we *can* -- and we *will*! This doctor told me this morning we could resume . . . you *Know*!" She ripped her dress and everything else free of her tiny body, threw it to the deck, fell on the bed, pulled me down on top of her and started working her hands up and down my back while she battered at my face with her perky, little breasts. "Oh, it has been so long! Do me, Clay. Do *things* to me!"

She did not have to make that offer twice!

After we got it all in one sea bag and were resting, wrapped like snakes in spring, I said, "That was pretty darned good for the first time in our new house."

"Oh, yes, much better than simply good!" She sighed, playing with things likely to get her into trouble again. So, I thought I'd tease her a mite.

"Patty, I don't want you to do things you don't enjoy. But it would be nice to make love again, say next week or the week after, if you can see your way clear to do that. I know you are sort of frigid and all but --"

She rolled on top and started working me over with her tiny fists. "Frigid! Me? Oh, you Henry Clay Berkeley! We just did *It* and, Sir, that single time will not be even close to the last time today! You grab onto what interests you the most and that had better be me -- all of me!

CHAPTER ELEVEN

DOLDRUMS AND HOLIDAY ROUTINE

I returned Yeoman Striker Grosnick to ship's office as I had told him I would, but had kept him a bit longer than the two months I promised because there was no one to relieve him until a new striker reported.

What I received in exchange for Grosnick was a near midget, black, female yeoman striker who did not look old enough to have completed junior high school. I strongly suspected the doctor who approved her enlistment physical read her weight and height incorrectly, or had sucked down some torpedo juice with his breakfast the morning of her physical. If she met the minimum height standards, it was by the thickness of a llama hair. She was a deep, dusky black with European features often seen in Ethiopians. She was as cute as a button is the best I can describe her.

Grosnick had done all required of him, and more, and I had written him an excellent evaluation, but he was no match for this ball of fire!

She barely reported before she was crawling beneath desks and other furnishings wiping dust and dirt from the most inaccessible of places. When that did not satisfy her standards, she borrowed a tall stepladder from the Spanish janitor and had at the lights and the overhead. When she had our two rooms spit shinnied like a battleship, she started reorganizing the contents of the file cabinets and desk drawers. After that, she submitted a dozen or so work requests to the public works department for refurbishment, repair or replacement of items such as chipped and discolored paint, gouges in the plaster, broken drawer latches, cracked light covers and other minor items that needed attention. All of this took her only about three days, after which she could be seen, when she had nothing else to do, with her nose buried in publications related to her rating.

After a week of working with her, I hunted down the senior chief yeoman and told him I considered it a waste of assets to assign a woman of her caliber to a billet that had little to do in the way of heavy administrative work. I further told him it would be cost effective to place her in a billet where he could use the vigor she radiated. He said he would be most pleased to do that, except his other new striker was also a water walker and one of the two had to fill the billet in my office I then proposed we exchange yeoman strikers two afternoons each week so the little striker could gain exposure to all aspects of her rating, rather than wait until she was assigned back to ship's office in three months. He agreed.

I returned to my office, called the striker in and explained how I had arranged to share her with ship's office. I thought she was going to cry!

"Is something wrong with that, Seaman Ingram?"

"You don't likes me, does you, Master Chief? You wants a white girl!"

I sat, stunned for a moment, before answering her. "No, I don't want either a white girl or a black girl. For that matter, I don't want a white or black male either. What I want is a *person* who can answer the telephone, do light filing and typing and run stuff around for me. I don't need a person of your high caliber in this job. I intended to transfer you back to ship's office so you could learn your rating, but found that the other newly reported striker was also of high caliber.

"I tried to transfer you, not because you are black or an inferior performer. I tried to return you because your potential is high and you would do one hell of a lot for ship's office and gain practical experience at the same time. You working in ship's office two afternoons per week will give you a step up when you take the test for third class. yeoman."

"You going to recommends me for *third class*?" she gasped.

"You don't have enough time in grade as seaman. You'll be replaced by another striker by the time recommendations are due for the February examination. But you will surely be recommended if you continue the pattern you've already set."

She gave me a perplexed look, then asked, "You soon has me as a blond, white girl?"

"Where are you coming from, Seaman Ingram?"

"Lots of folks don't likes black people. They don't want them 'round."

"Where were you raised? In the Mississippi Delta?"

"Chicago. In the projects, but I knows 'bout white people!"

"How many white people do you know?"

That put a studious look on her face, then she said, "Not many. Not 'til I joined the Navy."

"Did anyone in the Navy ever treat you bad because you are black, isolate you from the group, or any such thing?"

"No, Sir, 'cept one white girl call me a bad name in boot camp when we fussed. The company commander really chewed her out! And she chewed me too, for yelling back at her."

"Did you go ashore with any white girls in yeoman school?"

"No, Sir, I bided in the barracks and studied, 'cept I went to the base movies at night. I didn't have no truck with none of them white girls. There wasn't no black girl in my class. Wasn't no black man neither."

"I'll tell you what, Seaman Ingram. I think you heard too many tales in the projects! Sure, there are people who hate blacks, just as there are blacks who hate whites. Those types are few and far between in the Navy and we get rid of them when we find them.

"I want you to do something for me. I want you to look around this one command at the number of black petty officers and chief petty officers. They wouldn't have gotten to those ranks if people disliked or hated them. True, we don't have any black officers in this command, but there are black officers aboard the naval station.

"I once had a black first class postal clerk running my largest and most important recruiting station. She was also rated as the top recruiter in an eleven state area. She was competent to the max. I even used her to train newly reported chief petty officers prior to assigning them as recruiter in charge of a station. I could trust her to do right, regardless of what pressure somebody put on her.

"On the negative side, she could get right down mean! She got in my face more than once. I loved her like a sister, even if she did put me up a wall at times. Flat drove me nuts, sometimes, is what she did. She bad-mouthed all my girlfriends too, except the one I married. She helped engineer that!

"She was, overall, superb and it had nothing at all to do with her being black. She'd likely acted the same if she were white. I would have put her in for a commission, except for one thing. Her smart mouth and the way she popped off at people wouldn't have allowed her to advance past ensign! I do, though, expect to see her name on the next advancement list for CPO. I have no doubt she'll be a master chief one day -- and that rank is restricted to less than one percent of the entire Navy.

"I think you will find most people in the Navy don't much care what color a person's skin is, or where they come from, so long as they do their job. You will find that white girls don't just go ashore with white girls. You will find all sorts of girls mixed together. I want you to go to the Jolly Jack Club tonight and look. You tell me tomorrow if I'm not right."

"You telling me straight, Master Chief?"

"Do iron ships float?"

"Uh, yes, they does, but I ain't never seen no ship."

"Opportunities are opening for women in the Navy. Your chance of standing on the deck of a ship when you leave here is excellent. I want you to get out of that shell you've built around yourself and have some fun. Having fun, running around with friends and raising hell within the confines of acceptable conduct is part of what the Navy is all about -- and the reason many enjoy it. Morale would be really poor if the many ethnic groups in the Navy didn't get along.

"When you make third class petty officer, you come and tell me if you have learned what the word 'shipmate' means. I suspect you will understand it by then. If by chance you do not, I'll explain it to you. Shipmates, you will learn, are not confined to people of one color. Basically, it's the mixing of sailors with a common goal, but it is a *lot* more than that."

"Why you telling me all this stuff?"

"Because I want you to be happy here. I want you to be happy in the Navy. I had thirty recruiters looking for people just like you. They are hard to find!

"There is no limit to how high you can go in the Navy if you continue as you've started. I have not looked at your service jacket and I will not, unless we have some sort of trouble. I suspect, though, that your education is limited. Take some night courses at the University of Chicago Extension College here on base. There is a lot of potential in your little hull, but you will need a good, basic education to advance in rank at a good pace."

She reached across my desk and laid a hesitant, little pat on my bare arm. "You a good man, Master Chief. I knows that. I hopes you right 'bout white folks."

I was not much involved in operational matters as CMC and had no reason to weed daily through several hundred messages. The only messages slotted to me concerned personnel in the command or personnel related directives from On High. There were usually only fifteen or twenty messages per day that concerned me: rats, cats, dogs, rainy days, whatever. Classified messages of concern, and they were few, were given me by the CO, XO or OPS. Consequently, there was no need for me to come in early. I, therefore, kept shore working hours, coming in around 0730.

Seaman Ingram was always there with the night's messages and the morning guard mail neatly separated by subject when I arrived. The morning after our little talk was no different, except that she was humming to herself and sort of swaying around in her chair.

"Everything okay, Seaman Ingram?" I asked, pretty certain things were.

"Yes, Sir, they's pretty good."

"You go to the Jolly Jack last night like I told you?"

"Yes'um, I did."

"And what did you see?"

"I see'd folks sitting 'round together jus' like you said. I sits down and got me a Coca Cola and then I goes over and plays with them shuffleboard things. 'Long comes a girl and wants to play with me, so we plays 'til some girls come over and then we plays some with them. 'Long 'bout maybe eight o'clock they went to some place out in town called Kenny's and they taken me 'long. We listened to music and talked some and then some boys come in and started dancing with the girls to the jukebox. One of them boys axed me to dance and I did. He didn't do nothing 'cept dance, Master Chief. He was a nice boy."

"How many were white?"

'They was all white! I seen black folks sitting 'round, some all mixed with white folks and some not mixed with white folks, but none of them black sailors said nothing to me. Them white girls, they thought it was funny that I don't drinks nothing. I told them I don't do no drugs and I don't drinks no beer. Nothing 'cept Coca Cola. They said they don't do no drugs neither, but they liked beer and wine, 'cept they called it *cerveza* and *vino*.

"Master Chief, I had me a good time! They axed me to go with them to a playa on Sunday. What's a playa? Is it something good or something bad?"

"Playa means beach in Spanish." I think you better go. You'll enjoy it. You'll probably have to beat Spanish guys off you with a stick." I teased.

"I ain't having no truck with no Spanish!"

"Seaman Ingram, you are being as prejudice as you think white people are! Spaniards are high-grade people. You should make a point of meeting folks everywhere you go. You'll find you'll like most people and that they are really no different from you, except they speak a different language, or might be a different color.

"You will likely find yourself speaking Spanglish before long. That's what happens when Americans and Spaniards mix Spanish and English so they can communicate. They use words from both languages and even some made up words. You watch!"

"I'll watch, Master Chief. I thinks you knows what you talking 'bout."

"Not always. Now, listen. Somebody might say something racial to you, or call you a name. You take that as it comes and consider the source of who said it, unless it is something that really hurts your feelings. If they do that, or harass you, go tell your boss."

"You thinks that'll happen?"

"Sure it will, sometime. When I was on recruiting, I had a couple-three towns in West Virginia and Kentucky that had a small black population. One had a small college and there I was sometimes called honky, white bread, dead skin and the like. Black folks, young ones usually, who didn't like the cut of my jib - - my color, really, called me such names."

"You whip up on them, Master Chief?"

"No, I just considered the source and went on about my business. I did whip up on one fellow though, but not for calling me a name."

"What he do?"

"I stopped my Navy car at a stop light, the only stop light in that little town, and this guy run up, stuck his hand inside the window, grabbed me by the throat and said, 'Hey, White Boy, you gives me your stuff!' I pulled a piece of pipe I kept wedged between the seats and tried my best to break his arm. Last I seen, he was heading down the street screaming."

"What you carry that pipe for?"

"Not to beat black folks. There aren't many minorities in West Virginia. Kentucky has a good number, but both states have red necks who get loaded on stump juice, Mary Jane, or some such, and start feeling tough. Man needs a little equalizer sometimes."

She give me a sly, little grin. "I sure wouldn't mess with none of you I seen you walkin' down the street! You looks mean with them scars on your face. How'd you gets them scars?"

"Vietnam."

"By them VC, huh? That where you got all them big medals too, ain't it."

"Yeah. Well, back to work, Seaman Ingram. I'm glad you had fun last night. You have fun this weekend too."

"I sure going to try, Master Chief. I ain't had me no fun since I was a little kid!"

As serious as that girl was, I suspect she was right.

Patty and I spent the Christmas holidays in Madrid, seeing the sights. We did the usual tourist things by touring the *El Prado* Art Museum and The Valley of the Fallen, a majestic cemetery in the mountains beyond Madrid where veterans of the Spanish Civil

War lay buried. We visited other sites too, including one not usually visited by American tourists when we spent an entire day in the Spanish Maritime Museum.

Patty, as interested in history as I, would have willingly spent a week there. She was quite taken by the huge brass oil lamps that had once graced the sterns of Spanish men-of-war in the days of sailing ships and now graced the balusters on each side of each landing on the inside stairs. She was impressed by the sheets of Tiffany type glass that hung above each tier of steps on the wide, white, marble staircase, but wondered why an olive drab netting hung beneath each sheet of glass. She shivered when I told her it was to prevent glass from flying around in event ETA, or another separatist group, threw a bomb as they had done in government buildings throughout Spain.

Patty was quite surprised when the curator, a Spanish Marine I had met while stationed in Madrid, told her that Queen Isabella had not pawned her jewels to finance Christopher Columbus' trip to the New World as Patty had been taught in school. Rather, the money came via the sailing master of the *Santa Maria*. She bugged me all evening about how history books were wrong and needed correction. I stopped that tirade by asking what she thought about the pope dividing the New World in halves, with one half going to Portugal and the other half going to Spain, as she had seen when the curator showed us the *Carta de Santa Maria*, a chart of the world as it existed in the sixteenth century. Drawn in a straight line, across the chart, was a green line decreed by the pope to stop squabbling between the two countries. The pope had apparently not given a fig for the feelings of non-Catholic nations involved in exploring the New World.

Patty said she didn't care who discovered what, but the New World should have been divided among all nations who had done the exploring. She then retracted that statement and said it was very unfair that Spain had ultimately been done out of the vast majority of her holdings, considering that Spain did much of the work in discovery and exploration. When she wanted to discuss various points, I shifted her interest elsewhere by taking her to bed. Patty was big on using a lot of words!

I like to never got her out the Madrid *El Corte Ingles*, flagship of the *El Corte Ingles* department stores found in every major Spanish city. There was little of significance that could not be purchased in the flagship store, floor after floor after floor filled with crystal, brass and other items she deemed necessary to her life. Had I had a truck, she would surely have filled it. Lucky for me she was using her own money!

On our last day in Madrid, she dragged me back to *El Corte Ingles* where she again inspected a suit of armor, some related items of war and a fine, hand tooled saddle. When I asked if she planned to start a war, she said those items, less the saddle, would fit well in the library of our West Virginia farm house with the weapons of my ancestors. I wondered how a suit of armor fit in with an M1 rifle from World War Two, a 1906 Springfield from World War One, a Krag from the Spanish-American War, a Spencer from the Civil War and muzzle loading guns from the Indian and Revolutionary Wars plus a broadsword or two, some bows and arrows, tomahawks, and a couple of Indian war clubs. I decided not to ask that question. She would surely have told me and I didn't have enough time left on my leave for her to do it. Patty was big on words!

I did ask if she wanted the saddle because she intended to replace her riding horse that had died a couple of years before I met her. She said she might want a horse when we returned to West Virginia, but the saddle was for Emma, the bony, age-worn mule that was a member of the Patterson family.

Emma was only a couple of weeks younger than Patty. She had ruled as the major family pet from Day One and also functioned as Patty's playmate until Patty reached junior high school. The ugly mule did pretty much as she wanted. She butted her head against the kitchen door twice each day, as regular as clockwork, to get a slice of bread from Missus Patterson. If the bread was not forthcoming, she kicked the door, once removing it totally from its hinges. No matter what she did, no one ever got angry, not even when she ate an entire clothesline of bed sheets, or pulled the hasp off the corn crib, after which a herd of deer cleaned the place out

She followed Mister Patterson around the farm like a dog. She would rear back her head and let out a loud, braying rant as if her heart was breaking when he crossed a fence or entered a building she could not enter. Emma had never done labor in her life, except when Mister Patterson hitched her to a cultivator to work his vegetable garden. He had a couple-three tillers of various sizes and didn't need her for cultivation, but chose to use her because he said it made Emma feel needed.

I tried to explain to Patty that Emma was of exceptionally low caste, even for a mule, and that putting a fine saddle on her was akin to suiting up a red neck in a tuxedo, then turning him loose in a common slop chute. It would embarrass her. I expounded on that by saying it was a great waste of money.

She said Emma was way up in years and deserved a nice saddle. The fact that no one ever rode Emma did not impress her. Emma deserved a nice saddle no matter what. She also said she was not spending *our* money. She was spending *her* money earned by raising, selling and trading cattle when she was in school and college.

I surrendered, but I suspected when she attempted to fit the saddle on Emma's bony back, it would fly all the way from Jessie's Run to Big Otter when Emma kicked her heels in the air and bucked it off. Emma has been ridden bareback in her life, mainly by Patty, but she had never worn a saddle.

Patty went into a lengthy conversation in lisping Spanish with one of the managers. I knew in my military mind that all items purchased were destined for West Virginia via whatever means of shipment they dreamed up.

Patty's high school Spanish had improved to where she was speaking almost without revealing her hillbilly accent. Submerging herself in what I dubbed the Spanish-American Coffee Drinking, Pastry Eating, Shopping and Gossip Society permitted her to exercise her Spanish for several hours per day, five days per week

January brought promotion with Lieutenant Prince high on the selection list for promotion to lieutenant commander. The captain made a joke at the wetting down party that he would now have to nail his stern to his chair to keep the Machiavellian Prince out of it. Some of his officers didn't see the humor in his joke. They had lost their own sterns dealing with the crafty LDO. Prince was the 'Captain's Boy' and they all knew it.

Results of the February rating examination returned in April and most advanced. Forty-eight gained promotion in the administration, operations, public works and supply departments, including Grosnick and Ingram to Yeoman Third Class and Everett to Storekeeper Third Class. Personnel assigned to the naval security group department done equally well, if not better

The CPO selection board selected T. J. Elliot for Chief Petty Officer, maybe as a result of the special evaluation we had written on him prior to the selection board meeting in Washington

Except for an occasional liberty incident, a fistfight, a hair pulling contest, domestic squabble or the much more serious use of drugs, my little world remained relatively quiet. There was the random pregnancy of an unmarried sailor, but nothing like before. It was now uncommon to see a girl padding around in a maternity uniform.

Patty and I enjoyed our free time immensely and took every opportunity to travel through the local area and to Portugal on long weekends. I often thought how much I disliked shore duty before I met her and how much I now enjoyed it.

Shore duty had many benefits with Patty around. I ate fine, regular meals. I didn't drink much and had not smoked a cigarette in weeks. My uniforms and civilian clothing were well maintained with no effort on my part. My house was spit shinnied. The back seat of my car was free of hamburger wrappers, paper coffee cups and empty soda cans. Best of all I could get my hands on her 24/7 . . . even when I didn't particularly want to. Sunday afternoons, after church, she liked to, among other interesting things, parade around the house in her wedding night attire, which was zip!

Cruising with Patty in formation steaming mode was good!.

CHAPTER TWELVE

FORMATION STEAMING II

My next yeoman striker, not particularly good at anything, prone to wander off, squat, peat bog Irish girl from Boston with the good Irish name of Mary Louise Riley was a nice young woman with a bubbling personality. Her lax attitude frequently drove me up the bulkhead, but it was impossible to stay angry at her for more than a few minutes.

She stuck her head into my office just before lunch a few weeks after she started working for me to announce Petty Officers Grosnick and Everett begged a few minutes of my time at 1330. I told her to send them in when they arrived. She giggled and left. I wondered what was so funny

They showed up as nervous as the last two rats left alive in a laboratory. Suddenly, I feared the worst.

"Uh, Master Chief, Alice and me, that is, we, uh, got something to tell you."

She was knocked up for sure!

"Spit it out, Petty Officer Grosnick."

'Uh, Alice thinks, that is, she believes, or I . . ."

"Do you want to tell me something, or not? If you do, stop stumbling around and say it!"

"**Alice and I . . . we want to get married**!" he yelled. Alice turned bright red.

I thought about that for a moment or three, letting them stand there in a sweat.

"Want to, or have to?"

"We want to, Master Chief." Alice said, in a scared voice. "We really do!"

"Let me rephrase the question. It is absolutely essential that you marry say . . . in the next *six* or *seven* months?"

"No, Master Chief, but we want to get married as soon as we can. We waited until after the rating examinations so we would have enough money. Is there some reason we should wait? We will do so if you want." Alice asked, concern throughout her voice.

Then she caught on. Her face lit up like Baltimore Harbor on Fourth of July night. She grabbed Grosnick's hand. "Oh, you think I am pregnant? No! We've never done anything like *that*, Master Chief. All we've done is, well, you know . . . *touched*."

I was a dirty, old man. I had a filthy mind. I was scum!

When I got it all in one sea bag, had all my gear locker keys accounted for and stopped kicking myself in the stern, I stood, shook Grosnick's hand and hugged Alice. I then pushed them together.

"You don't need permission to marry -- you're both United States. citizens. You'll make a fine couple and I'm proud of you both. Is there anything you need I can help you with, getting blood tests through sick bay, getting you a license, anything?"

"We need a really big favor, Master Chief. Please do not get angry."

"I see no reason to get angry, Alice, not when two nice, young people want to get married. What do you need?"

"I want you to give me away, Master Chief, like you did for Commander Stoutmaster."

I gave them a disarming smile, then asked, "What do I look like, the Duty Giver Away of Brides? Is that what I am around here? Sure, I'll give you away, but you both have regulation parents, don't you? Aren't they coming over for the wedding?"

"Darrell's parents might come, but mine does not have the money. My three sisters married in the past four years. They don't have money left after that. And tickets to Spain are expensive. Far too expensive for my folks."

"Have you thought about taking leave and flying to the States in a military aircraft? Those flights are free. Then you could get married in North Dakota with both of your families present. Wouldn't that be better?"

"It would, except my parents would then feel obligated to spent money on my wedding like they did for my sisters. We are a really big family. There are dozens of relatives. That is a lot of food. It would cost a ton of money. My Dad works in a dairy. He doesn't have much money!"

I thought, then, that if I had a daughter, I would want one just like this one.

I hugged her again, nothing like a little friendly fraternization. "Sure, I'll walk you up the aisle, three times if you want. You just let me know when."

"Maybe a week from next Saturday, if the chapel is available. Would that be okay?"

"I guarantee it will be available, or the Sky Pilot will . . . well, let's just say that it will be available unless someone else has a wedding already scheduled. Let me know if you run into any road blocks."

"What can we do to the chapel? Are there regulations that concern decoration?"

"You can do anything that Commander Stoutmaster did, Alice. More if you think of something. You sure you have enough money?"

"Well, yes, I suppose. We've rented an apartment and we have enough left over for some flowers and I'll find somebody to take snapshots." Alice clapped her hands together. "My mother has worried about me getting married because I am sort of the family Ugly Duckling, compared to my sisters. She will be *so* happy! Imagine what the neighbors will say when they see my picture in the newspaper and read that I was given to my husband by a decorated naval hero -- the best man in the entire Navy!"

I made a call to Patty after they left, then went to see the XO . . . after I dried my eyes.

"Of course we will do everything possible for them. I will never forget what you did for me! I will round up what you want, but I feel for you, Master Chief. I really do. There is no end of crippled kitties in your life!"

"These kids aren't crippled kitties. They may not be pretty and handsome and they might not run with the popular crowd, but if we had a command filled with sailors of their caliber, we wouldn't have a job!

"Petty Officer Everett's parents have no money, and probably no social status at all, but they raised one hell of a fine girl. Grosnick is a good kid too. He's a bit nervous and ill at ease, but he's been better lately. Getting some confidence, I suppose, now that he has a girlfriend. I doubt either ever had a date before they met, not a real one."

"I'll accept your word that they're not crippled kitties, but if they were, you would still pull them out of the wet and stroke them, wouldn't you? Mean and tough? Hah! You're a faker. That's what you are, Master Chief. A faker. The Word is out!"

A man could totally screw up his reputation in a place like this!

Patty came zipping into my office not long after I called her, gave me a smooch and asked, "Where are the bride and groom to be?"

"Back at work, I suppose. I finished with them, Look, Patty Lane, I'm not going all out for these two. All I want is get them off my hands. You have to help me out here."

Patty lit into me and called me a mean, cold, unfeeling man, which topped her list of bad things to say to me. She then informed me that she would take care of the wedding, herself, if need be.

"Kitten, those two don't know beans about what they need. We need the chapel decorated nice. We need a place for the reception and we can't have it at the Spanish officer's club because they're not officers. Maybe in the Jolly Jack Club, fixed up with flowers and the like. I think one of the scratch bands we have around here will play just for the exposure. We will have to find someone who knows something about photography. We'll have to round up enough folks so the chapel doesn't look empty. Then there is the honeymoon, maybe a night or two at the Rock Hotel, or some such place and --"

"Who is going to pay for all this, Henry Clay Berkeley?" Patty asked, putting her tiny hands on her hips and looking me straight in the eye.

"Well . . . I'll get someone to pass the hat around the supply department and ship's office, the whole command, actually. I'll cumshaw a few things. The XO is going to borrow swords from the officers. Commander Prince will find guys and gals for honor guards. We'll borrow the captain's sedan. I'll get them a few pieces of excess furniture from base housing. I got a couple of bucks that's not doing me any good. Oh, hell! You know!"

Patty stood on her tippy toes and kissed me very softly. "Yes, I do know, Master Chief Henry Clay Berkeley. Would you believe a girlfriend in Big Otter once stupidly asked *why* I adore you?"

It all fell into place until the Monday of the week of the wedding when Alice came into my office almost in tears. I pushed the door closed, got her seated and inquired as to the problem.

"It's Darrell's parents, or rather his father. They are arriving Friday."

"I don't see the problem. You expected them."

"Darrell's dad sent him a telegram telling him to make certain he reserved them a room at the best hotel in Puerto Santa Cruz. We don't have that kind of money!"

"Can't he pay for his own room?"

"Oh, he could. Maybe he will, but Darrell is afraid he might not. I think he is mean!"

"Why do you think that? You don't know him."

"Master Chief, Darrell tells me his father could *buy* any hotel in Puerto Santa Cruz. I don't think he likes me and he doesn't even know me. He's just mean!"

"What does he do for a living?"

"He is a real estate broker in Connecticut, a really big broker, Darrell says. Oh, why did he do this to us?"

"Why doesn't Grosnick simply tell him to get scre . . . er, tell him to pay for his own damn room if he is so well off?"

"Darrell is afraid of him!" she wailed, and burst into tears.

Great John Paul Jones!

"Look, Alice, stop crying. If the ass won't pay for his hotel, I'll pay for it! Get him a room at the *Playa de la Sol*, one of the regular ones. They're all nice."

"It is not fair for you to pay for it, Master Chief. We should do that, but we don't *have* the money!"

"No one should expect that two third class petty officers would have that kind of money. Don't sweat it. It'll sort out. I'll speak with him when he gets here. Maybe he doesn't know what third class petty officers earns. Maybe he intends to pay for the room. Now go and get hot on all the things you need to do before Saturday."

I thought about Grosnick's father for a while, then called the CMAA to my office.

Senior Chief Master-at-Arms Powell was a nice man. He was quite different from many in his rating who act like mean, small town cops. A goodly number of CMAA's hassle the crew instead of enforcing good order and discipline while providing a firm, guiding hand.

Senior Chief Powell was a kind, mannerly man well versed in pomp and ceremony and he was exactly what I needed. If Alice was correct about Grosnick's father being mean, we needed to get him on the right track by displaying class enough to impress and overwhelm him. We needed to ensure he thought well of the Navy and the people in it from the moment he arrived.

Alice knew little about him, but seemed to believe that he was less than overjoyed at his son marrying a Navy woman. I hoped that wasn't true, but I feared it was. I realized some ignorant civilians believed Navy women were sluts and whores, when nothing could be further from the truth. They were exactly like civilian women, some were saints and some were sinners -- with the vast majority between the two extremes. Regardless, I flat wasn't going to put up with anybody causing Alice anguish, even a future father-in-law. She was far too nice a girl.

Chief Powell bounded into my office late Friday afternoon, followed by my yeoman who he gently edged back into her area, then closed the door.

"You're really going to like this Mother, Master Chief. He's a real sweetheart!"

"Of whom are we speaking, Sheriff, if I might be so bold to inquire?"

"Grosnick's Old Man! You look in the dictionary under 'Anal Passageway' and you will see a picture of him. What an ass!"

"How so?"

"Grosnick and I met his parents on the ramp in *Jerez* and it flat went down hill. His mother hugged Grosnick and kissed him. His dad grabbed him by the arm and asked where his girl was. Didn't shake hands with him, hug him, kiss him, or nothing. He just snarled at him.

"Grosnick went to stammering and stuttering about her getting things ready for the wedding and his dad started chewing on him about how she had damn well better start worrying about meeting *him*. Then he went off about how Grosnick was getting into trouble by marrying a girl he, his dad, not Grosnick, didn't know anything about.

"I had enough of that in about a minute, so I stepped up and told them their car was waiting, but couldn't set at the curb long, or the police would get after us. He ask who in the hell did I think I was to butt in when he was talking. I told him! He didn't like it.

"We got to the car with Riley standing at attention holding the rear door open, just like we planned. She gave them one hell of a snappy salute as a greeting! She looked really smart. He pushed her aside and threw himself into the rear seat and left his wife standing on the curb! I gave Missus Grosnick my arm and assisted her into the seat beside him. He gave me one hell of a dirty look

"He bad-mouthed all the way to the hotel. He didn't like a female driving him, the factories were small, the fields weren't planted right, the roads were too narrow, the traffic signs didn't make sense, the houses were all jumbled together. God, he just kept on and on. I finally had enough of that, so I pointed out the beautiful Domecq winery warehouses and told him they beat any warehouse in the United States. He huffed that off, then started in on Riley.

"He called her a Paddy, asked what cattle boat her folks came over on and a whole bunch of things that would have gotten his ass kicked by any Irishman I ever met. I was, to tell the truth, surprised Riley didn't stop the car and put some knots on his head. I know I wanted to!

"Nothing in the hotel was good enough for him. The room was too small, the reefer was too small, they didn't have his scotch. God, what didn't he moan about! His wife seemed terribly embarrassed and I could tell Grosnick wanted to find a hole to crawl into. I hated to leave Grosnick with the bastard, but I couldn't very well hang around, being that I was, by then, excess gear. I didn't even try to take them to the hotel lounge for a welcome to Spain drink like we planned. The way I felt by then I would have ended up with bleeding knuckles!

"You're really going to like him, Master Chief. He might be the original Ugly American!"

Neither the bride nor groom were what one would call popular, but they were well turned, inoffensive kids and everybody in the command seemed to take an interest in them having a nice wedding. Yankee Green Dollars flowed when the hat was passed. The shipmates of Alice and Darrell arranged a Friday night pre-wedding supper and dance at a Puerto Santa Cruz restaurant that routinely catered affairs for U.S. Navy functions at a reasonable price.

Mister Grosnick steamed importantly through the restaurant's door, twenty minutes before the appointed time, with Missus Grosnick tagging behind. Darrell Grosnick stood up and pulled out a chair for his mother, but his father sat down in it. That left things a mite confused. Darrell Grosnick recovered and seated his mother, which left her removed from adjacent to Alice's chair where we had planned to put her. Only a few folks picked up on that evolution. Most people were not yet there, including Patty who had disappeared with Alice in the early afternoon. I was becoming concerned about their whereabouts.

The more I watched Mister Grosnick, the more he reminded me of some animal. I had initially thought he looked something like a bear, but that was not really so. He was ruddy faced with heavy jowls and a heavy beard, but the upper part of his head was too narrow for his lower face. His neck bulged from the collar of a tight, blue shirt. His huge body had gone to lard. He, overall, looked sloppy. He looked nothing like a match for his plump, well-groomed wife. His manner was one of overbearing, unfeeling, uncaring belligerence. I wondered how such a man could sell anything to anybody, then realized that he didn't have to. He had men and women to do that, all of whom were probably kept beat down to parade rest. He was a very unattractive man, both physically and personality wise.

He started browbeating his son about why he chose to marry a girl he, himself, had never met and how he didn't have an opportunity to have her 'looked at by some people.' He then went to work on him about quitting college, wasting his time in the Navy and a host of other deficiencies with which he had grievances.

Darrell looked pleadingly at his mother several times, but assistance was not forthcoming. He squirmed in his chair and twice tried to stand only to be pushed down by his father. If this had been going on during Darrell's childhood and teen years, it was easy to understand the nervousness and ill at ease mannerisms exhibited by his son.

I went over, thinking to get Darrell a little slack, but Mister Grosnick gaffed me off! He just looked at me, turned back and started in again on his son. That made me somewhat less than happy.

He then grabbed a Spanish waiter and complained about the quality of the scotch. The Spanish waiter probably didn't understand much English, but he knew enough to understand he was being taken to task by a Mark One - Mod Zero Ass. The waiter hissed something that I didn't grasp, but which was surely one of the fine Spanish insults.

I knew I was going to have to put a stop to this, but exactly how I would accomplish that was unknown. Everybody, by this time, was looking at the fool -- the captain, XO, hell, everybody! Allen Prince locked eyes with me and gave me the raised eyebrow.

Unbeknownst to me, Patty had laid her tiny hands on Alice Everett and taken her under tow. Patty and her cohorts, both American and Spanish, had taken Alice shopping for some new attire after Patty discovered Alice had essentially nothing in the way of civilian clothing. They then took Alice to a beauty parlor where they supervised the entire rebuilding process from get to go while holding school call on proper application of make-up. Patty later told me Alice had never before set foot in a beauty parlor and knew very little about the use of make-up.

It was a different Alice who sailed through the door, followed closely by Patty and a host of other ladies. Her hair was cut in a stylish mode that filled out her slender face. Her thin lips now appeared full and her eyes were big and bright. She wore a dress of pale lime with a white scarf affixed across her shoulders in such a manner as to enhance what little she had to show. She had likely never before walked in heels that high, but she did it well, sort of gliding across the floor. She was poised, pretty girl!

Darrell Grosnick's eyes bulged out as though he had been poked in the stomach with a billy club! He shook off his father's restraining hand and walked to meet her. I doubt the boy's feet touched the deck!

He carefully slid his arm around her waist, almost like he was afraid to touch her, and led her to the head table where he introduced her to his mother and father. His mother leaped from her chair and hugged Alice to her, then kissed her on the cheek. Mister Grosnick stared at Alice like he was looking at some lesser form of life and said, "She's some better than I thought you'd find."

It was time for practical, hillbilly, master chief leadership! I zipped around the table, grabbed Mister Grosnick by the arm and hustled him through the scattering of tables and chairs and out the hatch. He was so surprised that he went, although dragging him around the building to a trash strewn patio was like hauling a tank with a jeep.

I had been in enough fights to know this huge guy could clear my deck if he got one good lick, so without further ado I sunk my fist and about eight inches of arm into his fat belly! Air whooshed from his mouth and he fell to the ground with a thud. I'd seen smaller men than him get up, so I kicked him in the same general area, just to ensure he stayed where I had put him. Then, I kicked him again.

"Grosnick, I've been around the globe a few times and I've met men I thought were pure scum, but I've never met anybody as low down as you! A chancre sore dripping green pus has more class than you! The devil's hemorrhoids wouldn't claim you as kin. A clapped up leper with acute syphilis and TB would run from you for fear of catching disease! A vampire would run through a garlic patch, kiss a cross and suck blood out of an angel before he would stick his fangs into your fat neck!

"You've insulted the chief master-at-arms and a nice Irish girl, pissed off a bunch of Spaniards, embarrassed your wife and bad-mouthed your son in front of a room full of his shipmates, degraded and humiliated him is what you done. But, God love me, what you just did to a fine young woman is nothing approaching what a human would do!

"Your son obviously wasn't Big Man on the Campus like you maybe were, but he's your son, even if he doesn't meet your expectations. Well, by God, he meets ours and ours is one hell of a lot higher than yours! He is of value to us and he is one of us. Despite you half-ruining him, he has done well in the Navy and will do one hell of a lot better in years to come!

"When you stop moaning and crawling around, you are going to get up, walk back in there and you are going to act like somebody! You're going up to that sweet little girl your son found and you are going to treat her right!

"One nasty word, one crude remark, or anything else I take the wrong way and you are going to find your fat, sloppy ass in that dumpster over there. If I can't put you in there myself, there is a room full of sailors and Marines who will help me! You've gotten everybody's attention, Toad Face. Every man in that room would be tickled to death to lay a dogging wrench alongside your thick skull.

"Now you get your fat ass up, before I decide to get you up!"

He stumbled to his feet, wiped slobbers off his lips and murmured something I didn't quite hear. "What did you say?"

"You sucker punched me!"

"Sure did. And stand the hell by for a high-grade thrashing if you don't act like a father meeting his future daughter-in-law for the first time!

"You don't need to have her investigated, or whatever you meant by wanting to have her 'looked at by some people.' She comes from a lower-class family when it comes to money. They have none. She didn't know Darrell's folks had any either, not until you sent that stupid telegram and he had to tell her. It must be nice when your own son is ashamed of you.

"Those two kids scrimped to get enough money to marry. They never asked for anything. They don't want much, just each other. You're going to feel pretty beat down if they have children you'll never see because you drove them off with your complaining and that piss poor attitude. Real nice little nest you've made for yourself!

"I'll tell you one more thing. Getting Alice is the best thing that ever happened, or ever will happen to your son. I'll never have a daughter, or a daughter-in-law. But if I did, I would damn sure be happy to have one just like her!

"Now, either swing at me or get your lard ass back in that room. You oughta wash off first. Remember, one ill word out of you for the rest of the time you're here and you'll think you've been taken under fire by a battleship! This might be the first time somebody has knocked your big, slimy ass down, but I guarantee it won't be the last if you act up!"

I hung around the patio with the idea that I would give Mister Grosnick time to wash up and get his sea bag in order. I realized that was a bad decision when Patty rounded the corner carrying a chunk of jagged concrete in one tiny hand and a wine bottle in the other. Following closely was the captain, Mister

Prince and a couple-three Marines and sailors. Patty let out a cry, ran to me, threw herself in my arms and started wetting down my best civilian suit.

"Hey, Kitten! What's wrong?"

"Oh, you . . . you Master Chief Henry Clay Berkeley! I feared he hurt you!"

"Er . . . why so? I'm fine. Never been better. Got it all in one sea bag." I rambled, trying to figure out why they were milling about smartly outside the building.

"Oh, I *hate* you, Henry Clay Berkeley!" Patty sobbed, kissing me all over the face at the same time.

"You all come tearing out here and my wife shows up with a fist full of rocks. What the hell is going on?"

Mister Prince shrugged his shoulders. "I tried to tell everybody you had it handled."

"Did you thump him, Clay-honey. Did you thump him hard?" Patty asked, wiping her eyes and sniffing.

It was no use to attempt to slide a lie past Patty. She could read minds, or something. I could, on occasion, sidestep her questions with some success. "No, not really. He ain't even a contenda!"

She gave me one of her direct Patty stares, "*Did* you thump him, Clay?"

"He understands the Plan of the Day now"

"But you *did* thump him?"

"Yeah, you could say that, maybe. He's not marked up."

"Good! Patty exclaimed, with passion in her voice. "But you really should have broken that cretin's legs, both arms . . . and mashed his mouth!"

And that from a girl who did not approve of violence . . . usually.

Patty had the same tendencies as a mean mama cat with kittens when somebody threatened me in any manner; hence, the items she was carrying when she rounded the building. She had intended to apply them to whatever surface of Mister Grosnick best suited to her purpose!

She had once armed herself with a crystal decanter at the Holiday Inn in Big Otter when a military-hating newspaper publisher spit at me and I opened a can of Whup-ass on him. When the ruckus was over, and his executives left holding their boss upright by both arms, I asked Patty what she had intended to do with the decanter. She replied, with some degree of heat, that she might be small, but she was not helpless and if the publisher's executives had jumped into the fray she intended to break some heads! I learned something about my new girlfriend that night. Patty Lane was not much larger than the average mouse, but God save the King and his Knights when she got wound up!

The captain looked me straight in the eye and said, "Well done, Master Chief. Well done!"

The restaurant was quiet when we walked back in. Everybody was looking directly as us, but no one said anything. There wasn't even the usual low buzzing one heard after an occurrence no one understood. Even the band didn't know whether to play music, or draw small stores. I badly needed a beer, so I walked to the bar, got one and returned to the head table where we were seated. Mister Grosnick didn't look at me, but the rest of the group certainly did. They stared. The establishment was flat quiet.

Not so very good, Buccaneer.

The captain moved uncomfortably in his chair for a few minutes, then clapped Allen Prince on the shoulder, and motioned him to follow. They stepped around the long table until they were standing directly behind Alice and Missus Grosnick, at which time Captain Keene announced, "It is my policy to start an evening by dancing with the prettiest woman present. There are so many of them here tonight that I had a problem deciding. Commander Prince, being the gentleman he is, offered to bail me out after I narrowed it to two. Other gentlemen present will have different opinions as to who they believe to be the prettiest lady, but I will not argue the point. I am going to dance with one of the two I picked and Commander Prince will dance with the other."

The captain slid the chair from beneath furiously blushing Alice as Commander Prince slid the chair from beneath a pink Missus Grosnick. Damned if it didn't look like they had rehearsed it!

The captain got the results he was looking for as the small dance floor filled with sailors, Marines and their ladies. I was born a mite slow on the uptake, but Patty rectified that by snapping me out of my chair and onto the dance floor where she then went into her belt buckle polishing routine.

Patty and I returned to our seats on the end of the table distant from the prospective bride and groom and his parents. I kept an eye on Mister Grosnick, just in case he decided to go off-plumb and ruin Alice's evening, which was undoubtedly the finest she had ever known, or perhaps even dreamed of. I noticed him occasionally saying something to Alice and his wife, now sitting where she belonged, but I couldn't hear over the rumpus and decided what he had said was okay.

A weak turkey could have knocked me from my chair with a dangling feather when Mister Grosnick stood, pulled Alice's chair from beneath her and led her to the dance floor. It surprised me even more that a man of his bulk was so light on his feet. It was, I decided, a damn good thing that I had sucker punched him. Otherwise, he might have danced around and cut me to shreds.

I had always admired the neat, trim look of a woman's body inside the naval uniform and Alice was no exception when I walked her down the aisle of the nearly filled chapel. Patty and her running mates had done wonders with Alice. She was now as pretty in her dress white uniform as she had been in civilian clothing the night before.

Darrell Grosnick, well, there wasn't much one could do with a kid whose ears looked like mud flaps on an eighteen-wheeler. I did wonder if the black, heavy-framed eyeglasses he wore didn't make his ears stick out more than they would have otherwise. I made mental note to have Patty hint to Alice that he would look better with lighter frames.

I felt paternal as I watched the marriage vows exchanged. I had, for better or for worse, thrown the two kids together. There was little doubt in my military mind that it would be for better, rather than for worse. I was, to be truthful, quite proud of myself!

After the chaplain finished issuing them direct orders for a lifetime of formation steaming, they walked from the chapel, down the steps and passed through the honor guard lining both sides of the walkway between the chapel and the street. They turned and waved. Yeoman Striker Riley snapped open the rear door of the sedan. They slid into the car to a hail of cheers and whistles. Riley closed the door, zipped around and into the driver seat and caused the sedan to slip almost silently away. It was done.

Things were going quite well at the reception in the Jolly Jack's Club, then Alice came to where I was standing and handed me an envelope marked: **'FOR THE NEWLYWEDS.'**

"Please look inside, Master Chief. Oh, I cannot believe *this*! What will we *do* with it?"

The only thing inside the envelope was a bank draft drawn on *Banco de Andalusia* made out to them both. The bank draft was for twenty-five hundred dollars! There was no indication of who had purchased the draft.

"Beats the hell out of me, Alice. I don't have a glimmer. Obviously someone intended this for you and Darrell, so keep it. You can sure use it. You did pretty well in gifts too, looking at the stuff piled on the table."

"*You* didn't do this did you, Master Chief?" She gave me a suspicious look.

"No, Alice, I didn't. Ship's company threw quite a bit of money into the kitty, like they do when a shipmate marries, but this didn't come from the crew. And I'm not out one penny."

Not entirely true, but close enough for government work. Patty paid for Alice's new wardrobe, a gown for her wedding night and undergarments so sheer an ant could have walked through the material and never touched a thread of cloth. She paid for Alice's overhaul at the beauty parlor too. The look of delight with herself on Alice's face when she floated through the door at the pre-wedding dance made it cheap, very cheap -- cheap at any price.

The sweetening on the porridge was that the money collected within the command was enough for them to have a week in Benidorm among tourists of their own age group, rather than a couple of days with an older crowd at the expensive Rock Hotel in Gibraltar.

If they did things right, and everything went as nature intended, hanging out with any age group would likely not be in their Plan of the Day. Except for meals, and maybe an occasional night running the discos, the majority of their time would likely be spent in bed. Those kids had a whole suite of unfamiliar equipment on which to conduct calibration, operation and evaluation tests!

They sailed off in a shower of thrown rice en route Seville to catch their train to Benidorm. Alice was so happy she was crying. Darrell looked like he had won the Spanish national lottery, *El Gordo*. I sincerely hoped the two fine kids would find a wonderful life to make up for what they had probably experienced growing up: unpopular, unsure of themselves, poor in Alice's case, and enduring a constant stream of verbal abuse from his father in Darrell's case.

I was about to do a reconnaissance to find Patty, when a hand circled my upper arm. "I want to talk to you, Berkeley!"

Hail, rainstorm, pestilence.

"Grosnick, you are going to be here until tomorrow and I don't want to ruin an expensive monkey suit, so let's reschedule this thing for tonight. I'll give you a rematch."

Grosnick looked strangely before answering, "I don't want to fight you, Berkeley. Oh, I might be able to take you if I didn't give you the first punch, but we could disagree about that.

"I'm not happy about you putting me down. That never happened before, but then I only ever had a couple of fights in my life. I'm so big men leave me alone and so did boys when I was in school.

"I want to thank you for what you did for Darrell. It's more than I did. I had the idea he wanted what I wanted. He doesn't.

"Look, I went to their apartment this morning to give Darrell an open-ended ticket I bought at the travel agent outside the base gate. The ticket was for them both to come home when they can." Mister Grosnick turned his head away for a moment and wiped at his eyes. "Darrell wouldn't take it

"Berkeley, I have a daughter-in-law who seems like a really fine girl that I am never going to get to know and my wife, who does not ever talk back to me, raised some kind of hell last night in the hotel. She has packed her stuff and intends to tour Spain, France and England by *herself*!

"Here, look, you take this ticket and you give it to Darrell and Alice. Tell them to come home, even if it is only so they can visit his mom, if she comes back. Will you do that?"

"I'll give it to them, Grosnick, but I can't guarantee anything. I wouldn't want to see you if I was your son, let alone a new daughter-in-law who had no option but to suspect you're mean before she even met you. Now, she knows you're mean! I wouldn't give this a whole lot of hope. I could say I feel sorry for you, but that would be a lie and a whopper at that. You just received some of what is coming to you, probably long overdue, in fact.

"I talked with your wife last evening. She seems like a really sweet woman. What does surprise me is why she put up with you this long, the way you disrespect her, push her around and probably bad-mouth her, although I never heard you do that

"There's no accounting for womenfolk's feelings. I'll never understand why a wonderful girl like my wife picked a messed up sailor like me, but she did and the world turned into a better place. My best friend told me if I didn't marry her, I'd turn into a sour, bitter old man, hanging out with barflies. That probably would have happened if she had not seen it fit to drag me in out of the cold. Your chances of being old, lonely and bitter are pretty good right now!"

"Yeah, that looks right, Berkeley. I ruined things and I don't know why."

"Well, you surely didn't treat your wife like you do now when you met her, or she'd have canned you on your first date! I hope to hell you didn't always treat your son like you do now either. I have no kids of my own, but I have had dozens and dozens, for all practical purposes, what with all the young sailors I've had working for me. I am not totally ignorant how to handle them.

"Sure, you got to have discipline and even put the hammer down at times, but browbeating them accomplishes nothing. They end hating you and at that point don't much care what in the hell you do to them. You got into that sort of fix with Darrell, unless I read the chart totally wrong. I have little doubt he joined the Navy to get away from you.

"I don't give you much of a chance of pulling this out, but I were you, I'd start treating my wife like she was something I valued more than my own life. I'd telephone my kid once in a while, write him some newsy letters and stuff like that. Would that work for you? I don't know, but it's worth you firing a few rounds.

"It might not be a bad idea for you to call the Everett family, introduce yourself and see if maybe they are not as fine a people as the daughter they produced. Might surprise hell out of you just how fine folks without money can be.

"I don't know if you have other children, I never heard Darrell mention siblings. If you don't, you might start wondering who is going to take over when you're gone. Darrell is not going to want anything you've got, not the way he feels right now. It'd be a shame to let the business you worked for goes to somebody outside your family.

"All I can say, Grosnick, is I wish you luck, mainly because of your son and new daughter-in-law, both of whom I happen to think a lot of, particularly Alice. Lord knows the way you treat people you don't rate any sort of luck, except bad.

"Let me tell you something about Alice. She declined to have her wedding at her home, although she would have loved to have done that. The reason she did is because she knew her folks would spend money on her wedding that they don't have. You tell me, how many girls of *any* background think like that? Maybe one in a big number."

"I didn't think it through, Berkeley. Hell, I thought she would be some cheap girl that Darrell told I was rich. That really worried me, but it doesn't now. I see what Alice is and how well they fit together.

"I didn't sleep last night, thinking of the names you called me, things my wife said and how Alice acted afraid while she was dancing with me. I won't sleep tonight either, not if my wife flies to Madrid this evening like she said she is going to do. I'll be worrying if she is ever coming home.

"Anyway, Berkeley, I don't thank you for hitting me, but I do thank you for your advice. I'll thank you even more if you talk to Darrell and Alice and tell them . . . Oh, hell, tell them I want them!"

Grosnick stumbled away, then turned. "I noticed the furniture they have in that crappy apartment. Darrell said they don't own it. He said you borrowed it for them from the base. I left them a bank draft in an envelope on the gift table, so they can buy some good stuff. Don't tell them where it came from. They might send it back!"

"Grosnick, I doubt you will understand this, but I expect those two kids will be happier in that 'crappy' apartment with Navy issue stuff than you in your mansion, if that's what you have.

"Oh, hell! Come on, damn it! Let me buy you a drink. Let's hunt down your wife and get her one too. We'll work into a conversation the nice thing you tried to do with the ticket and the money you left for Darrell and Alice. Who knows . . . she might forgive you a bit if you keep your act cleaned up and start thinking of someone other than yourself. If she does, you might think of taking her around Europe on a real long trip. You can afford it. Hell, in the situation you find yourself, you can't afford not to!"

"I appreciate that, Berkeley -- I really appreciate it. Hey, wait . . . who do I pay for the drinks I've already had? I didn't know they cost anything!"

"They cost, Grosnick. Oh, but do they cost! But you can't pay. They were paid for by sailors and Marines who have no money to speak of. It was a small payment on what each of us owe if we expect to be called 'Shipmate.'"

CHAPTER THIRTEEN

HAIL AND FAREWELL

With no warning, Captain Jefferson E. Keene received transfer orders to the billet of Chief of Staff, United States Sixth Fleet, one of the prime billets lusted after by every captain in the Navy with the dream of making admiral. Assignment to such a billet did not guarantee future promotion to admiral, but it lifted one above competing captains. There was nothing chiseled in stone, but it was widely believed that only graduates of the Naval Academy were ordered to such billets. That the vast majority of captains who had ever held such billets were naval academy graduates made this theory almost a fact. Jiffy Jeff was not an academy graduate.

Jiffy Jeff, a senior captain, was one of many who had served brilliantly, faithfully and honorably, but had failed promotion to the rank of admiral and had grown middle-aged, if not gray, in the service of their country. Captain Keene had expected, within a year or two, to be ordered onto the retirement rolls in the grade of captain. Now, suddenly, without notice, his star was rising and his career was back into play.

The relationship between Captain Keene and myself was one of mutual trust, respect and liking for each other. We'd known each other since he, as a commander, had served as skipper of a top destroyer-leader in the Pacific Fleet and I, a newly minted chief radioman, served him. That period, coupled with our time in Santa Cruz, made working together a pleasure. I wished him the best, but I dreaded to see him leave. There was no telling what sort of man we would get as his relief. There were a fair number of ill-natured, self-serving and/or nutty captains lurking about.

In that he was authorized no delay in reporting and did not have a relief, the next senior officer, Lucy Stoutmaster-Hunycutt, would temporarily fill the billet of commanding officer. She had recently failed selection to commander and had orders to the Bureau of Naval Personnel in Washington, D.C., likely her next to last stop before retirement on twenty years of service. Her career appeared dead in the water. That did not seem to bother her in the slightest, but she was bugging me to help her get her husband a set of orders to Washington. I didn't think I had the hook-ups to accomplish that. I didn't *do* officers!

Jiffy Jeff called me into his office the morning after he received his orders, gave me a mug of his good Navy coffee and went into a discussion concerning his orders.

"I've had sea daddies in my career, Master Chief, as I am certain you did. I sat on my patio last evening and went through two cigars and about one-half a bottle of *Gran Duque d Alba* trying to figure who hooked me up with this set of orders. Damned if I could come up with anybody, even with the help of the cigars and the brandy. Most officers who helped further my career are retired. I called the Bureau and checked who held down what senior officer detailing desks. I don't personally know any of them. Any ideas?"

"Not a darn one, Captain, not a one. I've heard of officers coming back to life in the career sense, but I've never met one. I don't know anybody I could call either. I don't have a hook-up in the Bureau, not with the senior officer detailing desk.

"I did see an interesting thing one time, but that was in a cruiser-destroyer group. A new admiral took over and folks were transferred without warning. You might want to get your ear to the ground and see if such a thing is going on at COMSIXTHFLT. Has SIXTHFLT been performing okay? Do you know?"

"I've heard nothing negative about SIXTHFLT. What happened on that group staff?"

"Well, I had not yet reported, so I have no first-hand knowledge of the competence of those transferred. What happened was a salty fellow, just promoted to admiral, relieved the incumbent who had stepped on his crank and mashed the pink part. He nosed around a few days, then some assistant chiefs of staff and below unexpectedly received orders and transferred, probably to lesser billets.

"The Word was out by the time I reported. The reason for the transfers was that the admiral had taken a look at his new command and decided there was a lot of deadwood holding down chairs. You know there are always some deadwood in large command -- small ones too, for that matter. Good men, but men to whom the Peter Principle applies. I guess Admiral Grayson thought he had more than his fair share of deadwood, so he transferred some -- maybe all of them.

"One transferred was the master chief radioman. I was a patient as Naval Hospital San Diego, on the list for promotion to master chief and just declared fit for full duty, so I got grabbed. I reported about three weeks after the admiral reported, so I doubt he had anything to do with picking me. I became available for assignment, that particular billet came open and that's where the detailer sent me. There were several newly reported officers and chiefs when I arrived. All were hot runners, as it turned out. How many were actually picked by the admiral I don't know.

"Admiral Grayson is a fine man, but salty. He was not easy to work for. He was a bear at demanding tasks getting done correctly the first time. He didn't tolerate people who waffle, or didn't take responsibility for their decisions.

"One commander, who must hold the Navy-wide record for getting fired, lasted nine days. He tried to blame something that went wrong on a subordinate. The admiral told him to pack his sea bag and catch the next boat going ashore. That was after he ripped his head off and rolled it down the passageway. Admiral Grayson has a temper! I got along with him fine, not to say that he didn't rip into my stern on occasion. I had *no problem* seeing the error of my ways after he finished chewing on me. Oh, by the way, Commander Prince worked for him on a destroyer years back."

"I worked for him too. I was his operations officer when he was commodore of Destroyer Squadron Thirty-One. He was a bear then! Was he your rabbi?"

"No, but he took to me for some reason and he really lit his boilers when the detailer talked me into going ashore on recruiting duty after I had served in his cruiser-destroyer group for slightly over one year. The only time he offered to help me was when he tried to get me a set of orders back to sea when I was on recruiting. That didn't work out."

"This is the first time in my career I received orders with no delay in reporting. It's good I don't have a wife. Any wife would be in a tizzy at having to move with a three day notice!"

"Well, Captain, to tell the tale, everyone in your command is in a tizzy right now, getting ready for the change of command. The XO will likely have a nervous breakdown before tomorrow morning. Scuttlebutt has it that she has been to church six times since you received orders, burning candles and praying your relief shows up before she has to take command!"

The captain lost it. When he stopped laughing, he said, "I've called the Bureau about my relief, but no one has yet been assigned. It certainly won't hurt Missus Stoutmaster-Hunycutt to spend time in a four-striper billet. It might even pull *her* career out of the doldrums!

"You're going to be lonely around here in before long. She's leaving. Prince is leaving near-term and so are several other officers and chiefs with whom you've been working. How much longer do you have here, a year?"

"About that. I'll be okay. Things are pretty much on an even keel. Both our lives have been calm since the commander took over as XO and Prince took over as OPS. Wonder who will replace them?"

"The XO is coming from a tour as CO of a tin can, the *Underwood*, and OPS from a department head billet in the cruiser *Halsey*."

The captain stood and grabbed me by the hand. "I'll say goodbye again after the change of command, but I want to tell you something. If, perchance, I make admiral down the way and I get a sea going billet, rather than getting stuck behind a desk, I want you as my master chief radioman. I'll hunt you down, Clay. I *know* where you live!"

I exercised my brain to the max that afternoon thinking about how to get Lucy-baby's hubby orders to Washington, or somewhere close to there. I knew about officers. I knew a *lot* about officers, but my knowledge of how they were detailed, how their sea to shore rotation worked and what tickets needed punched to promote was out of my area of expertise.

Ensign Hunycutt received shore duty orders to Santa Cruz after his selection to officer, rather than to sea as would have been the normal thing. Did that mean he had to transfer to sea as an officer when he left Santa Cruz? Would back-to-back shore tours mess up his chances for promotion, him not having had sea duty as an officer?

I considered chucking the whole thing, but gave up that idea. While I had not promised the commander that I'd try to arrange it so she could continue sleeping next to her husband, I did sort of tell her I would check around. For a master chief who didn't *do* officers, I surely spent a portion of my time doing just that. While I did know a few senior officers in Washington, I knew none in the Bureau of Naval Personnel. It was time to work the CPO brotherhood.

"Hey, Pens, congratulations on making master chief! I tried to call you when the results came out, but you were on leave." I told my old shipmate from *King*, then a chief yeoman.

"Yeah, took two week's leave and fished the South Bank of the Potomac. I didn't catch much, but then it is hard to find time to wet a line what with the pickup load of beer I took along. I couldn't let it spoil! I could have handled the beer and still caught some trout, but I fouled up during a moment of weakness and took a government lawyer with me. The fish got really lonely. I wrote them a letter of apology.

"Clay, she like to killed me! I learned that a sleeping bag does not equal a regulation bed, not for certain evolutions. They are made of material so slick you can't stay on it when things get active.

"Before you ask . . . I don't know why Jiffy Jeff got orders to COMSIXTHFLT. Some rabbi took care of him is my guess. I hope that billet makes him admiral. He's one hell of a guy!"

"Yes, he is. Regarding that fishing trip, old as you are, you oughta know that some things don't mix. Gals and serious fishing is one of them, in most cases. Hey, I need a hook-up!"

Pens gave a long sigh. "You always do! You've not paid off your past debts to the Washington Gulls yet. You still owe them about a pickup load of roses and five gallons of French perfume from the last dozen hook-ups they did for you. But, lay it on me, Shipmate."

"I have female lieutenant commander I inherited when I came to Santa Cruz. I'm not going to tell you how she got hooked up with a LDO ensign for a husband. It is so confusing I don't even know for certain. She has orders to the Bureau. I don't know what section or department. She's good people and she's an administrative and computer whiz. She fleeted up to XO here and done one hell of a fine job and now she's going to be skipper for a while. I doubt she's really in the running for full commander because she's been passed over once for promotion. Pens, I like this woman, both as a person and an officer. She's about as good as they get.

"She wants her hubby to transfer to Washington as soon as possible after she reports. I don't know if that is possible because a shore tour in Santa Cruz is his first officer billet. Could be that he has to go to sea. You know about officers, you used to take care of officer administration, records, transfers and such. Will you look in the manuals and tell me which way to jump? If he needs to go to sea, then that's where he should go and I'll tell her: 'Oh, so very, very sorry, Commander, but your ensign bed warmer goes to sea!'"

"I can tell you right now that there are no really hard and fast rules for rotation of LDO's, but I'll have to look into his exact status. Give me his name and call me tomorrow. Give me that lieutenant commander's name too. I have one who is transferring and he isn't worth a broken shackle! Maybe she is his relief. If she isn't, maybe I can fix it so she is!"

I hung up the phone, grinning to myself. My old shipmate's concerns would increase greatly if the commander transferred to his department. She now firmly believed that master chiefs were the world's problem solvers -- hers, in particular. This was compounded by the fact that I had been correct in my original assumption that her husband didn't have a lot more common sense then she did when it came to matters of a personal nature.

I didn't dislike her husband, but I really didn't like him all that much either. He seemed ill at ease around me and, while he never said anything, he seemed to dislike the close relationship I had with his wife. I wondered if he might harbor the mistaken belief that she and I had engaged in a little friendly fraternization before he arrived in Santa Cruz. The commander constantly dragging me into their personal business probably contributed to his uncertainly. It seemed I had taken them to raise.

The commander charged into my office early one morning just weeks after they married, eyes all red and her face looking like hail, rainstorm and pestilence had descended upon her. I closed the door and mentally prepared myself for yet another segment in the Stoutmaster-Hunycutt saga.

"Master Chief, Paul refuses to wear his uniform to the Navy Ball!"

"It's not required. Civilian attire is authorized, but most will wear uniforms because that is, really, more appropriate. He spill coffee on his monkey suit, or something?"

"I'm senior to him."

"And that is a problem, how?"

"He says it would embarrass him, me being senior."

"You were way, way senior when you two started rubbing belly buttons . . . uh, sorry, Commander, that just slipped out. Hell, you're senior. Order him to wear the uniform!"

"Oh, I *can't* do *that!*"

"Commander, you are not in position to do me good or bad, so I'm not blowing smoke up your as . . . er, at you, but you are way up on my list of good people. You're a good officer and one hell of a fine person. I have nothing against your husband, but I don't know him as well as you, not nearly. That being as it may, I don't see how our close relationship equates to me getting involved in every squabble you and Paul have. You two are crazy about one another. Anybody can see that. So little minor squabbles are all they are and you two ought to be able to resolve them by yourselves.

"Remember the chicken affair? You caught Paul looking at a neat female as . . . er, stern at the Navy Exchange and you immediately put Paul and yourself on a crash diet. Paul called me, complaining you were feeding him cold cereal with skin milk for breakfast and boiled chicken with plain lettuce salad for lunch, supper and midnight rations. He claimed to have eaten so much chicken that he qualified for flight pay! He wanted me to talk to you about that. Now, I ask you, Commander, how could something like that have gotten me involved?"

"You're *my* shipmate and you were wrong to take his side!"

"I'm not going to argue the point, Commander. Men look at women. It has been that way since Eve and The Snake trapped poor, old Adam. It has nothing to do with thinking their wife has a big stern or that anything else is wrong with her appearance. It's a man thing. Anyway, like I told you. You don't carry excess stern cargo."

Not entirely true there, Buccaneer.

"Patty says you don't stare at other women."

"Patty Lane fibs."

"What are you going to do?"

"About what?"

"This uniform thing!"

"Commander, look. Just tell him to wear his uniform!"

"Oh, I *can't* do *that!*"

It was a great mystery how the old-time Mormons managed to survive with more than one.

"Commander, what do you expect me to do?"

"Patty said you could call Paul and explain Navy customs to him. She said he would believe that wearing a uniform is fitting, proper and expected -- if it came from you."

"I might could roll a hoop down a hill and jump through it too, but I'm not going to."

"Patty said you *would!*" she exclaimed, firmly.

Well, that cut it! If I didn't resolve this flap, I'd have to listen to Patty push the project for days to come. She'd bug me when she fed me. She'd bug me when she brought me a beer. She'd bug me when she cuddled on my lap. If that didn't work, she'd bug me after she beat me down to parade rest in bed and I was laying there, totally worn out, at her mercy. She wouldn't nag. She never did that, but she'd keep bringing the subject up until such time as the situation was resolved to her satisfaction. That meant Paul had to wear his monkey suit to the Navy Ball!

"OK, Commander, I'll reason with him.'"

I got Paul on the telephone and I laid it on him.

"Look here, Ensign. I want nothing more than to stay out of your family affairs, but what with our wives being sisters-in-everything-but-fact, that is not working out for either of us. That said, you are way off-course about not wearing your dinner dress uniform to the Navy Ball and it has nothing at all to do with what is fitting and proper. Wait! I don't want to hear your side of it. I already have.

"First, uniform aside, you didn't let seniority bother you when you started sneaking around with a lieutenant commander while you were a first class petty officer. I'm not blaming only you. You were both equally guilty. Okay, so it worked out, but you put her through a lot of hell.

"There you were . . . sitting on a tin can in Mayport while she was catching all sorts of flack in Santa Cruz, her trying to pass off a story about how a dead husband had fathered her kid and God-World believing she was an unwed mother. What were you doing at the time? Taking telephone calls from her two-three times a week and telling your shipmates that it was a little country girl just begging to jump your bones. You owe her, Mister. You owe her Big Time!

"Now I don't care about your sensitivities about her being senior. You have a fine woman for a wife and I realize you know that. The least you can do is humor her desire to parade around in her dinner dress uniform with her on your arm wearing *your* dinner dress uniform.

"Look at it this way. Your captain pinned a Navy Commendation Medal on you for doing something magnificent to the ship's weapons system. She doesn't have an NCM. All she has is a couple of Navy Achievement Medals. So, looking at it that way, you've got more on your chest than she does." True, but only in the sense of something made out of cloth and metal.

"I'll do it, Master Chief, but I'll be embarrassed."

"Not as embarrassed as you would have been if she hadn't gotten you a commission! Somebody would have eventually found out about your relationship. Then you'd have been stood tall in front of The, Long, Green Table with some evil chiefs and officers glaring at you, about to kick your Navy-lovin' stern out into Civvy Street with you wearing an ill-fitting, prison-made suit in lieu of your uniform. Oh, yeah! The Navy would have taken away your uniform before they booted your stern out of the main gate. You ought to be running in front of her throwing rose petals so she doesn't hurt her little pink toes on stones, as much as you owe her!"

"Lucy said *you* arranged my commissioning."

"She had the guts to trust me, and it took a lot of those, her barely knowing me. She was adrift so bad she had to tell somebody. Anyway, the idea of getting you a commission originated with Patty. All Prince and I did, really, was push it along.

"Now please, in the memory of John Paul Jones and for the sake of your friendly, neighborhood master chief, start settling your little spats by yourselves and, please, please keep me out of it!"

Pens Larson came through yet again.

"Clay, I found I know the LDO detailer. We served together in *Keyes* more years ago than I care to admit.

"The ensign transferred to Santa Cruz as a single man, so he is scheduled to serve in Santa Cruz for two years, rather than the three a married man would serve. The detailer said he could cut that a mite, but not too much. He could leave Santa Cruz a few months after his wife transfers.

"Problem is the ensign has never had contact with his detailer. He has never spoken with him since he was commissioned. Is he dumb, or what?

"If he wants to slide around with his wife on bed sheets, he'd best make like a bunny and hop on the horn and get penciled in for one of the Dee Cee billets expected to be available when he transfers from Santa Cruz. There are a couple of billets coming open on bird farms in the same time frame, so he might find himself on an aircraft carrier if he doesn't get hot.

"Oh, I checked and she is, in fact, detailed to my department. I sure hope she is as good as you say. You, Old Timer, have been known to lie like a dirty dog!"

I thanked Pens, promised the roses and stinky stuff would be forthcoming for the Washington Gulls. My old shipmate really didn't expect me to do that, but I had, on occasion, sent flowers and candy to female government workers who helped Pens accomplish things I had needed. The story, the way I heard it, was Pens and other old shipmates, were keeping the Gulls happy in ways that involved The Snake.

I informed the commander of her husband's dereliction in never having called his detailer. I didn't have to explain the ramifications of that. She well knew the importance of keeping one's name in front of the detailer. A person who does not maintain communications with their detailer is merely a name on a sheet of paper and was likely to be detailed to the first billet that pops up, such as Ice Control Officer at Naval Air Facility Adak, Alaska.

When the ecstatic commander got it all back into one sea bag, she took up for her husband by saying, "He's new at this, Clay. He just didn't know."

"Yeah, right. I forgot they remove the brain when they commission an ensign or assign a person to a public affairs billet. You got to watch them both!"

She flashed her pretty eyes at me and gave me a sad smile. "What in the world am I going to do without you, Clay? You've been my mainstay since you reported, Shipmate!"

"I've been thinking about you needing a little advice now and again. Look, when you report to the Bureau, there is this Master Chief Yeoman, Frank O. Larson -- Pens, for short. What you do is . . ."

CHAPTER FOURTEEN

PROCEED ON DUTY ASSIGNED

I was just turning the corner to the quarterdeck, snickering to myself about the Stoutmaster-Hunycutt problem I had just bequeathed Pens Larson, when a stubby ensign charged through the double glass doors and marched smartly to the duty room counter. It happened that the person standing officer of the day was making a head call, leaving the CMAA present.

"Senior Chief, I must speak to the Officer of the Day!" the Ensign demanded, importantly.

"She's off somewhere, What can I do for you, Ensign?"

"I must speak with her!"

I caught the CMAA's eye and winked at him.

"Well, if you'd rather speak with a first class petty officer than with a Senior Chief, I can hunt her down." the CMAA replied, picking up on the wink.

"Look, Senior Chief. I have an urgent dispatch for a member of this command. Urgent, I tell you!"

"If you'll tell me who it's for, I'm fairly certain I can muster that person up."

"It is for a Master Chief Berkeley."

"Hello, Ensign. There's only one Master Chief Berkeley in this command. That's me. What do you have for me?"

"Master Chief, you are directed to report *on the double* to the VIP Lounge at the air terminal."

"Any particular reason?"

The ensign looked at the CMAA out of the corner of his eye, as if he thought Senior Chief Powell was a spy waiting to intercept his dispatch. "Maybe we should speak away from other people." he said, uncertainly.

"Rest assured that the Sheriff is cleared for everything except Burn Before Reading. What's the message?"

"I am not totally certain . . . A VIP aircraft is en route from Madrid with an admiral aboard who wishes to speak with you. It will be landing in just minutes!"

"What does he want? Knowing his name would be a hint."

"I was not told. We must go. Now!"

"Ensign, do you really believe I dash over to the air terminal every time an admiral wants to see me without knowing what he wants or even who he is? Do you believe that?"

The cheek muscles in the Sheriff's face were jerking like the sides of an electrocuted cat. He was having a hard time handling the puncturing of the ensign's swelled head without breaking into whoops of laughter.

"Uh, that is, Er, my God, Master Chief! It is an *admiral* who wants to see you!"

"Ensign, admirals shake the water off it the same way we do. But, if it will make you happy, I'll meet him on the ramp."

"He said in the VIP Lounge!"

"Right. I'll meet him on the ramp. You run along, Ensign. I'll take my own car."

"You *must* arrive before the admiral!"

"John Paul Jones couldn't stop me!"

The ensign, in his excitement, must have taken a wrong turn, consequently, I arrived at the air terminal before him. I was standing on the tarmac near the blue canvas canopy that ran between the aircraft parking pad and the entrance to the VIP Lounge, chatting with his commanding officer when he showed up.

He marched to his captain, executed a sharp left turn and saluted smartly. "Captain, I *told* the Master Chief he was to meet the admiral in the VIP Lounge!"

I thought for a moment the captain was going to pat the ensign on his head, but instead he gave me a quick, sideways grin. "Master Chiefs know where they want to go, Mister. You will learn that eventually.

"Any idea who this admiral is, Master Chief? The pilot only informed the tower they had a three-star aboard and he wished to speak with you."

"I really don't, Captain. I don't know a whole gaggle of admirals. I know a two-star and I knew one who commanded the Brown Water Navy in Vietnam when he was a rear admiral, but he has since retired, I think. I don't know a single three-star who would want to speak with me. Not a glimmer, Sir."

A sleek, white and silver Lear jet swooped down on a distant runway, taxied rapidly to the terminal and rolled to a smooth stop centered on the VIP parking pad. Two sailors wheeled a red-carpeted stairway to the side of the plane and the door hissed open.

Down the ramp charged Admiral Grayson, wearing three stars on the collar of his immaculate white shirt. He returned our salutes, shook hands with the Air Station CO and then with the ensign, which probably made his year. He then turned and slapped me on the shoulder. "Well, Berkeley, so they let you out of the brig! Let you keep your master chief stars too. Damn, this Navy is getting soft!"

The ensigns jaw dropped to near the first button on his shirt.

"You know how it is, Admiral. Good behavior and all. Congratulations on your third star, Sir. I didn't hear about it."

"The day you exhibit good behavior is the day to set up a spear concession near Armageddon! Reference the third star . . . I don't officially rate it yet. Not until I actually take command of the Sixth Fleet. My steward, you remember him, Jesus Gomez, was a bit over eager when he put my uniform together this morning."

Likely story!

"Thank you for meeting me, Captain. You have a great looking air station. I'm sure you have much to do, so I won't keep you longer. I'll listen to the master chief tell me sea stories, let's call them lies as they always are, and then I'll be out of your hair soon as they get juice in the plane. Take care, Captain."

Everybody again exchanged salutes and left.

The ensign would have quite a story to tell in the officer's lounge that night about an admiral who came to see a master chief who just got out of the brig and who told the admiral lies as a matter of routine. That would generate all sorts of theories among the junior officers.

Inside the VIP Lounge, the admiral started clinking bottles around in the small reefer. "They have a lot of stuff in here, must expect someone important. I'm going to have a snort of this Spanish Old Wildcat or whatever they call this dark stuff. What do you want?"

"I'll have a San Miguel, Admiral. Thanks."

"I told Jesus to take a taxi and get me some cigars. He better get his ass back so we can leave. Don't sell them on station, do they?"

"No, Admiral. I suspect U.S. citizens would take offense if the Navy Exchange sold contraband like Cuban cigars." I grinned, knowing the trouble he had getting the Cuban stogies he mostly chewed, rather than smoked.

"Stupid law! What difference does it make if we import a few cigars, except to the virgins who roll them between their silky thighs. They could use the money.

"Master Chief, there will be three officers and a CPO flying through here in the next couple of days heading to Gaeta via Naples. I told them to look you up if anybody tried to bump them off a flight or they ran into problems here."

So that was what he wanted!

"Sixth Fleet is a going concern. One little problem is some on the staff are not my kind of sailors. Got a few pantywaists who want to play tiddly-winks on a computer before anyone can get a decision out of them. I don't do business that way. So, there will be replacements.

"Your Captain Keene is replacement for a fine man who is the current chief of staff. Absolutely nothing wrong with the incumbent, except he wouldn't make it with me. He is a preacher type who does not believe in sex, drinking or cussing. He doesn't believe in anything sailors used to do before we got politically correct -- not that most have stopped doing those things. I'm too old and too beat up to put up with his sensitivities. I thought it better if he takes command of a cruiser, which is something he always wanted. He's likely a shoo-in for admiral later.

"Keene was once my operations officer. He is my kind of sailor. That's why I picked him. Maybe I can get him a star. He rates one. One thing for certain, my second in command will think like I do! I can cuss and yell and not hurt his tender feelings.

"The communications department is only fair. None of the officers have anything approaching heavy fleet experience. They, to the man, served two-three back-to-back shore tours or some such. None of them had a heavy sea billet before that. The master chief was pretty good, so I heard, but he got sick, drunk, or acted up like you are prone to do and got retired a month or so back. I understand the Bureau found a replacement with sea duty coming out of his wazoo, but he has kids in college and didn't want to go overseas, so he put in his papers to retire.

"I've had the occasion to speak with admirals who returned from recent deployment to the Sixth Fleet. One of their complaints was that none of the operation orders contained the needed number of frequencies for the number of circuits needed by a battle group. They also bitched that it took an awfully long time to get a response from the communications lads at Sixth Fleet and some of the answers were flat piss poor! I can see how that would happen what with none of them having experience in sea-going communications at the battle group level.

"I can't have fleet communications not purring along like a tomcat conducting breeding drills. A fleet commander and his battle group commanders have to have excellent communications in today's world, even to make a head call.

"So, Berkeley, you ready to shift your ass to Gaeta, Italy? I'll put you in charge of communications *within* the fleet. Your new boss won't cause you problems. By the time you report he will understand that your efforts will improve his reputation to where he'll likely make captain after his tour. The rest of them can do other stuff, work with NATO, liaison with foreign military commands, plan exercises, attend conferences, oversee shore communications support and the like."

That lightening bolt came from nowhere!

"Admiral, I'd be honored to be part of your staff. I really would. I enjoyed working for you the last time, except maybe when you were yelling at me. I'd love to get my hands on communications at the fleet level, but I've got to check with somebody before I commit."

"Don't worry about your detailer. I've got it all set up, although he was a little odd about transferring you. He seemed to think I wanted you as fleet master chief. Is he the same dildo I had trouble with when he ball sucked you into applying for recruiting duty?"

"Yes, Sir. Same guy. Master Chief Abraham Lincoln McGee -- Reb, for short. He's some sort of wheel in the NAACP, or some such organization and the Navy is never going to get him out of Washington! Admiral, I'm not concerned about him. I have to check with my wife."

"Your *wife*? You got *married*?"

"If I didn't, there is a hard-nosed preacher who lied and a little girl living in sin I sent you an invitation. I guess you didn't get it."

The admiral looked bad perplexed. "No, I never received the invitation. Damn yeoman! Always losing stuff! I thought for a minute you were trying to weasel your way out of sea duty, but you're serious! How did *that* happen?"

"I'm not exactly sure, Admiral. I met this little girl, and she is little, tiny really. The next thing I knew, four-five months later, I was standing tall at the altar beside this giant gunnery sergeant watching her walk up the aisle. The rest is history."

"You *wanted* to get married?"

"It didn't seem to make any difference what I wanted, Admiral. I don't believe I had much say in the evolution. Now, I wouldn't want to be anything else, except married to her."

"I'll be flat go to hell! A shackled down Clay Berkeley! Well, you run and ask her permission like a good little boy and you get back to me via message no later than tomorrow. I hope you will take the billet, for several reasons. One is: I've got to *meet* this little lady!"

"Uh, one more thing, Admiral. You don't have the Fleet Master Chief billet waiting in the wings for me, do you?"

"Not right now. The current fleet master chief is okay, far as I know. If the enlisted distribution sheet is correct, he's due to roll in eight-nine months, then we'll see."

"The communications billet would be great, but I'd rather not be in the running for fleet master chief."

"Master Chief Berkeley, do you remember, even during your dreams, of me ever *asking* you if you *wanted* to do a particular job for me. Do you?"

"No, Admiral. I can't say that I have, except now. I was your command master chief in your battle group, but I was double-hatted as communications assistant, which was okay."

"Wouldn't be asking now if you had completed your tour here. Your stern would be on that plane right alongside mine when it lifted off. Here's how it goes, Bucko. If I decide to make you fleet master chief, then you *will* be fleet master chief! I will double-hat you again, if that's what you want. We'll wait and see what the Bureau digs up for the current guy's replacement. I won't take a shore puke or a guy who spent his life in an airdale squadron. The guy I want has to swagger and roll when he walks!"

The crusty, old admiral gave the sly look he always exhibited before shocking hell out of someone. "Unless that doe you married has your ass worn ragged, exercising The Beast With Two Backs and dragged the fire out of you, you'll have everything in fleet communications squared away and be looking for something to do for a living in lot less than any eight-nine months. Hell, you'll beg me for the fleet job!"

The CO of the air station and a gaggle of his more senior officers lined the ramp and smarted smartly as the admiral's jet taxied away. They had all been waiting when we walked from the VIP Lounge to the aircraft. There wasn't an officer anywhere likely to miss the chance to get his face in an admiral's mind, if only for a moment. The ensign was absent. The CO had likely sent him out to play with the other kiddies.

Admiral Grayson had put me flat in the middle of a deep lake of kimchee! Patty wouldn't want to leave Spain and she sure wouldn't want me on a ship, not even a flagship that stayed in home port for lengthy periods. If I went, Patty would be unhappy. If I didn't go, the admiral would be angry and might grab me anyway, in which case Patty would believe I took the billet against her wishes. My options equaled that of a condemned man offered

213

a choice of death by burning at the stake, or drawing and quartering.

That night I took Patty to the worst restaurant in Puerto Santa Cruz, maybe the worst in all of Spain.

"Food pretty bad, huh, Kitten? Aren't you getting tired of this Spanish grub?"

"This meal is not good, but Spanish food, in general, is no different from what we eat in West Virginia. It is presented more attractively in Spain. Food is beautiful here." (Scratch one)

"Well, the pasta in Spain is sort of weird, not like in Italy. Pasta is great in Italy and they have dozens of kinds."

"I am not particularly fond of pasta." (Scratch two)

I took a sip of the wine and set down my glass as if disgusted. "Wine is much better in Italy."

"I have never had Italian wine, but it could not be better than Spanish. I consider French wine inferior to Spanish too. Plus, dearest, I read many Italian wines is nothing more than re-bottled Spanish wine. (Scratch three)

"Patty, you've seen the sights in Spain and Portugal. Wouldn't you like to see more of Europe? Beautiful cathedrals and buildings and famous paintings such as they have in Italy? Maybe even see the Mona Lisa? The pope even?"

"I am quite content here." (Scratch four)

"I stopped in our little bar this evening. The Spanish men were discussing Jarhead causing so many puppies in Puerto Santa Cruz. Maybe it is time to get him out of Dodge."

"They must have been discussing the family of Jarhead and the sweet Pekinese that lives near Red Square. Oh, Clay, you should see those puppies! They look like Jarhead, except they have long, silky hair and a sleeker body. Those puppies are the talk of the town! The owner of the Pekinese believes he has an entirely new breed of dog and has priced the puppies quite high. Several Spaniards have stopped by our house, asking if they can borrow Jarhead for a few days. (Scratch five)

"Patty, you never got much chance to teach school because I dragged you to Spain. You're going to have a difficult time getting hired when you return to West Virginia. Maybe you should study something and further your degree. Italian art, maybe."

Patty was beginning to look strangely at me. "I doubt I will teach again, dearest. I have a fulfilling life and there are only so many teaching positions available. I fear I might take a position needed by a person who has to earn a living. I would not like to do that. (Scratch six)

I mulled the dilemma while Patty jabbered about a children's party she and her Spanish running mates held at an orphanage in Cadiz. I was pretty well stuck. I simply could not get a rise out of Patty to where I could open the subject of our transferring to Gaeta, Italy. I couldn't very well hit her right between the eyes with the idea. Not a glimmer. I was pondering my next move when Patty spoke up.

"You came home early today, Clay. You never come home early on a workday. You've been constantly spouting about Italy. You want to tell me something and you do not know how to do it. So I will ask. Clay, when are we transferring to Italy and why?"

She really could read minds!

"Patty, I'm caught in a blight. If I take a job an admiral offered today, you are going to be pis . . . er, unhappy. If I don't take the job, he is going to be unhappy. He might fire a silver bullet and transfer me there even if I don't volunteer.

"I just as well tell you. You'd worm it out of me anyway. Patty, I want the job. Everybody I know in Santa Cruz is being transferred and I'm getting stale now that things are pretty much Bristol Fashion. But I won't go if you don't want to. We can hang here and take what happens when my normal transfer date comes next year."

Patty reached across the table and took my hand. "Clay, for a highly intelligent man, you can sometimes be so *dense*! Do you actually believe I would stand in the way of your career -- a career you had long before we married? Yes, I love Spain, but I love my husband more -- a whole lot more! Take the job."

What a wife!

"There are considerations, Kitten. It's sea duty, for one thing."

Patty's face crumpled. "Sea duty?   Away from me? Bugger the bosun!"

"It's not regulation sea duty where I'd be away a whole lot, like an aircraft carrier battle group. The rotation of the flagship is a month with the fleet, a month in home port of Gaeta, Italy, and a month visiting ports throughout the Mediterranean. Even the month with the fleet and the month running the Med are often broken up with short visits to her home port. I don't know how much of a given year we'd be parted, but it wouldn't be much, two-three weeks at a time, mostly. You could fly to most ports that the ship visits and we could steam around together. It's good sea duty. Much better than anything I'll get next year when we have to transfer from Santa Cruz."

"I always realized you would eventually return to sea duty, but it is hard to accept. I never realized how fantastic life could be until we married. I do not like being away from you, not even a few hours. I dread leaving Puerto Santa Cruz. I have never had so many friends. Wonderful friends. Almost family."

"Kitten, Gaeta is a small naval community too. It is fifty miles, or more, to the nearest naval activities, which are in Naples. Located in Gaeta is the flagship, itself, a small naval support detachment, a DOD school and some welfare and recreation stuff, such as a club and a small Navy Exchange. You'll need to learn Italian because you will purchase most of your groceries in the local open air markets.

"I only visited Gaeta once, some years ago, but I've heard a lot about it. Everyone ever stationed there claim to have loved the town.   Gaeta has, maybe, twenty thousand residents, but the population jumps a lot when the summer tourists come to hit the beaches. From what I hear, the Italians in Gaeta are great friends with the Navy. They look upon sailors and their dependents as a part of the community. There is no naval housing in Gaeta. Everybody lives intermingled with the locals, just like you and I do here. The Navy will put us up in a nice hotel when we arrive and we'll take our time looking for a place to live. I doubt we will find a cottage like we have here, but we will find something nice.

"I really hate to do this to you, Kitten, but that's the way it is in the Navy. You get settled in one location, then you move.

"Look, I love the Navy, but I love you ever so much more. If you're not happy in Gaeta and you don't think you can handle separation, I'll retire next year and we'll return to West Virginia.

"You will *not*! You will never leave the Navy because of me! I will never allow that. You have been Navy since you were a teenager. You would be lost without the Navy -- miserable and lost. You will remain in the Navy until such time as you, yourself, are ready to leave. Dearest, I am sort of in the Navy too. And, thus far, I love it! I love the people in the Navy too.

"We will proceed on duty assigned!"

CHAPTER FIFTEEN

POLLYWOG -- ARRIVING

Patty and I moved bag, baggage, bulldog and cat from Puerto Santa Cruz, Spain to Gaeta, Italy, home port of the Sixth Fleet flagship. Our life fitted nicely into the flagship's schedule: one-third of each quarter steaming with the fleet, one-third showing the flag (grip and grins) in the ports of Mediterranean littoral countries and one-third in home port. We were, in actuality, separated far less than two-thirds of the time because Patty routinely hired an animal setter and flew to ports-of-call of the flagship.

We happily played tourist in most every country bordering the Med. Watching tiny Patty waving madly as the flagship nosed slowly toward the pier always caused a lump in my throat and a tightening in my lions. I knew exactly what Patty had in mind the minute she could grab hold of me in whatever accommodations she had rented. I was as happy as a snake in a rock pile.

Then it ended.

Shortly after we completed our first year in Gaeta, Patty met me in Barcelona during a time when the usual belligerent cults and sects and hostile countries in the Middle East engaged in a cease fire, peace negotiations, stand down, whatever. At any rate, they were not working their customary hardest to make the lives of their citizens and the Sixth Fleet sailors flat miserable. Consequently, crises driven working hours reduced to something approaching that of normal humans. I snatched that opportunity and took leave for the entire inport period.

Patty and I burned my unexpected abundance of free time steaming about Barcelona. We sampled tapes and wine at sidewalk cafes, inspected wares in outdoor markets and bargained in small shops by day, then wandered arm-in-arm on *La Ramblas* as evening turned into night. We kept Spanish hours and dined late on roast leg of lamb so tender we could flake meat from the bone with the flick of a fork. We usually had an after dinner drink at a sidewalk café before shifting our Flag to our *residencia*. For ten nights, wrapped together like snakes in spring, we fell asleep listening through open windows to the late-living Spanish prowl the streets.

Patty flew home to Gaeta the morning the flagship sailed to join the fleet. When I returned to Gaeta seventeen days later, she was gone. A loving letter left in the villa failed to provide a reason why she had returned to West Virginia.

I pushed electrons through undersea cables, satellite shots, and landlines connecting Mediterranean basin countries with the Patterson farm on Jessie's Run, West Virginia. I expended my pay checks in phone calls, but Patty was not ready to return to Gaeta. She refused to enlighten me as to what she was doing in the States. I was one worried kitty cat.

Frequent letters from Patty provided information on all the happenings in Big Otter County, but contained no revelation to explain her absence. I remained more worried than a long-haired liberal in a Louisiana coon ass bar when, after nearly seven weeks, Patty called to say she was booked two days hence on a United flight to Rome.

I didn't get excited. I only charged to Art's Beef and Ale, bought drinks for every sailor and Italian in the place, then tore home to field day the joint. Jarhead and Blue Suit danced around the room when I told them Patty was returning. I danced with them -- yelps, yowls and such radiated. My Italian neighbors streamed across the courtyard and up the steps to investigate the strange noises emitting from the Berkeley villa. They broke out the vino when they discovered Patty was returning I got nothing cleaned that night, but it was one hell of a party. Jarhead was bad hung over the next day because Italians had kept feeding him beer.

The morning of Patty's scheduled arrival I reserved a table for two at the best seafood restaurant in nearby Formia, recruited my kindly landlady to decorate the villa with seasonal flowers and laid course to Rome to meet Patty's plane.

Patty halted just sort of where she would normally have leaped to throw herself into my arms. She whipped my face with her big, gray eyes before pulling the blanket from the bundle in her arms and saying, "Henry Clay Berkeley -- meet your son, Joseph Clay Berkeley. By damn-in-hell he is our son! I have nicknamed him Joe-Joe, for no particular reason, other than he looks like a Joe-Joe. But we can call him JC, Clay or whatever you wish."

When the smoke cleared, I discovered the little mouse adopted a newborn baby by using the General Power of Attorney I had given her for use when I was at sea, or in event something happened to me. Anyone who does not believe adoption is possible with a General Power of Attorney knows nothing about Patricia Lane (Patterson) Berkeley once she decides on course, speed and waypoints. Sir Winston Churchill wasn't scat when it came to bullheadedness -- not compared to Patty.

I didn't weep, wail or gnash my teeth. I didn't shift uniform of the day to sackcloth and ashes either. It was too late for that.

We enjoyed *fruita de mar* in Formia that night -- with Joseph Clay Berkeley in a basket donated by our landlady. He didn't cry during our seafood meal, nor did he cry that night. Good thing too, considering how long we'd been separated.

Patty kept trying to explain her reasons for adopting the baby, but I gaffed her off. I sulked until Saturday morning when she drafted me to watch the kid while she went to the outdoor market to replenish our nearly bare larder. She had barely cleared the courtyard when the kid made a strange noise. I bent over the cradle to see if he was choking, spitting up, cussing, whatever.

To my surprise and shock, the little devil reached up and grabbed me by the forefinger. I was afraid he'd start bawling if I pried him loose, so I lifted him out of the old Berkeley family cradle and fooled with him, which he seemed to like. It was the first time I had ever held a child, let alone a baby. This one turned out to be a pretty interesting little guy. He even took my total ignorance of babies into account as I messed with him.

By the time Patty returned, we were firm buddies. There was no doubt in my military mind that adopting him was yet another outstanding idea on my part. Patty teased that I played more with the kid that afternoon than I played with her. I teased back that wives were standard stock items and easy to acquire.

That night, Patty beat on me until I agreed to listen to her reason for adopting Joe-Joe. Her explanation, taken in its entirety, would have filled two-three shelves in the Library of Congress.

"Although you would never discuss our having children, I was certain you would care for any child our love produced. I believed that mainly because you certainly did not want *me* forever so long, but you were ecstatic once we became one. With the same reasoning I used to influence you to marry me, I decided to become pregnant without your consent. I remained certain we should have a child, even though you moped for days and days after I informed you I was pregnant. Oh, I was *so* happy when you exhibited interest in what the baby might be like when born.

"I nearly died of shame when I awoke in the hospital and realized I had lost our child. I felt so *useless*! Clay-honey, despite your efforts at reassuring me, I felt I had let you down and the end of the Berkeley Line was my fault. I refused to accept that I could never bear a child. It was simply too horrible to accept. I eventually realized God had reasons of his own. That created an enormous problem! I could not bear a child, yet I felt strongly we should have one.

"I pondered the problem for months. Then Mommy called for our bi-weekly gossip session and told me your distant cousin,

Helen Ashfield, was pregnant and unmarried. It further developed she had no idea who the father was -- and supposedly did not care. I almost fainted when Mommy said Helen intended to place the baby for adoption at birth. I knew immediately God had answered my prayers!

"I knew something of the adoption process because an older sister of a college classmate adopted a daughter. I knew a child, if adopted near to the date of delivery, was issued a birth certificate listing adoptive parents as birth parents. So, knowing in my heart that her baby was intended for us, I flew home. I could not tell you what I intended because you would have forbidden it. I was not certain you even knew you had this cousin. I never heard you, or anybody else, mention her.

"Mommy and Daddy tried very hard to discourage me. They said Helen suffered a terrible reputation. She was some sort of street person and supposedly a heavy user of drugs. They were *really* against the adoption when they discovered you knew nothing about it. They made every possible argument, including the probability the baby would be born addicted to alcohol or drugs, or both! Once they understood just how serious I was, Daddy arranged for his lawyer to arrange a referral in Huntington where the baby would be born.

"Mommy and I arrived in Huntington five days before Joe-Joe was due to be born. I had told myself I would take the child regardless of condition, but after seeing the terrible state of your cousin, I was much afraid Mommy and Daddy were correct concerning the baby's chances of being born normal.

"Helen was in terrible shape! She was extremely skinny with little flesh on her bones -- skeleton like, really. Her thin arms and legs were covered with tattoos, bruises and scars. Her skin was translucent with veins showing from beneath the skin. Her eyes were dull -- almost lifeless.

"She *detested* her baby! I realized she experienced a very difficult life, but considered that no excuse for her being so cold and cruel toward the baby she had carried for so long. She relinquished all claim to her future baby without tears, no show of emotion at all, really.

"As the birth approached, I worried so much I became ill. I do not have words to tell you how happy and relieved I was when the doctor pronounced the baby normal and free of anything that could cause long-term damage. Pediatricians puzzled at the excellent condition of the baby, considering Helen's physical condition and the alcohol and drugs she ingested while pregnant. Dearest, I can only attribute Joe-Joe's excellent health to the mercy of God!

"I now realize I was wrong to think Helen cruel. I believe she understood her lifestyle would ultimately result in death. It did too. She departed West Virginia against the wishes of her parents and returned to the evil streets in Seattle as soon as she left the hospital. She became ill there and developed pneumonia. She died something over one week after giving birth.

"Her family arranged for her body to be shipped home. Mommy and I attended her funeral in French Creek. We were the only ones present, outside of her mother and father. That was quite sad. She caused her parents untold anguish since she was a young teen, so I was told. I suspect she willingly engaged in horrible acts, but she accomplished something in her life by leaving such a wonderful person behind.

"Clay-honey, Joe-Joe is part Berkeley, regardless of who the father is. Your distant cousin's mother, being from the Berkeley side of the family, makes this true!

"No one, including Helen, had the slightest idea who fathered Joe-Joe. That does not worry me in the least. He will grow to be the same kind and gentle and courageous man as Henry Clay Berkeley -- his *real* father!

"Oh, honey, please, please accept that God has blessed us. He first gave us each other. Then he gave us a child!"

What with the troubles in the Universe, I suspected God really didn't have time to put his fid into the affairs of the Berkeley family, but it was not for me to question Patty's rock solid faith in the Lord and in the degree of His power and concern. She could be right. She usually was.

Life remained good. Patty and Joe-Joe continued to meet the flagship at most ports-of-call. I carried Joe-Joe around dozens of Mediterranean cities until he was older, then toted him on my shoulders. Patty maintained the places I took him in Gaeta would result in barfly qualifications before he reached kindergarten, but she never made me quit taking him to the family orientated Italian bars. He became my running mate for several reasons, one being exposure to our Italian neighbors and their children enabled him to speak Italian like a native -- arm waving and all. My Italian was terrible. God never intended hillbillies to speak Italian.

CHAPTER SIXTEEN

SHELLBACK -- DEPARTING

My billet remained both enjoyable and interesting. Captain Keene selected for rear admiral and transferred to a billet in the Pentagon. Admiral Grayson picked up his fourth star during his second year as COMSIXTHFLT and left to assume command of the Pacific Fleet. He was relieved by Vice Admiral Ferrell, another fine man.

Disaster then struck on two fronts.

Admiral Ferrell slipped and fell while crossing from the gangway to his barge and injured his left hip to the point he required a lengthy period of hospitalization and therapy at Naval Hospital Bethesda, Maryland. An admiral I disliked the very first time we spoke relieved him. There was an aura of sleaze around him that tripped my trigger. My long naval service told me to stay as far as possible from this guy.

I was having a cool one with the staff heavies in Art's Beef and Ale about one week after the admiral took command. The new admiral was, of course, the prime topic of conversation. I listened to fellow staffers discuss how friendly he was, how understanding he was, and how he left work early most afternoons. Finally, I went into my Popeye mode. I couldn't stands no more!

"You all believe what you want, but my gut feeling is he will be the last man standing." I told those clustered around the bar in the small room.

"What do you mean by that?" the Marine colonel questioned.

"I've worked with two admirals at COMSIXTHFLT, not counting this one. I've known others too, but not well. Here's how I see it.

"None of us walk on water and most of us have made errors on our own or we participated in a group project that crashed and burned. Grayson and Ferrell beat us severely about the head and shoulders for fouling up, but they took heat generated outside of their command. This guy won't. Embarrass this guy, and the only hint of you left aboard will be your name in the deck log when you check out of the command."

A barrage of voices disagreed with me. That did not upset me. I'd been disagreed with before. I'd been wrong before. I hoped I was this time.

Moans and groans circulated the staff and the flagship within one month.

The admiral informed the flagship captain that he did not intend to walk around dirty, unsightly crates and ordered him to move several crates of just delivered repair parts from the pier side deck where such things were routinely staged awaiting inventory. This was a lengthy process because each item had to be accounted for prior to stowage. Storekeepers and personnel from other departments worked long into the night, moving the heavy crates from the starboard side to the port side of the ship so the admiral would not have to walk around them when he boarded the ship the following morning.

The admiral ordered the flagship's electronic material officer to install a fish finder in his official barge, a sleek, high-powered, thirty-foot boat. The EMO tactfully informed the admiral it was against regulation to modify any craft without approval from Naval Ship's Engineering Command and that approval would certainly not be forthcoming to install civilian equipment on a navy-owned boat. The admiral went totally off-plumb! When the EMO asked for the order in writing, the admiral threw him out of his cabin. He then summoned the flagship captain and cussed him out too. The flagship captain ordered the EMO to install the fish finder, but wrote the admiral's order into the ship's log.

The admiral relieved the air officer for cause after the Spanish complained that a flight of carrier aircraft dropped the wrong type of ordnance on a bombing range in Central Spain. That the admiral was reminded he was made aware at morning briefing about the type of ordnance to be dropped that day did not sway him. The relieved officer was sent ashore to await orders, his career probably at an end.

An expensive china cabinet in an Italian store caught the eye of the admiral's wife. She requested the Officer in Charge of the Naval Support Detachment purchase the cabinet for the admiral's ashore quarters, for which the OINC was responsible. The OINC politely explained that the quarters had a full allowance of furniture and that no funds were available to purchase the cabinet. The admiral complained to the OINC's parent command in Naples that the OINC was not properly supporting him. Naples ordered the OINC to purchase the cabinet ASAP!

The OINC delivered the cabinet to the admiral's quarters where, in keeping with regulations, asked the flag steward sign a property custody sheet. The flag steward notified the admiral that the OINC was pressing him to sign custody documents. The admiral called the OINC to the flagship and admonished him. The actions of the flag steward and the admiral told the OINC that the admiral intended to keep the cabinet as part of his personal household goods when transferred, rather than leaving it in the quarters. The OINC notified his parent command of his suspicions that the transaction had great potential for fraud and abuse. He was relieved of his billet and transferred.

When the balance in the travel fund account dropped below that needed for a trip the admiral wanted to take to London, allegedly for a conference, he requested the logistics captain move funds from another account to the travel fund account. The captain informed the admiral that appropriated funds could be used only for the purpose intended. The admiral then made his request a direct order. The Naval Supply System Command noticed the transfer of funds in a later report and COMSIXTHFLT received a nasty, *What the Hell?* message from Washington. The admiral ended paying several thousand dollars for the London trip out of his own pocket, mainly, because he and his wife stayed in a very expensive hotel near Hyde Park. The admiral relieved the logistics captain for a variety of alleged faults.

Barely any week passed when the admiral did not cause problems for one or more members of staff or the crew of the flagship.

Not three months had passed when the Marine colonel slapped a Danish beer on the bar in front of me at Art's Beef and Ale and asked, "Master Chief, how did you know so quickly?"

"How did I know what, Colonel?"

"How did you know the admiral was a stone ass and a slimy creature?"

"Colonel, I don't know what tipped me off. Maybe it was the fact that he smiled the entire time I was briefing him on my billet as command master chief of the Sixth Fleet, but his eyes were not smiling. I could tell he was listening to nothing I told him. He simply was not interested in the morale and well-being of Sixth Fleet personnel. I guess, maybe, old, beat up CPO's just have a feeling for that sort of thing." I grinned at him. "I'm surprised that an old, beat up Marine colonel didn't pick up on him early-on."

"I did, Master Chief, but it took me longer than you. Tell me, are you going to report him for fraud and abuse? Someone needs to."

I understood exactly where the colonel was coming from. Everybody of importance on the staff now knew the admiral was slimy, but no one wanted to jeopardize their career by reporting him. I could understand that too.

"Colonel, I'd damn sure like to, but I'm caught in a bight. He has done nothing directly to me. Every wrong he allegedly committed is second or third hand information to me. I couldn't prove a thing. You folks are going to have to sort this one out. That said, if he ever gives me an illegal order, or tries to involve me in some sort of fraud and abuse, then I damn sure *will* report him! I have absolutely nothing against a hard nose, so long as he is a hard nose all the time, like Admiral Grayson. Fact is, I prefer them. Guys like this one? Far as I am concerned, they make my Navy look bad!"

Things were changing rapidly in the Navy and, in my opinion, for the worst. A considerable number of chiefs and officers seemed to value their careers more than their duty. Many appeared to have lost the desire to take care of subordinates. Young sailors in ships I visited were not receiving the guidance I had received as a young sailor. People in positions of leadership seemed to want people to like them and would not take corrective action even when they knew a person had done wrong, particularly if that person was a female or a minority.

A minor liberty incident, such as a fight ashore, required the immediate transmission of a message to God-World to report the incident in detail. Why a fight between sailors was of interest to the Seat of Government is a total mystery to me. Common sense told me the heavy brass in Washington had much more important things to do than read about fights between sailors. There were allegation after allegation of sexual assault and racial abuse, many of which turned out to be unfounded. Officers, chief petty officers and petty officers throughout the Navy were unjustly issued bad fitness reports and bad evaluations. Some suffered captain's mast or court martial when the actual evidence dictated neither were applicable.

It seemed those in command of the Navy greatly feared the slightest rebuke from the civilian controlled Seat of Government. Nothing seemed important enough for them to speak out. They put their own interests ahead of those of their subordinates, their Navy and their country I knew of no high-ranking officer who resigned or retired because he believed those above him issued faulty orders or direction.

I heard of some of the more salty admirals being passed over for another star, or a more important command. There were, however, likely 'shadow' retirements in which a high-ranking officer simply quietly retired, rather than put up with orders he could not stomach. Admiral Grayson was probably one of them, although I had no concrete knowledge that he was one. No one I knew expected him to retire when he did. I certainly didn't.

I had, a dozen or more times, attempted to discuss personnel and/or morale problems with the admiral to no avail. He simply gaffed me off, or gave me lip service. Nothing was ever done to correct any of the problems.

I, armed with a cold beer, conducted a weeping, wailing and gnashing of teeth session our balcony while watching the setting of the sun across the bay. I told Patty a sinister cloud had descended upon the Navy, bringing things partly from civilian life to which I could not subscribe. When the Navy placed a person's feelings above accomplishment of the very reason for the Navy's existence, it was time to consider swallowing the anchor.

"You love the Navy, dearest. You would remain in the Navy until your death if that were possible. But I see worry and discontent in you. You are not sleeping well and you are cranky . . . well, you are just not you!

"I would never advise you to leave the Navy, but if the Navy expects you to do things in which you do not believe or which makes you uncomfortable, then I believe you should enter the Fleet Reserve. You have enough time to do that, more than enough time. I do not want you to develop ulcers or worry yourself sick. I want you around for a long, long time. *Forever*!"

We kicked it around for the better part of the evening before I decided I'd hang around the Navy, at least for a while. Unfortunately, I remained unhappy at what I was seeing and the fact I could do nothing to change it. It was time to go.

"I'm submitting my papers for the Fleet Reserve tomorrow, Kitten." I informed Patty the evening after the presidential election. "Get ready to pack out in three or four months. We are going to West Virginia!"

Patty burst into tears and threw herself into my lap. "Oh, I hate this. I simply *hate* it!"

The shrill of a boatswain's mate's call and the double clang of boat gongs filled the air when I swallowed the anchor on a bright, spring morning by passing between ranks of chief petty officers acting as side boys, saluting the officer of the deck, then the national ensign snapping above the fantail in a stiff breeze.

"**Master Chief Berkeley, United States Navy, departing!**" boomed through topside speakers.

The boat gongs sounded a single clang as I stepped from the gangway to the pier with Patty clutching my arm. That final clang informed the ranks standing on the helicopter flight deck and those inside the skin of the ship that I had departed the United States Navy forever.

Then something happened I had never before seen done at a retirement ceremony, not even for an admiral.

"**Ship's company! Right Face!**"

"**Hand Salute!**"

With that last unorthodox honor bestowed upon me, I entered the Fleet Reserve after serving twenty-two years, one month and eight days.

Patty, carrying the bouquet of roses in the crook of her arm that the staff had presented her, guided me toward the black, Navy sedan waiting at the head of the pier. I could barely see through the tears in my eyes.

The End:

Author: F. L. H. Hudkins

ABOUT THE AUTHOR

Author was raised on a hillside farm in West Virginia. He had his first paid job at the age of seven, riding ancient horses engaged in pulling hay shocks from meadow to stacking point He worked on his parents' farm and on neighbors' farms until he enlisted in the Navy at seventeen.

He was double-hatted in his last Navy billet as Command Master Chief of the United States Sixth Fleet and Communications Readiness Officer. He shipped as Radio Electronics Officer in the United States Merchant Marine after retiring from the Navy.

He is married to the former Agueda Caceres Perez of Madrid, Spain. They have five children.

THE CRUISE

www.ingramcontent.com/pod-product-compliance
Lightning Source LLC
Chambersburg PA
CBHW060427180626
46817CB00007B/2695